GOODNIGHT STRANGER

GOODNIGHT STRANGER

MICIAH BAY GAULT

PARK
ROW
BOOKS

PARK
ROW
BOOKS

Recycling programs
for this product may
not exist in your area.

ISBN-13: 978-0-7783-0870-6

Goodnight Stranger

ParkRowBooks.com
BookClubbish.com

Printed in U.S.A.

For Jeff

GOODNIGHT STRANGER

I

Baby B was our brother, and he'd been dead all our lives. For a long time I thought I'd see him again, but by the time I was twenty-eight, I believed that the dead stay dead. I knew that the space he left in our lives would have to be filled in other ways.

That summer I was working in the information booth on the landing, as I had every summer for ten years. It was August, which meant that humidity and the smell of dead sea animals hung in the air like fog. Masts clanged and seagulls cried out in the harbor. The water was blue, green, and gray, and the sight of it made me thirsty.

The ferry was a little white toy as it rounded the tip of the island, growing larger and more substantial as it lumbered into the landing and let down its planks. Passengers descended, blinking and lugging suitcases, and I leaned back to await their questions.

I recognized everyone who stepped off the boat. They all fit into one of three categories: tourist, islander, returning visitor.

I was an expert on tourists. They didn't know me, but I knew them. With a glance, I could tell why they were here. Some arrived armed with cameras and pocket money, trying to capture the island, fit it onto a scrapbook page. Some came because they loved beauty. Some came to remember the past, or to refuse the future.

And then there were those of us who were born here and never left. That was me, and my brother Lucas, and about half the class we graduated with from the tiny island high school, and the old fishermen, the Portuguese and Cape Verdean grandpas and their sons and grandsons, and the shop owners, the barkeeps, the waitresses, and hotel clerks. The people who stayed had various and complicated reasons for staying. For me it was because of my brothers—Lucas, the living brother, who needed me to look after him, but also my dead brother in the little island graveyard. They held on to me the way families do—that love-anchored gravitational pull.

I felt a shadow and looked up to see Eddie Frank standing by the information booth. The crooked expression on his face was completely familiar to me, one eyebrow up, one corner of his mouth raised in a half grin. I'd known him all my life, like almost everyone else on the island. We'd been in the same classroom from preschool on. When others from our graduating class had gone, we'd stayed behind on the island together.

He leaned on the booth. "You coming into the bar tonight?" he asked. "It's been a while."

"I told you—"

"You look like you could use a drink."

"I'm trying to be a good person, okay?"

"That means no drinks?"

"That means no drinks with *you*."

"Sometimes a drink is just a drink," Eddie said.

I shook my head and he went away, back to the bouncer's stool outside One Eyed Jack's, the bar across the street from the information booth. I watched him as he went, his broad back, his already thinning hair. I put my head down, closed my eyes.

That night my brother Lucas didn't come home after work. I opened the mail, swept the kitchen floor, and read the first few pages of a novel recommended by Elijah West, our new librarian. When Lucas still didn't show, I retrieved a folder I kept hidden on the top shelf of the pantry, under a waffle iron we hadn't used in years. This was something I couldn't let Lucas see—so I worked on it at times like these. I took the brochures out of the folder, the applications for scholarships.

I didn't intend to hide it from him forever—just for now, while I completed the applications. There was always the chance that I wouldn't be accepted, wouldn't get enough scholarship money to make it possible, and then Lucas would never have to know.

And if I were to be accepted… When I imagined it, I felt something like a wave breaking in my chest, a crash of joy and fear. For so many years I'd known that out there beyond the bay, people were living busy, complicated lives. One of those busy lives was supposed to be mine, and I wanted to go—wanted off this island. It was one of my earliest memories, longing to leave, dreaming I'd burst past the edges of this little sandbox, leave it all behind.

Footsteps outside. I hid the college applications in the pantry and slipped into the yard to greet Lucas. But it was the Grendles next door, opening and closing their garage. They were ancient and grouchy, and had been my neighbors since I was born.

"Lydia!" I heard Mrs. Grendle call. "What are you doing out here? Spying on us?"

"I heard clanging and wanted to see what was going on."

"Not a goddamn thing," she said, "except we needed the wheelbarrow."

I made spaghetti and ate it alone. I slipped onto the screened-in back porch overlooking Bhone Bay. Growing up, Lucas and I preferred the porch to any other room in the house. Our bedrooms felt lonely and far away. The living room was the realm of adults: books with no pictures, dark paintings of lighthouses and cliffs. The porch was where we set up forts, devoured books, napped, ate our meals. I always had the impression that our parents resented us for not making better use of the rest of the house. They had bought it to be filled with kids and traces of us—not for us to be separate, unto ourselves.

I looked out at the sailboats, bare masts swaying, at the houseboat that had been in Bhone Bay for as long as Lucas and I could remember: tiny, red, rocking like a cradle all night long. We used to pretend it was ours.

At nine it was dark, the house too quiet. *Fuck*, I thought. Where was Lucas? I didn't want to worry, but I had to worry. That's how it was with my brother. I grabbed a sweater off a chair in the kitchen and left, letting the door slam and echo over Bhone Bay.

On the shore, the air smelled of beach roses, and the bushes were covered with the plump shadows of rose hips. I saw shapes in the water and started, but they were only seals. On Clara Day Street, a few lingering weekend tourists walked up and down with ice-cream cones and baby carriages. A group of teenagers was skateboarding in the street and a car honked at them. The old wooden door to Jack's was propped open, and Ed Frank was lounging on his bouncer stool outside.

"You came after all," he said. "Guess what I heard. Kevin Bacon's on the island tonight. Supposedly."

"So?"

"So...it's Kevin Bacon. *Footloose?*"

"I never saw it."

"Where were you all those years? In a cave? He's on the island, but I don't know where he's staying."

"Listen, have you seen Lucas?"

He shook his head. "I'm glad you're here, though. Let's go in. I'm buying."

"I have to find Lucas," I said.

"Uh-oh," he said. "Is everything okay?"

"Oh, it's fine. I don't know where he is, but I'm sure he's fine." I turned to walk down Clara Day Street and then pivoted back to Eddie. "Lucas has been really happy lately," I told him.

Which was true enough. He was happy in his own way. Lucas had too many fears, too many anxieties to ever experience the kind of happy-go-lucky contentment other people did. The psychologist he went to when we were little called it pathological shyness. But calling it shyness was like calling a hurricane a frisky breeze. It felt more like a fear, a phobia, of people. I didn't understand it. But when you love someone you don't have to understand them, you just have to accept who they are, and that was who Lucas was.

What it meant was that all the small things one does to take care of business on a daily basis, Lucas was incapable of doing. The mere thought of talking to a teller in a bank left him shaking with dread. He couldn't go to the grocery store. He never used the telephone.

In other ways he functioned like any other adult. He went to work every day, did half the house chores, made a reasonable baked chicken. But he didn't have friends, and never girlfriends. And if it weren't for me, I'm not sure how he'd get food into the house. If it weren't for me, he might actually die of loneliness.

That was why I was twenty-eight years old and only just getting around to finishing those college applications. It wasn't that Lucas was any more capable of taking care of himself now than last year, or the year before. But increasingly, I'd been feeling that my chances were running out—that it was now or never, that if I didn't leave soon I would literally sink into the sand of this island forever.

Mady's Diner wasn't open. Lucas wasn't at Island Pie or the Island Inn, but I hadn't thought he would be. It was after ten when I returned to the dark house. I wrapped up in a chenille blanket on the back porch and waited. I looked at the bay, the tops of the waves pearly in the moonlight. I worried, the way my mother used to worry. Lucas at the top of the lighthouse. Lucas slipping on rocks, slipping under the black water. And then there it was: the same old irrational thought, that I was to blame, that the act of filling out college applications had somehow led him into danger.

At eleven, I picked up the phone. I cradled it against my

chest, listening to the drone of the dial tone. Then I called the island police. I almost hung up, but George Samson answered on the fourth ring, very sleepy, very grumpy, and then it was too late.

"It's Lydia Moore," I said.

"Not again," he said.

"He's not home. I'm worried."

"I'll let you know if I find him," he said.

In bed, I listened to all the sounds of the island, a whole orchestra. The wind scratched the door, tapped the windows. A raccoon clanged the trash can lids together. Someone stood on the sand waving a conductor's wand, a tall and regal woman. My mother. I could almost see her, on the outer edge of every dream. "I'm sorry," I said to her, as she turned slightly in my direction. "I'm trying to take care of him, I really am."

Then I heard the front door. I heard fumbling in the fridge. He was getting a beer. He was sitting alone at the kitchen table. I could see it as clearly as if I were in the room with him. I grabbed for the phone and called the island police again.

"George," I whispered. "He's home. I guess I was overreacting."

I heard him yawning. "Okay. Happy ending," he said.

"Did you even go out looking for him?" I said. "Or did you go back to sleep?"

"I'm awake," he said, yawning again. "I looked for him! But, Lydia, you know as well as I do that when he doesn't want to be found, there's no finding him."

It didn't matter. Lucas was home. I told myself I'd tear up the college applications. I told myself I had all I needed right here. I knew it wasn't true, but I was euphoric with relief. I took a deep breath and dived headfirst into a deep sleep.

———

2

Voices pulled me out of my dreams. A kind of pure white light reflected up from the bay, filling the room. The voices belonged to the ripples of light on the wall, then to the waves out in the bay. Then I was fully awake, and the voices were just voices.

I slid out of bed and pulled on pajama pants. Crept down the stairs.

Not voices—music. I paused to make sure it wasn't the record player, the old Nina Simone album—because that would mean things with Lucas were worse than I thought. But it was Leonard Cohen, which meant things were okay. Lucas was making scrambled eggs. His hair was tousled, sticking up, as if he'd slept on it wet. This time of year, late summer, his skin was brilliant and brown, and his shoulders and cheeks glowed with sunburn.

"You were out late," I said.

He slid a plate of eggs in front of me without a word.

"Were you at the lighthouse?"

He sat across from me, fixed me with his earnest stare, his complicated amber eyes. Lucas was a child of the earth. He was all rocks and bricks and dirt, sun-warmed things, molten things, dust and leaves and pollen. One of his eyes had a dark brown stripe through it, the other a single fleck of gold.

"Well?" I said. "Were you?"

"Don't you ever miss him, Lyd?"

"Who?" I said, but I knew.

"I just want things to be the way used to be," Lucas said.

"He's been dead all our lives, Lu."

"The way things were supposed to be, then."

That was a dangerous line of thinking. How did anyone know how things were *supposed* to be? Our destinies weren't like clothes laid out for a party, they weren't some one-size-fits-all costume to slip into. But I understood why Lucas was thinking about Baby B and how things should have been. That was the turn thoughts took when loneliness grew too big and unruly. Island Loneliness was more terrible than regular loneliness. Loneliness could be just sad, sweet solitude. Island Loneliness was solitude with wind and crashing waves, and it wasn't at all sweet. Island Loneliness meant looking toward the blue edge of the world and longing for something that existed only on the other side.

"I'm late," I said. "I have to go." But I turned back from the doorway. "Let's do something fun together tonight. You and me. I don't know what. Make a big dinner or something."

"I could get clams?" he said.

"Yes, let's have a feast. Just you and me."

I hurried along the beach to the landing, the sky above me pearly like the inside of a shell. The red houseboat rocked lazily in the bay. A white egret was stalking in the shallow water, and cormorants perched on every rock, turning their heads one by one to watch as I walked by. Their necks bulged as if they'd swallowed a string of beads. They threw their heads back and the beads slid deeper.

Wolf Island was smaller and plainer than Martha's Vineyard and Nantucket. We were the girl-next-door island. No gingerbread houses. No bakery with a line around the block by eight in the morning. No kitschy restaurants that sold more T-shirts than food. Clara Day Street was only a few blocks long, and most of the stores were for us, not the tourists: grocery store, dry cleaner, pharmacy, Mady's Diner, One Eyed Jack's, Island Pie. The high school, community hall, and post office were at one end of the street in old slanty buildings. The ferry came in at the other end. From the information booth, I could see all of it, every gray and shingled roof, every widow's walk and weathervane. Roses climbed up all the fences. Gulls circled overhead, their wings vanishing into the sky.

Instead of going straight to my information booth by the docks, I went into the Ferry-All office building on Clara Day Street where Jim Cardoza, my boss, was working at his desk, surrounded by picture after picture of his daughter Mary-Ann, who had moved to New York and never visited.

"What's going on?" Jim said. "Why are you late?"

"Long story," I said. "Lucas was out late, and I—"

"Is he sick? Why was he out so late?" Jim's mother had died suddenly a year ago, and he was sure disasters were about to befall everyone he knew.

"You worry too much," I said.

"There were people here at nine," he said. "You missed everyone."

We glanced out the window. The landing looked like a

ghost town. It looked the way it looked in winter. We shivered. And then we laughed. Jim's laughter sounded very much like crying.

The streets were busy again by lunchtime. I watched from the info booth as tourists filed off the noon boat, a huddle of energy in sunglasses and baseball caps, tugging at suitcases and snapping open brochures. A dad pushed babies in a double stroller. A college kid was bringing his girlfriend home for the first time. He loved his home and wanted her to love it, too. An old woman and her husband were here to visit their children. They couldn't wait. They spent all year telling stories about their kids, and then for one glorious week each summer they became characters in the stories they told. Two boys with dreadlocks clutched cell phones in their hands like protective amulets. I didn't have the heart to tell them that cell service was almost nonexistent on Wolf Island.

It was a comfort to sit at the information booth and dole out information—a kind of currency. I told tourists which of the two inns was better for children. I told them where the aquarium was and warned them not to expect more than two sad seals and a tank of lobsters. I told them who had the best clam chowder. When the whale watch cruise left. Where there were mopeds for rent and where there were bikes.

These were the questions I knew how to answer.

Eddie came over from One Eyed Jack's. He was wearing a T-shirt that said, "Wolf Harbor: A Quaint Little Drinking Village with a Fishing Problem."

"You want to get lunch or something?" he asked.

"I'm kind of busy right now," I said, handing over a map of the island to a young couple with a baby in a backpack.

"After it clears out," he said.

In high school I'd worshipped Ed Frank. I was still trying

to get over that, if I'm being honest, even though he'd gotten married a few years back to an island girl, Kim, who had been three grades behind us in school. Marriage had changed him somehow, aged him, but when I looked at him I still saw Ed Frank, seventeen years old, his face flushed from running, his head thrown back laughing—and maybe he saw the girl in me, too. I don't know what we still wanted from each other, maybe just to hold on to the people we used to be. Despite Kim, and the fact that we'd known each other forever, it seemed somehow a natural progression—expected even—that we'd end up seeing each other secretly. I wasn't proud of it, I didn't like sneaking around, but it was hard to stop. Eddie, his warm belly, his clumsy hands.

But I'd made up my mind to end all that.

"You seem tense," Eddie said.

"I guess I am."

"I know some good massage techniques."

"Thanks, Eddie, but I don't think that will help."

"Shiatsu," he said.

"I'm just thinking about the future," I said.

"Well, there's your mistake," he said. "Be in the moment."

I looked around me. I loved the island. Loved it the way you love home. Which meant that sometimes I hated it, love and hate being two sides of the same coin. I looked at Eddie, felt a little volcano of anger. *Be in the moment.* Easy for him to say; his future was one he'd already chosen, with Kim. Sometimes my past, present, and future felt more like stories being told to me than a life I had any power over. "I'm sick of the moment," I said.

"What you need is a distraction," Eddie said.

And that's when the stranger stepped off the boat.

I noticed him immediately because he didn't fit into any of

my categories. He was carrying a *New York Times* and a black duffel bag. He was handsome, and he seemed like an island himself, not in any way part of the commotion around him. He looked like someone coming home, but I knew everyone who grew up here. He wasn't a tourist either, not on vacation. He didn't really fit anywhere.

He stood at the bottom of the plank and heaved his bag over his shoulder, looking up and down Clara Day Street. He wore a white shirt and dark jeans, had dark eyes and dark hair, too. His shirt was untucked, and his black hair was windblown, but he still gave the impression of neatness, formality, and precision. He looked around him with a complicated expression—I couldn't read him, but it seemed at once hungry and content, a contradiction.

He noticed me. I straightened. I was messy, unbeautiful. My hair was tangled, the color of sand. Lucas got the golden hair and amber eyes. I had sand-hair and mud-eyes. What was soft and sensual in Lucas's face was just ill-defined in mine. But still, there was something about me that some men liked: sunburn, scratched skin, those little signs of danger and disorder. There was something pitiable about me, I knew, island girl, trapped here at the mercy of storms and boats. Some people spent all their lives looking for a girl like that. They wanted to be the one to give her the brave new world.

The stranger lifted his hand, waved. I waved. Then he turned and walked away. I watched him disappear down Clara Day Street. I realized I'd been holding my breath.

"Who the fuck is that?" Eddie asked.

"No idea," I said.

I wondered where he'd come from, pictured those possible cities and towns. Throughout the day, I scanned Clara Day Street for a glimpse of him. A distraction. I imagined running

into him on a dark street—maybe in the rain—sharing an um-
brella, talking all night. Eventually, unable to part with me,
he'd ask me to come back to whatever city he came from: long
streets, tall buildings, buses and taxis and brick and bridge.
What's more important than this love? he might say. Only that
was the wrong question, because the answer was: the other
love, the first love. That's what's more important. Family.
Brothers. The living and dead. Lucas. Baby B.

What was wrong with me? I was hopeless. I couldn't even
fuck a stranger in my imagination without first thinking about
my family obligations.

That night Lucas brought home a bucket of clams, and we
prepared them with corn on the cob. Our feasts were simple and transcendent. "Lucas," I said, looking up, butter and
lemon sauce on my fingers. "What would you do if I were
to go away someday—I'm just asking hypothetically here."

"Like on a trip?" he said.

"Yes. A trip."

"I don't know," he said. "Same thing I do now, I guess.
Plus wait for you to come home."

"You might be pretty lonely."

"I'd survive."

"How would you, I don't know, shop for food?"

"You could shop before you left."

"Right but—" I didn't know what I was hoping he'd say.
"What if you got a roommate or something. Someone to stay
here—while I was away—to shop, and keep you company."

Lucas laughed. "I don't want a roommate, thank you. I'd
be fine on my own. It's not like you've never gone away."

"That was different. Mom was here."

"If you want to go on a trip, go ahead," Lucas said, suddenly uneasy.

"I don't want to go on a trip," I said. "I told you, it was just hypothetical. You know what I will do, though? Go out for a drink."

Lucas shrugged. "Fine with me. Have all the drinks you want."

We cleared the dishes in silence, stacked them in the sink. The night hadn't gone at all as I'd planned. I had wanted to feel that old sense of connection with Lucas, but now I felt more alone than ever, and maybe Lucas did, too. I left through the kitchen door, headed for the beach. It was already dark, and the slapping of the water was amplified—little crashes over and over. I followed the noise down to the dock. But it was only the rowboat, nudging against the pilings as the water got choppy in the wind.

From inside I could hear faintly the scratching of the record player. The unmistakable piano, like breaking glass, of Nina Simone, "Here Comes the Sun." This was a bad sign—I could see in my mind Lucas bent over the record player. I could feel the intensity of his longing. I felt desperate to escape the sound of it.

The lounge at the Island Inn was scattered all around with soft armchairs and little low tables. There was a small dance floor by a grand piano near the bar. A pianist in jeans and a Hawaiian shirt was playing "Take the A Train." I wouldn't normally come to this bar—I liked Jack's where Eddie worked. But I thought I might see the stranger here, and I did.

He was with the tourists at the bar. He was watching the room, taking it in with the same almost-possessive look I'd seen at the landing. *Mine, all mine*, his look seemed to say—to everything in the room, armchairs, barstools, piano, pianist.

I crossed the lounge and sat next to him.

"Hi," he said. "I recognize you."

"From the information booth."

"No, from—" He shook his head. "Actually this is convenient, because I'm in need of some information."

"I thought you might be."

Laughing, he said, "I find islanders very accommodating."

"Some of us are."

I ordered scotch, which was what I liked to drink. I loved the way it burned, the way each sip seemed illicit, even long after I turned twenty-one. The stranger paid for it. Already, that force was blooming between us, a kind of invisible presence, air pressure, humidity, the fullness before a storm. The way the air around you grows arms and legs, a beating heart. He was here from New York, he said, not on vacation, more like a retreat. His name was Cole. He had no wedding ring. He smelled like salt, like corn flour.

"What kind of information did you need?" I asked.

He thought for a moment. "Best lobster roll on the island?"

"Drake's."

"Best pancakes?"

"The diner. Mady's."

"Bookstore?"

"No, sorry. Library."

"Affordable hotel—for a possible extended stay?"

I shook my head, considering. "The Sea Breeze is cheap. But you can stay here for the same cost if you ask for room eleven."

"What's wrong with room eleven? Haunted?"

"Yes."

"I can't wait to find out what that means," he said.

"Do you already have a room?"

"Number five."

"I've never seen that one," I said. "I'd like to."

I watched his eyes dilate, that sudden opening to the light, darkness creating space for desire. But he shook his head. "I would offer to show you. But everything is...everywhere. It's a mess."

"I like messes."

"Do you have a room?"

"I have a house."

"I would love to see *it*."

"But—I also have a brother, and he will be there."

"I like brothers."

"You won't like mine."

"I'll risk it."

I held his arm on the beach. We bumped against each other's shoulders. I felt reckless, like someone else, another girl. Lucas could hide in his room all night. He could sleep up on the attic bed. He could spend the night at the lighthouse. I wanted to forget him, just for one night, for an hour or two.

"Oh," Cole said, suddenly. My house was in front of us, and he stopped and stared at it. He looked over his shoulder as if orienting himself. The houses of the island all perched like seabirds on the sand—squatting gulls nestled against the wind or long-legged herons keeping safe from waves on rickety stilts. Our house was among those, looking out across the bay, over Vineyard Sound, toward Martha's Vineyard and Cape Cod. It was a rambling house with big, generous windows, shingles the color of the sky on a cloudy day. Now its windows were dark except for one upstairs bedroom, and the kitchen.

"Is something wrong?" I asked Cole.

"Nothing." He shook his head. "I think I noticed your house from the ferry today, that's all."

"Impossible. The ferry comes in on the other side of the island."

"I guess a lot of houses look alike."

Inside the kitchen, he took my wrists and pulled me toward him. I closed my eyes, waiting to feel his mouth. But a moment went by and when I opened my eyes, I saw that he was studying me, examining my face.

"Is this an inspection?" I asked. "Am I going to pass?"

"Sorry," he said. "I was just—you're beautiful—"

"I already invited you home with me, so you can relax with the flattery," I said.

And then the door from the living room swung open and Lucas walked in.

I hated watching Lucas freeze when he encountered someone new, his shoulders hunching into little mounds. I saw his body go rigid, his posture tense like a rabbit. He dropped his eyes. I waited for him to back out of the room, disappear.

But instead, Lucas seemed to see something—I saw the little jerk of recognition. He pointed at Cole's legs or feet. He moved toward Cole, and then bent over to examine his legs.

"I'm guessing this is the brother," Cole said.

"Lu?" I said. "What's going on?"

"Are you…?" Lucas looked into Cole's face. Then he turned to me. "It's him," he said.

"Who?" His eyes were suddenly glassy, and I felt a tremor of fear, something rising up from the earth, through the floorboards, entering the soles of my feet, and racing through my veins along with my blood as it hurried toward my heart.

"Lydia," Lucas said, "it's Baby B."

3

Our family wasn't like other families when it came to this lost brother, and how we grieved for him. We talked about him so much growing up that it sometimes felt as though he occupied a more elevated spot in our family's hierarchy than Lucas and I did. My mother didn't just grieve for him, she longed for him. I longed for him, too, and so did Lucas, and for Lucas, the longing ebbed and flowed like some internal tide of his nature, rising, raging, crashing into something pathological every few years.

The three of us were born together, triplets. Baby B's name was Colin, but my mother often called him Baby B, as she had during the pregnancy, and so we called him Baby B as well. It reminded Lucas of a nursery rhyme. *Big A little a, Bouncing B, the Cat's in the Cupboard and Can't see me.* To me it seemed to rely on some simple, undeniable system of categorization.

Baby: the very title of what he was. B: his place in the order, after me, before Lucas.

My mother and father had married late in life, and at first hadn't thought they wanted kids at all. My mother spent her twenties trying to break away from her own family, a dysfunctional cadre of Catholics from Chicago, whose enthusiastic mingling of love and guilt and—sometimes—violence was forever in her memory along with the scratchy sound of Bing Crosby on the record player. She'd had more than her fill, she always said, of the noise and the guilt and the God and the Bing.

When she got married she decided my father was all the family she needed. They did all the things you do when you have no kids: threw elaborate late-night parties, up until dawn playing guitar, reading Edward Abbey and Tom Robbins and Jack Kerouac; the only ones for them were the mad ones, they agreed. They moved from Chicago to Denver to Atlanta to Boston, taking jobs at self-impressed liberal arts colleges, teaching literature courses or working in admissions offices. They spent holidays at the cinema watching *Jaws* and *Carrie*, congratulating themselves on how nimbly they'd escaped the life they didn't want, which dogged them all the time: commercials with aproned mothers and suited fathers and children agog over fat golden turkeys on checkerboard tablecloths. They ate lasagna on Christmas Eve and made a big tofu and broccoli stir-fry on Christmas Day.

But it was on Christmas Day my mother started thinking about kids. The way she always told it, she was watching *The Sound of Music*. She didn't like that Maria gave up her goal of being a nun, but my mother, along with Maria, succumbed thoroughly to Captain von Trapp's stern enchantment, and felt elated when he kissed that lovely governess and sang about his wicked childhood.

It was the movie's ending that did it. The von Trapps climbing through the Alps to escape the Nazis, a unit of togetherness, a family. The way she presented it to my father was, we don't want to be alone when we're old, do we? No, my father agreed, we shouldn't grow old alone.

She spent two years trying to get pregnant. No luck. And then she was forty, and suddenly hungry for babies, starved for babies. She began taking human menopausal gonadotropin—a new drug at the time—to encourage ovulation, and it worked. At forty-one she was pregnant, not with one baby, not with two babies, but with three babies. Just what she'd wanted! She prepared to sew matching play clothes cut cleverly from curtains.

Both Mom and Dad had small inheritances, which they combined to buy the house on Wolf Island. Their dream house, they said, even though the wind blew through cracks in the wall, the floorboards were full of sand, the roof sagged and leaked. They liked the huge kitchen overlooking the bay, the big lawn with a tire swing already tied to the branch of a tree. A house with plenty of room. A house meant for children.

They were moving to a place that was gloriously out of the way. What they liked best was the sense of adventure. They would have three children, but they were young at heart. No suburban cul-de-sac. No PTA potlucks and Tupperware parties! My father would commute to Boston, where he'd been appointed dean of a tiny college. Eventually he hoped to write full-time.

We looked like beans on the ultrasound monitor, she told us, three little beans of light in the dark. They called us Baby A,

B, and C. I was A, Lucas C, and the other baby was B. We were born too early, at thirty-two weeks, struggling into the world: me, then Colin, and finally Lucas. We were skinny, our stick-bones visible through translucent skin. Lucas and I weighed less than four pounds, and Baby B was even smaller. Our miniature mouths didn't yet know how to nurse. Doctors dripped milk into our stomachs through tubes in our noses. Our lungs were reluctant to breathe out of water, but only Baby B needed a tube for that as well.

For weeks, our mother believed we were dying. She sat in the NICU day after day, her hair turning gray, her bones losing density.

After one month in the NICU, we turned some corner finally, our lungs and hearts and stomachs working efficiently in our tiny bodies. We drank from bottles. We grew. They brought us home to Wolf Island. And we lived all together in the big house on the bay for three weeks, until Baby B developed pneumonia, which was common in premature babies, the doctors told my parents.

He died in the night. My mother was alone with him when it happened. She'd tried to take him over to the mainland on the evening ferry, but he didn't make it to the hospital. I didn't like to picture him in her arms, seven weeks old, the cold wind as the ferry ripped along, all of them—mother, baby, and boat—chasing his disappearing breath.

They buried him in the island cemetery and lady's slippers sprang up on the mound of earth under the shady branches of the encroaching woods. The flowers returned year after year, their delicate swelling like some sad secret the earth was telling. They were beautiful in a way that nothing else we knew was beautiful, their pale fleshiness, dark pink veins. In childhood, we went every year to plant more, transplanting them from the woods around the Day Estate, even after we didn't need to. They flourished, spread, a lovely rash creeping from Baby B's earth to the other grassy graves, the color densest beside the headstone that said SON~BROTHER.

He had broken my mother's heart, that was clear to us. Although his body was buried in the earth under all those flowers, he never really *passed away* the way the dead should. He hung around on the fringes of our consciousness all the time.

In the dimly lit kitchen—only a single bulb over the sink—I watched my brother's eyes, huge, glassy. "It's Baby B," he said.

The stranger held still as if afraid to break a spell. His eyes moved from me to Lucas.

"Lucas, Baby B is dead," I said.

"I've been dreaming about him every night," Lucas said. "I could sense him getting closer, and I thought there was something I was supposed to do. But it wasn't me after all. You were the one who had to bring him here."

"He's a stranger, Lu. I met him tonight at the inn."

"Then how do you explain this?" Lucas pointed at Cole's ankle—at a small tattoo I hadn't noticed. "Lady's slipper."

We both looked at Cole. "I got that when I was twenty-one," he said.

"Why that particular flower?" I asked.

"Why? Because it's beautiful, and rare. And it was someone's favorite flower—someone I loved. Sorry, what is going on? Who's Baby B?" A flush had risen from his neck to his cheeks. His eyes black, bright.

"He was our brother," I said. "Sorry, maybe it's time for you to go."

"No," Lucas said. "Don't go! Here, sit down. I'll get a beer for you, and we'll tell you about Baby B. We'll tell you the whole story."

It was disorienting to see Lucas talking with a stranger, Lucas who sometimes couldn't even say hi to Eddie, or the Grendles, or Jim Cardoza, people he'd known his whole life. I felt dizzy, as if the room were tilting around me.

"I'm always up for a story," Cole said, sitting at the table. Lucas popped the tab on a PBR and set it in front of Cole.

"I need to sit, too," I said, and they pulled out a chair for me.

We were up all night, and the biggest surprise of all was that Lucas talked most of that time. It was as if something had come uncorked, and stories were pouring out of him.

"His name was Colin," Lucas said. "I mean even your name is similar."

"That's just a coincidence," I said.

"Did you feel anything?" Lucas asked me. "When you first saw each other, I mean? Did you have any idea?"

"I did," the stranger said. "I felt something right away."

"Of course I didn't feel anything," I said. "Because there's nothing to feel."

"Don't worry," Lucas said. "She's always like this at first."

"Like what?" I said. But I knew what he meant. Practical— trying to tether him to earth. He resented that. But look what happened when I slipped up, when I forgot myself for one night, tried to bring a stranger home. It was like I was pretending to be someone else, someone without responsibilities. Look how that worked out. I felt my heart beating, felt warmth crawling up the back of my neck, sweat prickling my scalp.

Just before sunrise, Cole went away down the chilly beach

promising to come back later that day. Lucas and I stood on the screened-in porch, watched him disappear down the shore. Just before the second jetty, he stopped and found a stone in the sand, skipped it even though it was too dark to see its skittering path through the water.

"Did you see that?" Lucas said.

"It doesn't mean anything. A lot of people skip stones."

"In that exact place?"

As long as I could remember, Lucas had stopped at the second jetty to skip one stone. For good luck. For Baby B. I never knew why he did it. But in my memory, I could see him at all these different ages, five years old, ten years old, eighteen, twenty-five. That same flick of the wrist. Stone after stone.

Lucas tipped his head back and finished his beer. For some reason neither of us wanted to go to bed. We sat on the porch until the grainy light of dawn made visible the dock and the jetties and the boats in the bay. I looked at Lucas and felt a deep ache in my chest—love swelling to enormous proportions inside my ribs. I loved him so much. I wanted to give him everything he wanted. A brother returned from the dead. Our parents, too. If I'd known how to do it, what to sacrifice, I would have without hesitation.

It was ironic that our parents had decided to have children so they wouldn't be alone when they were old. It turned out they didn't need to worry about growing old at all. Dad had a heart attack when we were in seventh grade. Mom died eight years later from breast cancer. Ever since, just Lucas and me. Alone on the island, alone in the big house they bought for us and Baby B.

Early light crept into the porch where we sat, lighting up the table and chairs, the wicker sofa, chenille blanket, potted plants. Everything was in place, but everything felt different. Bhone Bay was out there doing what it always did, tide creeping out, revealing damp raw sand, black seaweed. The red houseboat was anchored where it always was. The light was the same light. The sound of the bay was the same sound.

But we felt different now, already revised in some indefinable way. How amazing the change one day can bring, one chance meeting. Or—maybe it wasn't so amazing. After all, we'd spent a lifetime longing for something—or someone— we could never have. That longing had created a space in us, in our lives. And Cole, in ways I didn't yet understand, seemed to fit into that space, filling it like a missing puzzle piece.

4

Our relationship with Baby B had been complicated, and it changed over time like any relationship, but one thing remained constant: he was always real to us. We knew about him as soon as we were old enough to know anything. We had four photos of Baby B, but only one of the three of us together, the ultrasound photo, which my mother had stuck up on the fridge with magnets. She used to point to the little beans and say, "There you are, and there you are, and there's Baby B."

My mother never seemed to fully recover, from losing a child, or from having them. Our existence exhausted her. We were never the von Trapp family, not Lucas and me. We didn't sing, we cried. We howled. We were messy. We had bad dispositions. As we grew, we sometimes caught a look of disappointment on our mother's face. Then we thought the same thing: the other baby would have been lovely, neat, affectionate. The other baby would not have disappointed her.

We were too young to know that what we were seeing on her face wasn't disappointment, but lifelong sorrow, the kind that chisels its way into every movement, posture, and expression. It was all too easy to project any feeling of unworthiness onto Baby B. We saw so clearly what life would have been like if he had lived. My mother's perpetual exhaustion would lift like fog burning off the water. My parents would stop looking at us with mystified, resentful expressions. They loved us, we knew, and they loved each other, but they were unhappy on some level that we never made sense of.

From the moment we could dream, we dreamed about Baby B. In Lucas's dreams he was bright and alive, but nonsensical. He slid down banisters and snake holes, drove giant cars and reindeer, hid in cellars and knotholes. Lucas followed him through rooms that opened into other rooms. Chased him along strange beaches, where he disappeared into a series of underwater caves, his feet—or maybe fins—flashing behind him.

My dreams were logical, like me. In my dreams, we were in a classroom and a teacher was calling roll, and Colin was there along with the other children, raising his hand, saying *here*. My subconscious was forever trying to line us up, put everyone in order. Lucas's subconscious was attempting to break the rules of reality, create a world in which Colin could return. Those were the ways we dealt with loss, even as children.

But it wasn't just that we missed him. There's a kind of peace in missing someone you'll never see again. We didn't have that peace. There was always a sense that we might see him again. Lucas believed with all his heart that Baby B would come back to us. And he wasn't alone. My mother believed it, too. And maybe I did as well, some small unruly fraction of my psyche that rebelled against order and logic.

"He's a spirit now," my mother used to say. "He lives in the air all around us. He's waiting to be born to us again."

We'd thought she meant she was having another baby.

"No. I can't have any more babies," she said.

"That's okay," Lucas said. "He can wait for Lydia."

The notion that our brother, Baby B, who we knew from dreams, could exist inside my body, having somehow gotten *in*, and needing someday to get *out*, filled me with panic and—because it's the nature of humans to be conflicted—longing.

"No, thank you," I said.

"In Japan, they're called *mizuko*," my mother said. "Water babies. They float around us in the spirit world, waiting for a chance to be born again. I feel him everywhere I go."

"Water baby," Lucas said, laughing.

"Water baby," my mother said.

I couldn't stop thinking about it: the idea of sex, that wondrous, frightening unknown all mixed up with the idea of pregnancy, and all of that mixed up with the idea of a hovering baby brother who haunted us, wanting to be born.

"He's patient," my mother told us. "He'll wait until the time is right."

This was how Lucas learned to believe the unbelievable, from our mother, a champion believer. After we were born, and Baby B died, she not only believed in psychotherapy and chiropractic, she believed in acupuncture, homeopathy, past life regression, and soul retrieval. She believed in the power of yoga, astrology, tarot, and craniosacral therapy. Each belief replaced the one before. When she moved on to a new belief—soul retrieval for instance—her fervor for the previous belief dimmed and gradually faded out of the framework of her life. This search lasted until she died. She had an entourage of women her age who were looking for health, meaning, a sense of well-being, power, purpose, or reassurance. She was always searching, scouring—for something we couldn't give her.

I was a teenager when she was at the height of her self-searching. The things that glowed bright and holy for her never did for me. But I learned from her that belief was a way of exploring the world. Belief brought you to the edges of what might be, rather than keeping you safe in the insular *is*. It was an act of courage to believe, she thought. Lucas thought so, too.

No wonder Lucas spent so much time trying to bring him back to us. Lucas began turning lights on for Baby B when we were still tiny. Three years old. Four years old. He left a night-light on in the hallway in case Baby B came back in the night. Then he started leaving the bathroom light on. Then the hallway light, the kitchen light, the closet light.

"We can't sleep when the lights are on," my parents told him.

"How will he find the house in the dark?" Lucas asked.

"He doesn't need to see," my mother said. "It doesn't work like that."

"Do you know that for sure?" he asked, and of course she didn't.

Then he would forget about the lights for a while. A couple years later, the lights would be on again. He'd turn them all on after my parents had gone to bed. Or he'd play music for Baby B. Lucas opened all the windows and blasted Nina Simone—"Here Comes the Sun" and "Mr. Bojangles" because those were the songs Baby B liked. How did Lucas know Baby B liked those songs? Good question. We were ten when he started playing Nina Simone. Always with the windows open, as if Baby B were a bird who might alight on the sill. Always full blast. "He's not deaf, he's *dead*," I used to tell him.

Or he would bake for Baby B. Cinnamon cookies, the spice of them filling the kitchen, drifting out the open windows.

The lighthouse was like the world's tallest candle. Lucas climbed up to be closer to his brother. He climbed to be closer to that light calling him home. He was a sucker for a beacon.

My mother didn't exactly encourage him, but she had her own rituals for remembering Baby B. She lit candles, burned incense. Sang to him on our birthday. The way I saw it, they were complicit. She said she could feel him close by sometimes, and Lucas believed her.

What did I believe? I wasn't sure. When the stranger came, we were twenty-eight years old. We'd been orphans for almost ten years. We'd been happy, but we'd been lonely. We'd both longed for more.

Cole came to the booth at lunchtime. He leaned his elbows on the counter. I made a mental list of what I saw: jaw stubble, Adam's apple, bitten fingernails, crease between his eyes from squinting or from worry.

"Maybe this goes without saying," I said, "but given the turn of events, I think we better keep things—friendly—between us."

"Oh, I see," he said. "Very disappointing."

"I'm sure you'll survive the disappointment."

"We'll see."

"And I'm sorry about Lucas—"

"I like Lucas."

"I just mean all this stuff about Baby B."

He shrugged. "I don't know. I'm intrigued."

"That's good, because I have a favor to ask you."

"Now I'm really intrigued."

"He's just so happy," I said. "I mean the happiest I've seen him in…well, maybe ever. I'm asking you to—go along—just for a little while."

"You want me to pretend I'm Baby B?"

"No! I know that's crazy. But maybe you could *not* mention to Lucas just how crazy it is."

"And you think this is good for him?"

"It's not good for him to sulk around at home day in and day out, that's for sure. I mean, if you'd seen him before—"

With one finger, Cole touched the top of my hand. "Stop," he said. His fingertip was hot, burned a little spot on the skin of my hand. I felt strangely close to him, as if we'd been through something big together—me, and Cole, and Lucas, too—an adventure, a trial. "I've already told Lucas I'm coming for dinner," Cole said. "I'll see you, too."

"Well, thank you," I said. "I mean, this will mean a lot to Lucas."

After the four o'clock ferry left for the cape, I walked home along the beach. This was the time of year when afternoon lasted all evening. The sun was still warm, and I cast a long shadow on the sand. Those moments on the beach as I walked home always seemed to me bright and angular, moments of intense order and symmetry. In front of our house, I stopped with my feet in the warm sand, picturing what I might find inside—Cole, Lucas, conversation, laughter, the opposite of loneliness. Who was this man, who swept in like an intimate storm, changing the atmosphere of our home? How could a stranger bring about this kind of sea change?

They were in the living room watching football. This was remarkable since Lucas had never watched football in his life. When Dad had thrown us a football, we'd studied it as if it were a bird with its wings pulled in tight against its wobbling body. "Catch it!" Dad had yelled. "Why are you just looking at it?"

Now Cole said, "He's big but fast. That's what people don't realize. They're worried because he's a rookie, but he has the arm that's going to win us the Super Bowl. I have a premonition about this."

"Hi, Lyd," Lucas said. "We're watching the game."

Cole said what sounded like "giant eagles" and looked up at me as if I'd know what that meant.

"This is our team now," Lucas said.

"Preseason," Cole said. "Watch this. Oh man, he threw that ball away."

"You mean it's Cole's team?"

"Well, we didn't have a team," Lucas said.

"I didn't know we needed a team."

"Everyone needs a team," Cole said. "Believe me, you won't be sorry. These boys are good. And this is their year. They can't lose."

They leaned forward in one synchronized motion. I was struck by the ease between them. Lucas was smiling, his shoulders relaxed. Carefree, happy.

I imagined for one minute that my mother was here, and my father, too, that this stranger really was Colin. That he'd come home from his life somewhere else—New York City, London, Tokyo—for a family vacation. I imagined us all standing together in one room, everyone drinking beer from cans, toasting each other. I yearned for that family that didn't exist anymore, that had never existed.

I wandered out to the dock and sat on the end with my feet hanging over and watched the movements of the water. A school of fish swam by, embroidering the surface. The sun turned orange and slipped lower. The objects around me took on a bright-edged insistence, the old splintered boards of the dock each separate and unique, the white sails in the bay popping out from the background.

I heard the screen door and turned to see Lucas coming toward me.

"Cole wants ice cream," he said.

"We haven't had dinner yet."

Cole strode out the back door. "I like ice cream after a game," he called to me. Lucas hurried after him.

"We haven't had dinner," I said again, but they were going, and I jumped up and followed them.

We sat on a bench down by the ferry landing and looked out at the lights of Martha's Vineyard. The late ferry would be coming in at nine. I knew that boat as if it were my own body, I'd been watching its comings and goings for so many years.

"I'm going to look," Lucas said.

"Good luck," I told him.

Cole and I licked ice-cream cones and watched Lucas crouch by the water and poke the sand with a stick, searching for phosphorescence.

"We couldn't get a better night if we ordered it from a catalog," Cole said. He leaned back and surveyed the water. I noted again the way he looked at everything with an expression of ownership—as if it were already his.

"I don't really order my nights from catalogs," he said. "That's a good way to get the wrong size. No, the way I do it, I go to the store, I try a bunch on, see what fits, what feels right, then put it on the credit card."

"Mine are hand-me-downs," I said.

"Really? Who had them first?"

"My mom. Lucas. Baby B. I don't know. I don't even know why I said that."

Cole licked the drips around the bottom of his scoop of ice cream, put the rest of the cone in his mouth. "I could eat another one," he said. "I'm basically always hungry."

I looked at him through the dusky light and felt a familiar feeling rise up. A desire for something out of reach, something in the past, or the future, something lost to time, or not meant for me.

"You know," I said, "all this will probably make things harder for Lucas when you leave."

"I'm not planning to leave anytime soon."

"Just to be clear, *I* don't believe you're the reincarnation of my dead brother."

"You say *believe* like it's a filthy thing. Don't you believe in anything?"

What did I believe? I didn't believe he was Baby B, but I did see something almost familiar in him, one small thing that made even a stranger recognizable. Cole also longed for hidden things to rise to the surface, wanted something more, something deeper, something buried. I remembered the feeling of his hands on my wrists, how I'd opened my eyes to find him examining me, as if he were trying to find someone, something.

Then Lucas was there, his hands full of sand, and when he moved his fingers, the luminous phytoplankton lit up like stars, and then went dull and dead. The water was so dark behind him, a thick green-black, the air chilly. The air held something else that was harder to describe, something I couldn't see or hear or touch. Something that emanated from Cole, light, or frequency, or pheromones. Whatever it was, I recognized it, and it recognized me.

5

I sat at the bar at Jack's until Eddie abandoned his bouncer stool and sat down beside me.

"So, Lyd."

"So, Ed."

"I saw you tonight," he said. "With this new guy." He spun around on the stool and surveyed the bar. The same CD was playing that was always playing in Jack's. It belonged to the bartender, Eliot Moniz. A girlfriend had made it for him years ago, and he kept listening to it, long after she broke up with him and moved off the island. It was all Van Morrison and Tom Waits, sad, romantic songs. I'd begun to associate those voices with the smells and tastes of the bar, the salty scent that permeated the air of fish, both fried and fresh, the thick, heady stench of spilled beer. "I guess that's how it's going to be. That's the end of us." He stared morosely at the bar where something had spilled earlier, leaving a long, dark streak.

"I already ended things between us," I reminded him.

"I'm trying to be happy for you," he said. "This guy looks nice enough."

"I hope he is."

Ed looked surprised. "You hope so? Don't you know whether he's nice or not? If the guy's not nice to you, Lyd, I can help you out."

"It's not like that."

"If I'm being honest, I got a weird feeling when I saw him," Eddie said. "I thought something might be a little off. You don't have to take shit from him or anyone. You want me to talk to him?"

"It's nothing serious. I'm not fucking him," I said. "Or dating him, or whatever people do."

He looked relieved. "Everyone's been saying you met him on the internet," Eddie said.

"I don't even know him, Ed. He just showed up. Honestly. He and Lucas think they know each other from a past life."

"That sounds like a load of bullcrap."

"It's more complicated than that," I said.

"What makes it so complicated?"

"Lucas is crazy about him. And you know Lucas. He doesn't usually warm up to people." Imagine you had a brother like mine, I wanted to say, a brother who liked imaginary people best, who was always longing for some impossible happiness, a brother who suddenly grasped on to something, some*one*, with ease and joy. The way he was with Cole. Laughing and talking. I'd never seen this before. Not with anyone. Not in all these years.

"You know about my brother Colin?"

"Only that he passed away when he was a few months old."

"Weeks old," I said.

"Oh man," Eddie said. "Poor little guy."

"But for Lucas he was always really present. Even years later. I know that sounds crazy. Lucas thinks this guy is *Colin*, you know, reborn."

Eddie whistled.

"I know," I said. "It sounds so wild. But listen, Eddie, you don't need to worry about me. This isn't your problem."

"Please," he said. "Your problems are my problems."

"No," I said. "I've been trying to tell you. They're not anymore, okay?"

"You know what I'm going to do?" Eddie said. "I'm going to stop by and see you and Lucas. Just to show my face. I haven't been over in a while."

I couldn't remember Eddie *ever* stopping by to see us— we tended to see each other in the storeroom of Jack's after hours, in the stacks at the library, the Biography section where no one ever went, or—once—in the bathroom at the drugstore. I knew by offering to keep an eye on Cole, Eddie was being overprotective, jealous even, but Cole was, after all, a stranger, and I wanted him to think there was someone looking out for us.

"Anytime," I said to Eddie. I touched his big hand just to feel something real, and warm, and safe.

He went back out to the bouncer stool, and I waited for Lucas and Cole, who had gone home to eat dinner, while I'd come straight to Jack's, not hungry. At this time of year, when the rest of the island restaurants were full of tourists, Jack's was often a haven for islanders. A few locals sat at the bar: an old fisherman named Sebastian, who'd sat at that barstool every night for as long as I could remember; a couple named Stephan and Steph, who I'd gone to school with. They'd been in love forever, since childhood, or maybe before. They sat there at the other end of the bar, and Steph put both arms around Stephan's neck, and they looked like they were on their first date, so much in their own world. I couldn't imagine being that in love for so many years. What would that feel like? Weren't they exhausted?

The whole place was full of people I recognized, the people I'd gone to school with, the people who took care of the island, serving its food, and cleaning its rooms, and patching its roads, and sweeping its sidewalks. They sat at big tables with barrels for seats and ordered pitchers of beer and laughed together.

"I haven't seen you in here in a while," Eliot, the bartender, said to me. He nodded at my empty glass. "But I guess you needed a night out."

"Lucas is meeting me here," I said.

"Lucas, your brother?" Eliot looked incredulous.

When the door of the bar next opened—I heard the jingle of bells like the tinkling of shells in the waves—Lucas and Cole walked in, the door swinging shut behind them. Everyone looked up, surprised. Lucas didn't often go out in public, not since we were in school, and even then it was pretty touch and go. He'd even been homeschooled for a while. When we had the funeral for my mom, he'd hid in the woods the whole time.

"There's Lydia," I heard Lucas say.

He cupped one hand around his eye, a kind of half blinder, and made his way across the room. He sat on one side of me, and Cole on the other. Lucas stared at the floor.

"What would you like?" Eliot asked Lucas from behind the bar, and Lucas looked up, startled by the question.

"I'm just going to bring you a really good beer," Eliot said.

"You were right," Cole said to Lucas. "This is a great bar."

Eliot brought their beers and Lucas and Cole took long sips.

"It is a great bar," Lucas said. He looked at me and smiled, and I felt inexpressibly happy. I felt the kind of happiness that goes along with fragile things, little shells, dried flowers, beautiful in part *because* they're fragile. I felt the weight of that complicated feeling, as if I were holding gorgeous, crushable things in my hand.

Beside me, Lucas lifted the beer to his mouth, an unselfconscious action, like any other man, like someone else's brother. I took a long sip from my drink and felt it burn my mouth, my throat.

I pointed out Steph and Stephan, and told Cole about how they'd been in love as long as we could remember, since third grade, second grade. Cole introduced himself to Eliot. Lucas drank a second beer and laughed when Cole pretended he could read the scratches in the wooden floor like hieroglyphics. The rest of the bar lost interest in Lucas pretty soon and went back to their own stories over their own tumblers.

Later, drunk, we walked Cole back to the Island Inn. Lucas was chatty, nostalgic. He remembered Eddie finding Lucas's lost harmonica in second grade. He remembered when Eliot's mother drove her car into Hiram's Bounty, the grocery store, right through the big glass door. He remembered eating at the Island Inn restaurant with our parents, the waitress bringing him maraschino cherries in a cup. I listened to Lucas, to the waves rolling onto the sand. I wanted Lucas to talk forever. I wanted to stay for a long, long time in that moment on the beach, with the warm air and the rhythmic shushing of the waves.

We stopped before we got to the inn, near Tame Jaw Beach, and I watched the two men walk toward the water. The air was humid, shimmering with moisture, and I was still drunk and thinking about the past. "You know what I don't understand," I said. "What about the dreams?"

"What dreams?" Lucas turned toward me.

"The dreams about Colin. We know exactly what he looked like. And it wasn't anything like—"

In every dream, his hair and complexion had been dark, almost oily, and his eyes amber like Lucas's. He had a smooth dark head and a sleek nose. The whites of his eyes glowed, as if he had to light his own way through our dreams. I held out my arms for a moment, as if I could see him away across the water.

Lucas shook his head. "In your dreams Baby B looked the way he would have looked if he'd grown up with us. But after he died, he was born in a different place, to a different family. Cole doesn't look like us. He doesn't share our DNA."

"Then how is he Baby B?"

"Soul," Lucas said.

My mom had believed pieces of the soul could splinter off over time. You didn't notice it happening, but from that point on you were—in small ways—crippled, going through life without the benefits of a whole, intact soul. A shaman could lead you back on the path of your life, looking for the missing parts.

My mother had found her missing part in a dressing room in Saks Fifth Avenue. Her soul was seven years old and had been in the store trying on hats for fifty years.

Lucas went to the very edge of the water, and lifted his shirt over his head, let his jeans fall to the ground. Naked, he walked into the water, vanished. Cole and I sat down on the sand, watching the dark surface, waiting for Lucas to reappear.

It was almost midnight, a clumsy swollen quarter moon overhead.

"Have you moved to room eleven?" I asked.

"Not yet. But I put in a request. The clerk looked horrified."

"You don't seem like someone who's afraid of ghosts."

"Depends on the ghosts, I guess."

Far out in the water, I saw Lucas's head. Wind picked up, ruffled the surface.

I watched the spot that was Lucas, small and unremarkable. Could have been a seal or a rock.

"All my life I've had dreams," Cole said. "About certain places. About this place."

I felt suddenly sober, the celestial feeling of scotch in my bloodstream dissolving into a kind of foggy humidity. "You dream about the island?" I asked.

"And about certain people," he said.

"What people?"

Lucas was swimming to shore, he was standing in the shallow water. He was moving toward us, naked, beautiful, sea-creature, moon-creature.

"Shit!" he said. "Cold!"

"What people?" I asked again.

Lucas pulled his clothes on, shivering, exhilarated. He was grinning. He looked like he might take off flying, unfold surprise wings and lift into the darkness.

Cole laughed. He turned to me. "Ignore me," he said. "I'm drunk. I'm drunk and nostalgic. I'm having déjà vu." He touched my arm, and I felt warmth radiating from that spot, star, starfish, sunspot, gold.

6

When I woke in the morning the house was empty. I felt haunted by a dream, something that lurked at the edge of my memory just out of reach. Lucas's bed was a tangle of sheets. There was a note for me on the kitchen table in Cole's unfamiliar handwriting. *We have gone together to seek our fortunes,* it said. *Meet here for lunch?* I went to work, but after the noon boat had come and gone, I felt restless. I'd thought Cole would stop by the booth. I'd looked for him. I wanted to see him. When I left for lunch, I didn't even tell Jim Cardoza I was going.

From the beach, our house looked shabby: the missing shingles we hadn't bothered to replace in the roof, the faded paint. I wondered how it looked to Cole. Where was Cole, and what had he done all day while we were at work? Was he at the inn, or was he here in the house waiting for us? I pictured him opening the doors of our house; I imagined his fingers touching the old pages of our books; I saw him looking into all our mirrors.

I stood in the doorway of my home. "Hello?" I said. The house was quiet and sunny, dust suspended in light coming in the living room windows. I crept upstairs and peeked in all the bedrooms.

From my bedroom window, I could see the lawn and the dock and the bay. And I could also see Cole, who was sitting cross-legged at the end of the dock.

He was centered on the dock, his back straight and tall, one hand on the back of his neck. My heart gave a strange small jump, because for a moment he reminded me of my mother. This was the place my mother used to go to meditate, and this was exactly the way she sat, with one hand on her neck. I remembered her fingers in her hair. I touched the window screen. I watched him for a long time, but he didn't move. He was like my mother in that way, too—a heavy, unmovable stone with Lucas and me dancing around her in the current.

Downstairs, I let the kitchen door slam so he would know I was approaching.

His eyes were closed, his face lustrous from sweat. His body was not a body used to being in the sun. I got a sudden flash of Cole behind a desk, unhappy, bored, rolling from place to place on his office chair, his hands full of blindingly white paper. Here he was different, peaceful.

"Meditating?" I asked.

"You could call it that." He tilted his face toward me, his eyes squinted against the afternoon sun.

"Why do you sit like that?"

"Like what?"

"With your hand on your neck."

He dropped his hand and turned toward me completely. "I don't know," he said. "I guess because it's comfortable. Why do you ask?"

"It's how my mother used to sit," I said.

He raised his eyebrows. "Your mother," he said. "Do I look like her?"

"No, not at all. She was blonde. You just—remind me of her sometimes. Or remind me of someone."

"You remind me of someone, too," he said.

"Who?"

"I don't know," he said. "Someone from a dream."

I sat, letting my feet hang over the edge of the dock. Down below eel grass waved and silversides darted past. Barnacles covered the legs of the dock like gooseflesh. Cole stretched out on his back beside me. His ribs rose like the arches of some city. I didn't know what to say to him. I reminded him of someone from a dream? What did that mean? I would have laughed a week ago, but now I didn't feel like laughing. Instead I changed the subject.

"What did you and Lucas do this morning anyway?"

Cole pushed himself up on one elbow and shielded his eyes from the sun so he could look at me. "Lucas took me clamming. Dinner will be a feast."

I could feel the heat radiating off his body as if his skin were saturated with sunlight. I could *see* light shimmering on him. I looked away.

The water was blue-black, the little red houseboat sweet and forlorn by itself out there. When we were little, a family had vacationed in it. There were two kids our age, a sister and a brother, and we could see them from the dock or the porch, hanging out their towels and swimsuits on the railing, sitting in little folding chairs in the sun. The parents seemed silent and detached. But we thought we would like the kids. The boy wore a straw hat all the time, even in the rain. The girl had short hair like Peter Pan. I thought about swimming out to meet them, but I was too shy.

And then—the sister died. She drowned. Not here, but off Block Island at the end of one summer. The family came back the following summer, but it was different. They were too sad, even from a distance we could see that. The boy spent hours alone on the deck of the houseboat staring at the water, the horizon, the shore. That was the last we'd seen of them. The boat had been empty ever since.

I shivered.

"Someone walking over your grave?" Cole said.

"I'm still alive."

"The place where your grave will be. Haven't you ever heard that?"

"Where did you say you live?" I asked. "New York?"

He paused for a moment. "Yes," he said. "But I gave up my apartment there. There was no reason to stay."

"So you're just planning to start over...here?"

"I don't know," he said. "Maybe. It depends."

"Won't you miss city life?"

He gave a dry laugh. "Not really. I'll miss the coffee at my favorite diner. What's worth missing? Stuff? No, just people."

"That's true, I guess." But I was thinking of the college applications hidden in the pantry. There were things to miss that weren't people, and weren't stuff. Experiences. Dreams for ourselves. There were things I missed, was missing every day.

I looked over at him. The skin of his stomach was so taut, it folded when he sat, like a hem. My chest tightened into a tough twist of sorrow that I didn't quite understand, a long-ing for the past, the future, a longing for him in some com-plicated way I didn't like at all.

"You don't need to be afraid," he said.

"I'm not afraid."

"I can see your heart beating."

I clapped my hands over my chest. "I'm not afraid."

I felt an electric sensation coursing through me, as if I'd swallowed ocean water bright with bioluminescence. I could feel those water-stars gliding up and down the avenues of my body.

All evening, I felt electrified, my nerves raw. I cut my finger chopping vegetables for dinner. I put my finger in my mouth and the taste of the blood reminded me of rocks pulled out of the sea. I was transported to a time when my young self—five? six?—lifted rocks into the sunlight, smooth or slick with green growing things, and I tasted the salt and greenness. The act of recollection flooded me with pleasure. The sorting and cataloging of those old thoughts, collecting again, *recollecting*. Rocks, saltwater, the starburst of light on the surface of the water.

But then the door from the living room opened suddenly, and I knocked over a glass of water.

"What's wrong with you?" Lucas said.

"I cut myself." I held up my finger.

"I'll get a bandage."

He carefully wrapped a too-big Band-Aid around my fin-ger and then mopped up the spilled water.

Cole entered the room, and my chest tightened and relaxed and tightened again, a bird trying out its wings. He looked at us, the spilled water, and the cut finger.

"Is everything okay?" he asked.

"It's fine," Lucas said. "Just Lydia being Lydia."

"Hello, hello!" Eddie didn't bother to knock, just stuck his head inside the kitchen door. Behind him, his wife, Kim, was holding a jean jacket closed at her throat, though the night wasn't cold. I beckoned them in and dried my hands on a dishcloth.

"Hi," I said. "You're here. I didn't think you were really going to—"

"We wanted to come," Kim said. I was surprised that Kim had come along, and I tried to read her face. Was she just looking for a chance to observe Eddie and me together? But no, her expression was inquisitive but not suspicious as she glanced around the kitchen. Islanders were innately wary of newcomers, and Cole had burst so suddenly into our lives, I didn't blame her for being curious.

"I haven't been over here since—" Eddie broke off.

Since when? I wondered. Since Eddie and some other kids from middle school came over to do yard work, a way to offer condolences when my father died? I had watched from an upstairs window while they raked leaves into piles, too scared, too sad, too shy to go down.

"Where is he?" Eddie said.

"Cole? He's in the living room, but please don't—"

Eddie walked through the swinging door, with Kim scurrying behind. Cole was looking through the *New Yorker*. Lucas was bent over the table in the corner where he kept material for making elaborate little faux-insects for fishing. Cole put down his magazine and looked at Eddie in a friendly way.

"This is Eddie," I said. "And Kim. Sit down, you guys."

"I will do that, Lydia. Thank you so much," Eddie said. He turned to Cole. "So I hear you've been reincarnated from these guys' dead brother."

Cole laughed, glanced at me, at Lucas. "That's one way to put it."

"I have to tell you, my friend," Eddie said, "I'm suspicious of all this."

"I don't blame you," Cole said. "It sounds wild, doesn't it?"

"It sounds," Eddie said, "like you're trying to pull the wool over somebody's eyes."

Lucas gave me a terrible look.

"Eddie, you've got it wrong," I said.

Cole held up his hand. "I think Ed and I should talk privately. Would you all excuse us? Just for a moment."

"It's okay, Lyd," Eddie said.

What were they going to do? I wondered. Fight? Lucas scooted out of the room, and Kim and I followed him into the kitchen.

"They're going to walk out here in a few minutes best friends," Kim said. "He just has that way with people."

I felt the familiar feeling Kim always evoked in me. I hated her for marrying Eddie. But I also didn't want to hurt her, and felt guilt and regret and resentment squeezing the walls of my throat. "Want some wine while we wait?" I asked.

I found a bottle in the pantry and Kim and I sat at the table drinking out of mason jars. We used to have wineglasses, but they broke over the years, and we never replaced them.

"Cheers," I said to Kim, holding up my jar. She laughed. She was a laugher. She finished every sentence with a laugh, whether it was funny or not. She made everyone happy.

Lucas leaned on the counter, too shy to sit down next to

Kim, too interested in what was happening behind the living room door to leave the room altogether. We heard their voices, but not what they were saying. A word or two floated at us, but never enough to make meaning.

"Why would you tell him?" Lucas asked after a while. Kim looked at me with interest, but I didn't answer.

They were in there for half a bottle of wine. I microwaved some popcorn and we were snacking on that when they appeared through the swinging door.

"Sorry I can't stay longer, Lydia," Eddie said. "I promised I'd get back to the bar before nine." He turned to Cole.

"Glad to have had this talk," Cole said.

"Likewise," Eddie said, and they shook hands.

"Okay," I said. "I'll walk you guys out."

I stood with Eddie and Kim outside in the dark and the wind. The night had grown chilly after all. I pulled my hands into the sleeves of my sweatshirt.

"What was that little one-on-one about?" I said.

Eddie shrugged. "I just didn't want him to think you were all alone," he said. "And I'm glad I came over. Because, Lyd, something's not right."

"What's that supposed to mean?"

"For one thing, he wouldn't say a word about where he came from. He just said he's looking for family."

"What's wrong with that?"

"Nothing on the surface, but it's what's under the surface that worries me."

"I think you're worrying for nothing."

"There was another very weird thing, Lyd. We were chit-chatting. I told him he had to try all the island cuisine while he's here, you know just trying to be friendly. And I started listing my favorite places. And then—I don't even know why I said it—I told him he should try the Quahog Pit."

"The Pit? They closed ten years ago."

"Yeah, but I told him he couldn't miss it. And he said, *Just look for the giant quahog, right?*"

"That sign's been down for ages," Kim said.

"Righto," Eddie said. "So how did he know about it?"

"Was he joking?" I said. "Like just guessing that someplace called the Quahog Pit would have a giant quahog out front?"

"It didn't sound like he was joking. Or guessing. It seemed like he knew the place."

"Well, that doesn't make any sense. Unless Lucas told him about it."

"Can I ask you a question…?" Eddie hesitated. "I don't want to offend you or anything. This isn't something I would have thought of normally, but Kim and I were talking last night—"

"We were," she said.

"About Lucas, and if you guys ever, you know, had him looked at."

I felt instantly deflated. "You're wondering if he's crazy?"

"No, shut up. I wouldn't say that. I just know he has some challenges…"

"There's a whole history," I said, a little sharply. "We have had him *looked at*, if you really want to know."

"I didn't mean to say it like that," he said.

"Things just come out wrong for Eddie," Kim said. "It happens all the time."

"It's just anxiety," I said. "Like in social situations. The same thing a million other people have. For Lucas it's just really intense. My mom—well, you knew my mom—she was adamantly against medication of any kind. My dad was always pushing to get, you know, a psychiatrist to help him. With his shyness. Do you remember my dad?"

"Of course. Who didn't love your dad?"

I looked at him. "You loved my dad?" I said. "How did you even know him?"

"You're kidding, right? He was our Scout leader."

I looked at him blankly.

"Boy Scouts?" he said.

"My dad?" I said.

"For like three years. The whole troop loved him."

"How did I not know this?"

He shrugged. "Well, it was for boys, so you wouldn't have been there. And Lucas never wanted to do—"

"No, he wouldn't have."

"Don't you remember at his funeral?" Eddie said. "We were all there."

"I thought you were just being neighborly or something."

"I cried," he said. "He was the first person I knew who died."

"And then my mom," I said.

"Oh, by then a bunch of other people had died," Kim said. "Remember Mrs. Ainsley? And a couple grandparents had already gone. And that fourth grader who had leukemia?"

I nodded.

"The point is," Eddie said, "Kim reads all those medical magazines. She says there are basically drugs for everything and anything now."

She nodded solemnly. "There *are*."

"All that stuff with the lighthouse," Eddie said.

"Listen," I said. "I'm not going to *drug* my brother. There hasn't been any stuff with the lighthouse for years. He's, you

know, quirky, yes. But he doesn't need drugs. And there's
nothing to worry about with Cole. You're just—"

I was going to say *jealous*. But I stopped myself in time. I
glanced at Kim, and she nodded at me, her eyes big and trust-
ing. Poor Kim. What was wrong with me? I immediately remembered Eddie's hands on my hips, and felt my neck go hot.

"He says he's trying to start over," I said, looking away
from both of them.

Eddie shook his head. "Be careful, Lyd. That's all I'm saying. You don't know anything about him."

The wind blew a branch against the back of the house over
and over. A few pale clouds scuttled across the dark sky. The
evening felt full of secret things, skunks, and fireflies, and
sudden gusts.

"I'm always careful," I said, a little stiff.

"Are you mad at me?" Eddie asked.

I was. Or mad at myself. Or at Kim. I knew there was
something strange about Cole—the way he said he recognized
the island, what he said about knowing me from a dream.
Maybe he was caught up in Lucas's fairy tale—and that was
my fault. I'd asked him to play along. But I wasn't scared, and
I didn't want Eddie giving me advice about Cole, or Lucas,
or anything else.

Cole was at the kitchen table when I slipped back inside. I
stood with my back against the door, wondering if he'd heard
us talking. "I like that guy," he said.

"Everyone likes Eddie."

I sat down, he slid a mason jar toward me, and I raised it
to my mouth and drank. When I set it down, Cole was already reaching for the bottle to refill. The wine fell into the
jar in a bright stream, and Cole tipped the bottle so the last

drops could rain down, and the action was like something we'd memorized long ago. I put the jar on the table and ran my finger around the rim, faster and faster.

"Where's Lucas?" I said.

"I don't know." Cole looked once around the room as if Lucas might have been there the whole time without his having realized it. "He'll turn up if he wants to. Meanwhile, tell me about Ed Frank."

I laughed. I felt my anger disappearing. I forgot about the Quahog Pit. I guess I liked his attention. When was the last time anyone had said to me, "So tell me about...?"

"I used to be in love with him, if you must know. When I was twelve. And thirteen and fourteen and fifteen."

He leaned back in his chair, waiting for me to go on.

"He was just a big deal in high school. Like huge laugh, huge personality. And, I don't know, he always seemed kind of grown up, even when he was a kid. Like he always asked about my mother, the way adults do. He would tell these really dirty jokes and then look abashed when he realized there were girls listening. Like really filthy jokes."

The truth was I'd longed to be the one to make him laugh. I used to imagine his big hands touching my face. Kissing him under a streetlight. Or in front of a fireplace. I imagined kissing him so often and so vividly I couldn't actually stand to be near him. He would definitely know what I had been thinking. That love, which I kept to myself for as long as possible, was the longest love of my life.

By the time we graduated I assumed nothing could happen between Eddie and me. Then a few years years later he started going out with Kim, who was seventeen and pretty, with a long ponytail and the kind of smooth, round features no one remembers. She laughed at everything he said. Of course he loved her. Of course he married her.

But maybe that explains why it was so easy to be with him years later—old loves don't die easy. But now—well, it didn't feel at all the way I'd imagined.

"He never knew how I felt, and please don't tell him," I said to Cole. "That would be incredibly awkward now."

"I'm sure Kim wouldn't like to hear it. But I don't think he would mind," Cole said. He looked at me. "I would want to know—if it were me you loved. I never would have let you go to begin with. If you were mine."

We sat in silence for a long moment that gradually became more and more uncomfortable, until I stood, suddenly tongue-tied.

"That's my cue," Cole said, and stood up as well. "Sweet dreams," he said. He slipped out the kitchen door. From the window I watched the dark shadow that was him moving away from me along the beach.

7

I went away to college when I was seventeen. Everyone forgets that. They think I'm one of the islanders who never left, and sometimes I think of myself that way, too. But I had almost an entire semester in Providence before I came back to the island.

I took four classes. Intro to psychology, intro to Shakespeare, library research, and a freshman seminar about modernism. I had notebooks labeled with the name of each class, and very little in life had given me as much joy as all that blank paper.

I liked school. I liked my professors. I liked my roommate, who struck me as supernaturally uncomplicated. She was sleepy when it was time to sleep, she woke up when it was time to wake up, and she was hungry when it was time to eat. When it was chilly she said, "I'm chilly," and put on a sweater.

I liked campus, all the old brick buildings with their domed windows and iron gates. The buildings I was used to on Wolf Island felt like extensions of the island itself, gray and brown wooden things, driftwood and bone. But in Providence the buildings were massive red and gray boxes, with pretty roofs and orderly windows.

Mostly I liked the town itself, with its brick sidewalks, its galleries and coffee shops. There was a footbridge I walked over almost every day so I could look down into the Providence River and think about how it ran into Narragansett Bay and then opened into the ocean.

One night in September I stumbled upon a tradition I hadn't known about before. The river, I found, was on fire. At least one hundred tiny bonfires were blazing on the river itself, lit by men and women in gondolas with long torches who floated silently past, leaving fire in their wakes. Water fire. I felt the shock of it deep in my system, the beauty of the flame and the cool water reflecting it. I'd never felt a contradiction so viscerally before.

I was only seventeen. Everything was new to me, and not just the buildings and the river and the classes. The sensations were new. The feeling of being alone in the world. I missed my mother, and I missed Lucas, but even missing them was a good feeling, because unlike missing Baby B or my dad, I would see them again, at Thanksgiving.

But when I'd been at school for almost six weeks, my mom called to tell me that Lucas was on top of the lighthouse.

"Again?" I said.

I was alone in my room, Amanda having gone to the library before dinner. I was in my bed, that narrow dormitory bed that I already loved. This was only the first of many rooms I was going to sleep in, I felt sure. I meant to see the world. And more than see it. Know it. Fall asleep in rooms and wake up in rooms and smell their scents and notice how light illuminated those rooms.

Light fell in stiff lines through the venetian blinds of my dorm room, deep gold afternoon light, the light of October at four in the afternoon. It put stripes on the wall across from me, the warm orange stripes of a tiger cat, and I'd been watching the stripes lengthen and widen all afternoon as the sun sank swiftly. Already I knew this room intimately. It smelled of peppermint tea, and coconut oil, and pencil shavings.

"He's been up there for hours," my mother said.

"He's up there now?"

"And the police got involved, so he's scared to come down."

"Call them off," I said. "He'll come down when it's dark."

She sighed. Just hearing her voice on the phone transported me from my dorm room back to the rooms I'd known best and longest. I could smell my mother's sandalwood oil, which she dabbed on her skin and threw in with her laundry. The house's perfume of mildew and wood.

"Now it's a breaking-and-entering issue," she said. "I can't call them off, my friend. We'll be lucky if they don't arrest him."

"I don't know why you're calling me," I said. "I'm trying to write a paper, and it's due tomorrow. And I still have to go to dinner."

"Forgive me for thinking you'd want to know."

We were both quiet, and I listened to her breathing. Her posture—I could see it clearly—would be perfect yoga posture. She was a tall woman to begin with—a full inch taller than my father, who himself was tall. Her yoga practice seemed to increase her height, or the impression of height, a full inch or more. She towered. When she sat, she rose from the seat like a pillar. When she stood, she reached the sky, an oak tree, a mountain. Her spine was the envy of middle-aged yogis everywhere.

"I'm not coming home," I said.

"I wasn't asking you to."

"I'll be home at Thanksgiving. He can stay up there until Thanksgiving if he wants to be stubborn. I'm not coming now."

"You know it's not stubbornness. And I wasn't suggesting you come home," she said again. But of course, that was exactly what she was suggesting. She was a woman who fiercely defended her independence while handing you her shopping bags to carry. She was used to being taken care of—first by her big family with four older brothers, then by my father, then by Lucas and me, but she told the world a different story and expected us to corroborate.

I felt a surge of anger, which seemed to gallop in alongside my own growing sense of independence. If she was going to pretend to be so independent, so capable on her own, then I certainly wasn't going to race to bail her out.

"You'll just have to figure it out yourself," I said. "I have to go."

Lucas did come down. Fell down, actually, some time in the night when I was sleeping, or lying awake in my dorm room, which felt smaller after that conversation. Lucas broke his wrist when he fell, but saved himself from being arrested since the police on the scene felt guilty about his injury. They drove him to the clinic and waited for him while Dr. Lyle set the bone. Then they drove him home, and literally, I'm not making this up, they gave him a lollipop.

That fall at Brown when Lucas was in trouble and I didn't come home, that was the first time I took a stand against my mother. That was my rebellion. It's funny to think about it now, my arrogance. As if I were somehow stronger than the forces that pull us together in this life. As if I could make a plan, a guess, a reasonable estimate of what life would hold for me.

Late that night, the night I hung up the phone on my mother, I went to the river. The river wasn't on fire, but it was still beautiful, aglow with the reflection of the city's streetlamps and headlights and lit windows. I walked over the footbridge and then back again. I touched the railing of the bridge, felt the heat from the day.

I sensed someone beside me, and turned uneasily—I was still young, and this was a city and totally new to me. The girl standing there was someone I recognized only slightly. She sat behind me in one of my classes; I'd noticed in passing her thick plastic glasses. She was pudgy, doughy in the way some little girls are, and she wore her hair in pigtails, with thick overgrown bangs hiding her forehead. She was my age, I knew, but she looked like a little girl in every way except one. She had a small scar like a tiny star on her cheek, and this gave her a sophisticated look, as though it were a beauty mark. I took all this in, the way I took everything in, saving it all for some later moment when I'd have time to analyze and make meaning out of what I'd seen.

"You want to go in?" she said, nodding at the river.

"No," I said.

"Come on. Let's get closer."

We crossed the bridge and scrambled down its edge and made our way through the thick growth of jewelweed and knotweed growing there. We scrambled to the very edge of the water, and stood together looking at the cold reflections of the city.

"I don't think we better," I said finally. "I don't think it's supposed to be very clean."

We heard the sound of the river lapping against its shore. We heard the city all around us, the gentle roar of cars.

"If we don't go in, we might regret it when we're old," she said.

I turned and looked at her. This thought appealed to me in a profound way. Even as a child I thought about the past with an intensity that bordered on brooding, obsessively categorizing memories in order to hold on to them for as long as possible—forever I hoped. And because I was seventeen, I thought a lot about the future, too, what it might hold for me, who I would be then, in the unknown places of my life. But to combine the past and future like that, to imagine the present moment as I might *remember* it in the future, this layering of time, this positioning and repositioning myself in relation to time: it felt like a gift this girl was giving me, and I looked at her with gratitude.

Her name was Mary. We *did* go in the river. In some future world, our future selves smiled and were pleased that we did it, even though the shock of the cold water and the difficulty of exiting a swift current onto slippery, weedy banks made it far more dangerous than we'd expected.

We had stashed our clothes in the brush where we'd gone in, and then drifted swiftly in our underwear far from that spot. When we climbed out, naked except for bras and underwear, cold and shivering and laughing and scared and full of adrenaline, we had to creep along the banks looking for our clothes in dim light. The moon, the water, the lights reflected in the river, all contrasted with the trash along the river, the old fast-food bags, and newspapers, and plastic cups, and the shapes we glimpsed in the brush we thought were homeless men in sleeping bags.

We were so cold when we found our clothes, we couldn't

stop shivering, but even that felt good. The danger of the night felt like something our future selves would approve of. In intro to psychology the next day—that was the class we shared—I sat by Mary. And even this felt new and strange, this making a friend. On the island, we'd all known each other for so long, we were more like some big extended family of cousins, forced to play together, than like friends who'd found each other. But Mary was a friend I'd found, or who had found me. I imagined all the memories my future self would have of Mary and me, our adventures. Maybe we would backpack across Europe together the way my parents had. Maybe we would move into an apartment together when we graduated. We would be maids of honor at each other's weddings, godmothers to each other's babies. Our husbands would be best friends, as would our children.

I could see the future, as clearly as I'd ever seen anything. It was full of love. And it was mine alone, not Lucas's or my mother's. There was a freedom in that thought as sweet and forbidden as the October swim in the Providence River.

When my mother called a few weeks later to tell me she had cancer, I went home right away. I had to this time. I only mourned the one lost semester, the spring, somehow thinking she'd get better fast, that I'd be back next fall.

My mother never mentioned the lighthouse to me again. But she told me again and again that I had to look after Lucas. The sicker she got, the more desperate she sounded. *You take care of him. Don't leave him alone.* Of course I was going to look after Lucas. I wasn't a monster. She got smaller and smaller, her head tiny-looking with its wispy crown of hair. And when she died, like Baby B, she continued to hang around. Lucas said he saw her in the bathroom mirror. The smell of sandalwood sometimes wafted through the house, a ghostly cloud of it. He said he felt her embracing him just as he was falling asleep.

Please stop, I told him. I knew there was no ghostly mother hanging around. There was no one hanging around. The smell of sandalwood was everywhere, but that didn't mean we weren't suddenly and terrifyingly alone, or that our future plans hadn't been obliterated with swift and absolute disregard. When she died and her body was gone, the silence in the house was overwhelming. Whole systems of movement and vibration evaporated. It felt wrong, like the air before a storm, to be without parents.

We were twenty when she died. We had no college education, no way of making money, a house three times too big for us, a mortgage, and a sudden necessity to readjust everything we thought the future held. The only thing I understood clearly was what my responsibility was in regard to Lucas. I could not leave him alone. Never. What kind of sister would do such a thing?

There was no alternative, so I gave up thinking about alternatives. Anyway, I was happy on the island with Lucas. Loving my brother was the biggest feeling I'd ever had. It was a ferocious feeling, almost angry. It was bigger than anything I'd felt at school, I told myself. Who was Mary, a friend I'd had for a few weeks, compared to this relationship between brother and sister? And Lucas wasn't an ordinary brother.

When my mother told me to take care of Lucas, it was because he honestly needed taking care of. Despite his shyness, or because of it, as kids we were always together. He needed me to talk for him. Even with the islanders, he was rigid and reserved. And with new people? He turned pale; he trembled; he broke out in a cold sweat. He could barely breathe. He was afraid of other people. Or afraid of how they made him feel. My parents made him see a psychologist for years—but he never learned to like people. Only me. I was his sister, and his friend. And after Mom died, I was his mother, too.

He was happy that way; at least most of the time. He knew the deserted stretches of beach. He knew the hidden forest paths. He began his job as a landscaper at the Day Estate the summer after we graduated high school, and he'd worked there ever since. The plants and seeds and sod and mulch and leaves and moss and old stones never tried to make conversation.

He wore an old sun hat when he went out, so he could pull it down over his eyes when he passed someone.

That summer, when Cole came to Wolf Island, Lucas and I had been alone in the house for almost ten years, and I'd been looking after him all that time. The desire to leave the island—to go back to college—was usually smothered by another force: the need to take care of him, which was strong and palpable, a physical pressure in my chest. Sometimes when I remember those years together alone, I think: we were happy. Sometimes I think: we were dying of loneliness. With Cole, I felt the arrival of a new force in our lives—a new desire—and I had the strange feeling that we'd spent our whole lives preparing for this change.

Everyone has their own way of dealing with loss. Lucas saw ghosts and went to the lighthouse. I read books and organized drawers. I gave out information, piece by piece. Everyone finds a way to cope with grief. So what if Lucas's way seemed eccentric? It was only music. It was only light. The cinnamon cookies were excellent. *That's his way*, I told myself. *He has his way and I have mine.* What harm could come of it?

8

Cole stayed for three days, four days, five. It felt like a miracle—a brother returned to me. And I don't mean Colin, I mean Lucas. He bloomed and flourished, was confident, happy. It was as though Cole made him into a different person altogether: someone who could interact with the world without fear. I might have worried more about this brotherly infatuation—except that Cole seemed to have nothing better to do with his time than whatever Lucas wanted him to do.

They went clamming, fishing. They went to the movies. Cooked dinner together. I felt like I was watching an after-school special.

I didn't ask him how long he planned to stay, but he gave no indication he was thinking of leaving. He moved to room eleven at the Island Inn, but there were no ghosts, he said, with disappointment.

"You're the ghost," I told him.

Sometimes I thought about what he'd said about dreams, about the Quahog Pit, or about the coincidences with the skipped stone, the way he sat like my mother. Those were strange little flags, asking me to pay attention. But it was so much easier to pay attention to other things. How he laughed at what I said, making me feel funny and bright, like a different girl, someone like Kim. How he asked about the islanders as if they (and by extension *I*) were fascinating exemplars of human complexity. The way he paid for groceries, made dinners for us. If he was a guest, he was a very pleasant guest. If he was a ghost, he was a sincerely helpful ghost. And anyway, I was used to being haunted.

I sometimes asked myself what he was getting from us, what he was hoping for. That seemed like the right question, but the answer was tricky. I had a realization about him on the second Sunday of his stay. On Sundays Lucas and I always cleaned the house, dividing up the chores, and that Sunday, Cole offered to pitch in. He cheerfully dusted. He vacuumed. He said he preferred not to do bathrooms.

"I prefer not to do bathrooms, too," Lucas said.

I said, "Someone has to do them."

"I don't even live here," Cole said.

"Fine." Lucas held up his hands. "I'll do them."

All morning it rained. The inside of the house was dim and cool. When I gathered up shopping bags in the afternoon, Cole said, "Grocery shopping? I'll come." And he slid off the kitchen stool and fell into step beside me.

I backed the car out of the garage and Cole watched from the doorway, then darted toward me through the rain. It was a rust-colored 1983 Volkswagen Rabbit. He eased into the passenger's seat. "I wondered if you ever drove this thing," he said.

We passed Mr. and Mrs. Grendle next door; I saw them through their kitchen window. Did they see me? Did they worry, seeing me with a strange man suddenly after so many years?

The rain drummed on the roof of the car. The grocery store was a mile inland, part of a knot of ugly boxy buildings where South Street intersects with Hatch. The store was called Hiram's Bounty, a name Cole found amusing.

I had been terrified of Hiram, not because he was mean, but because he'd had a tracheotomy and spoke with a mechanical voice through a little box attached to his throat. That voice seemed to issue straight from a nightmare. He'd died maybe twenty years earlier, and someone else owned the store, but the name stayed. That was the unspoken agreement among islanders: we will do our utmost to keep time at a standstill. The same sand will sit on the same shore for a million years. Hiram's Bounty will forever remain Hiram's Bounty. Children won't grow up. Parents won't die. At least that was supposed to be the agreement. My antiestablishment parents were never good at following the rules.

"Where's the shopping list?" Cole asked. He held a shopping basket firmly at his side. The place was small and cramped. All around us, multicolored packages were stacked precariously on tall shelves. You had to climb up step stools to reach the tops. I had the impression of children's blocks rising in castles on the verge of tumbling down. It smelled like childhood, too, like the inside of a refrigerator.

"There's no list."

"How do you remember what you need?"

"I just know."

"How do *I* know what you need?"

"You don't know," I said. "I have to tell you. Milk, for starters."

He peeled off and found the dairy section and then found me again down a crowded aisle of canned things, and I sent him back with his two percent and told him to get whole milk, and then to look for olives and tomato sauce. For a while we shopped like that. I moved in solid lines and Cole circled back to me, each time with a heavier basket.

We ran into my old piano teacher in the bread aisle. I'd stopped taking piano lessons when I was fifteen, but Mrs. Mabe wrapped her arms around me in a hug and demanded I tell her every little thing I'd been up to.

"Nothing new," I said. "Except, I guess, this is Cole. A friend of Lucas's."

"Lovely," she said.

"A pleasure to meet you," Cole said, taking her hand in both of his.

She gave me a conspiratorial look and mouthed the word *cute* when she said goodbye.

When we got in line to check out, Cole said, "Here. I'll get these groceries." He pulled several bills out of his pocket. "But, question for you—why introduce me as Lucas's friend?"

I picked up a pack of gum and then put it back. "You'd rather I say you're the reincarnation of baby Colin?"

"I don't mean that. I mean, why Lucas's friend? Aren't I your friend?"

He tilted his head, looked at me, unsmiling, and I felt a sudden warm rush to my cheeks.

Later that day in front of the Lobster Claw, our hardware

store, we saw Allison Ferrera, who had been two years behind me in school. Both her kids were crying by the wheelbarrows. She waved at me and then stared at Cole the whole time I was talking. She'd always been pretty, but a little stupid, and disproportionately beloved, in my opinion.

"Who's this?" she said, nodding at Cole. I introduced him as an old friend of mine from college. I'm not sure why I lied, but Cole looked at me approvingly when I said it, and I felt a surge of warmth, the two of us connected, creating something together, even if the something was a lie.

"I thought you didn't go to college," Allison said.

"I left early because my mother died," I said.

"Oh, I'm sorry," Allison said. "I put my foot in my mouth, didn't I?"

"We met freshman year," Cole said. "That sounds right."

"Sounds right?" Allison said.

"Who can remember freshman year?" I said.

"What class was it?" Cole asked, snapping his fingers, as if trying to remember.

"I think it was psychology."

"It was history," he said, suddenly serious, almost angry.

"Well, it's good to meet you," Allison said. "Welcome to Wolf Island. The prettiest, most boring place on earth."

I had the sense something important had just taken place, and I looked at Cole's face for a clue, but it was pleasant and impassive again. It was as if I'd just seen a flash of his desire, what it was he wanted from us. The story. The lie. It didn't make any sense.

That week Cole walked me to work in the mornings. He began to meet me for lunch. He accompanied me to the post office, the bank. Everyone stared at him.

When I introduced him, he told an increasingly detailed story of how we met freshman year. "There was a train somewhere near campus," he told my boss in the Ferry-All offices. "And we could hear it from the dorm. Do you remember that, Lydia? The whistle of the train? And all the crows in the fall? The sky black with crows."

"No," I said. "I don't remember that."

"It slips away from you, doesn't it?" he said. "Memory."

Here's what I realized that day. *Memories* were of special interest to him. He collected them, studied them, as if the thing he wanted from us was our memories, as if memories could make a man rich.

But I couldn't tell if he was trying to take memories away from us or offer them to us.

The memories of train whistles and crows, the history class in college—maybe that was his way of being generous, offering me a gift in his favorite currency. But I wasn't sure I wanted this gift. I only had a few memories from that semester in Providence, and now they blurred, ran together with Cole's fabrications. Now, when I thought back to my dorm room that fall ten years ago, I heard the train. I saw the shadows of crows.

When we were eight, my mother took us to watch *The Wizard of Oz* at the little cinema inland. During the Munchkins' song, she leaned down and said something in my ear.

"What did you say?" I asked her.

"This is the part you're going to remember," she repeated. Even then I felt resentful. I would choose my own memories, thank you. But the funny thing is that that *was* the part I remembered, for years. It haunted me and I wondered if she had somehow, powerfully, created the memory, or if she were simply prophetic.

How would my mother have responded if Cole had shown up while she was still alive? I put her face together carefully, not leaving anything out: her heavy, pale hair, her orange lipstick, the way she pushed her reading glasses up on top of her head. I tried to remember her as she really was: my mother, not some dream. I imagined her in the doorway, with Cole Anthony standing across the threshold. She watched him carefully. He told his story. Something stirred in her face, but she didn't make a move yet. Some fissure in her belief system needed to widen before this new belief could enter. Her breathing got fast. The fissure widened. The belief entered her completely. She gasped. Opened her arms. Pulled him close.

In some ways it was like that for me. Slowly, day by day, hour by hour, almost without my knowing it was happening, I allowed Cole Anthony into the inner circle of trust where really only Lucas had been allowed before. He didn't talk about his past, but I slowly began to accept that there were private—justified—reasons for that. Maybe he was recovering from a broken heart, from a large and powerful grief. Maybe he really hadn't liked the person he used to be and wanted nothing more than to start over. In some ways he was just like everyone else who came to Wolf Island—he was looking for something. Memories, I thought. A new story, a new past. Or maybe a future.

I liked having Cole around for a few reasons, but when I was honest with myself I saw that a primary reason was that he took some responsibility for Lucas. For the first time in so long, I wasn't always needed. If I didn't come straight home after work, they simply made dinner without me. I could leave early in the morning, and they would make breakfast and Lucas would go ahead to work without me. It was like some vista opening up. I could see farther than ever before. I could see into the future, a future where I could make choices for myself.

A week turned into two weeks, and then into three weeks, and September was in full glow and Cole was still spending every evening with us. Here, conveniently enough, was a brother to take care of Lucas in my place. We don't choose our prisons, but we do come to love them. I loved Lucas deeply and honestly; I hardly knew who I was without him. But—I knew I was someone; I knew someone was there in me, some sliver of a girl who hadn't had a chance to grow up yet. That was why in unguarded moments when asked my age, I still immediately thought eighteen. Or sometimes thirteen. Or even, ten. As if I were trapped in time. Sometimes I felt a passing sadness for that girl, the one I'd been, or still was, frozen under a magician's spell.

In Cole, I saw that girl's release.

Lucas is happy with Cole here, I told myself. *And so am I. What else matters, really?*

I fell asleep watching a movie with Cole and Lucas. When I woke, Lucas was gone. My feet were pushed up against the outside of Cole's thigh, and when I pulled them away, groggy, blinking in the light, he reached out for my foot. His warm hand enveloped my foot, and the heat traveled to my ankle, my calf and shin, my knees, my thighs. A current of danger. I tried to remember how long he had been here. Exactly how many days. He came in August. I remembered the heat and the smell of the sea.

"How long are you planning to stay?" I asked, removing my foot from his touch.

"A long time. As long as it takes."

"As long as it takes for what?"

He didn't answer. The movie was still playing, a dirt road, two boys running away. Dust and weeds along the edge.

"Isn't there anyone waiting for you?"

"I told you, there isn't."

Outside, moths were banging against the screen. It was dark and still, but every now and then a fierce wind would rise up and shake the trees. I wouldn't want to go outside, not this late, not on a windy night.

"You can stay here tonight," I said. "We have a guest room."

It was actually Baby B's room, and no one had stayed in it for a long, long time. We always joked that it wasn't a guest room so much as a ghost room. "I'll show you," I said and led him upstairs. It was still furnished for a baby. There was a little twin bed against the wall, a dresser with teddy bear knobs.

He stood in the doorway. I wanted to explain to him why I hadn't invited him before this. I wanted him to know what it was like for me—needing to protect Lucas, watching out for him. "I'm not sure you understand what it's been like since our parents died. We only have each other. There's no one else. We're it."

Cole nodded. He looked kind, almost sorry for me. "I'm not sure you understand," he said, "how much things have changed. Now he has me."

The words chilled me, a strange mix of relief and fear.

"Goodnight," he said.

Goodnight brother. Goodnight ghosts. Goodnight shaky old wonderful house. I climbed into my own bed. Goodnight memories. Goodnight moon. Goodnight stranger in our ghost room.

9.

I heard a small sound coming from the hallway, a weak little cry. It was the dark, quiet hour before dawn. I got out of bed, and stood at the top of the stairs. There were all the usual nighttime sounds, the whine of the refrigerator, the sound of wind outside.

Once I'd heard my mother crying in the night. I was six, maybe seven. I'd walked down the hallway and stood listening. She came out of the bedroom and shrieked when she stumbled over me.

"What are you doing up?" she said.

"Are you crying?"

"I'm fine," she said. "I had a dream, that's all. I dreamed he came back, and I was happy."

"Then why are you crying?"

"Because I woke up."

It was like that. We all missed him. It was so easy to miss

him. Baby B was everything we wanted that was just out of reach. This was true even today, Lucas and I all grown up.

The night was chilly, the house quiet, and whatever I'd heard was apparently from a dream.

But then I noticed—or felt—something that didn't belong. Light, or movement, a disturbance in the equilibrium. My mother's bedroom door, ajar.

I crept to her door, stood on the threshold, listened for my mother, or Colin, listened to hear which ghost it was. I flipped the light switch on. No ghost, of course. It was Cole, shading his eyes from the sudden flood of light. He raised himself up from the bed where he'd been lying. The bed wasn't made, just covered with an old quilt. He lay on top of it.

"What are you doing in here?" I asked. "Were you sleeping here?" My mother's bed! Her quilt. Her room was a space we hardly ever entered, following an unspoken decision to leave it alone, pristine. I felt a wave of anger and moved as if to pull him off the bed.

He swung his legs over to sit up. Rubbed his face, disoriented. "I sleepwalk," he said.

"Your room is across the hall," I said.

"I'm sorry." He stood. He was shirtless, his eyes unfocused. He walked out of the room. "I sometimes sleepwalk," he said as he passed me in the doorway.

"I heard you the first time," I said.

He shuffled into Baby B's room, closed the bedroom door with a small click. I didn't go back to my room. I was wide-awake now. Instead I sat on my mother's bed, felt the warmth there from Cole's body. I looked around the room carefully.

The closet door was ajar. The top bureau drawer was open an inch. Had it been open like this before tonight? I couldn't remember. It might have sat open for months, years. I crossed the room and opened the drawer, ran my hands over the little cardboard jewelry boxes. I took out each little box, pulled out necklaces, rings, bracelets. Shook the tiny silver casket that held our baby teeth. Little tooth rattle. In the closet a few of her dresses still hung, sandalwood in the folds. I closed the closet door, closed the bureau drawer.

I went to Lucas's room.

"Move over," I said. I stood at the edge of Lucas's bed. In his sleeping face I saw the combined pieces of our parents that were there in my face, too.

"In the garden," he said. "Under a toadstool."

"Wake up."

"What?" He lifted his head. "What's wrong?"

"Nightmare."

In our family, it had always been acceptable to wake someone in the night to tell them your nightmare since the telling of the nightmare was the best power over it. I never minded waking or being woken. I didn't even mind the nightmares. My mother's bed was the best reward. In the night she was warm, comfortable, happy. Maybe I liked her best when she was half asleep. She would pat my back, then fall asleep with her hand heavy on me.

I crowded into Lucas's bed and lay on my back looking at his ceiling. I couldn't see much, but it didn't matter. I'd memorized his ceiling, which was different from my ceiling only in the shapes its rain stains had taken.

"What was it?" he asked. "What'd you dream?"

"I dreamed that Cole wasn't Baby B," I lied. "I dreamed that he was a stranger after all."

"It was just a dream."

The sound of the bay was part of the darkness somehow, some inner organ pumping out tremendous quantities of darkness. As long as we'd been alive, we'd heard the bay outside our windows all night long.

"You know what I've been thinking about?" I said. "Those parties at the golf course."

"In high school?"

"Remember we would go, but then we would just stay in the woods watching. No one knew we were there."

"It was better to watch than to be down there talking to people."

Outside I heard splashing. I went to the window and peered out but there was only darkness.

"How are you so comfortable with him?" I asked. "I've never seen you so at ease with a person. How can you just talk to him like—"

"I've been talking to him all my life."

"Lucas—"

"He remembers things. He knows things only we could know. He knew how to turn the hose on, even with the spigot hidden under the porch stairs. And he knew the trick for opening the shed. And when I asked him how he knew, he had no idea! He just *knew*, that's all."

I thought of how he sat at the end of the dock with his legs crossed, the way our mother used to sit. With his hand on his neck, in his hair, how he looked so much like her.

"This morning," Lucas said, sitting up, "he grabbed that old net with the long handle and started spinning it the way I used to. Remember I would do that for hours."

"How does he know that stuff?" I said. "If he were Baby

B, he wouldn't be able to remember any of that. He was a few weeks old."

"You can trust him," Lucas said. "I know it."

"I just found him in Mom's room," I said. "I think he was sleeping in there. But I don't know. The closet was open, and the top drawer. He says he sleepwalks."

"Then he sleepwalks," Lucas said.

"It feels like there's something else going on. Like he's not telling us the whole story. My heart is telling me not to trust him."

"Then our hearts are at war," Lucas said.

"Jesus Christ, Lu. Don't say things like that. No one's at war. I want what you want!"

That was a lie, though. Lucas wanted to go back in time. I wanted a future. But the problem was the same for both of us: we were stuck here—the two of us together—perpetually in this present moment, this tender scene, a page ripped from a calendar, a little childhood.

I returned to my bed but only to sit awake looking out the window as the bay became visible, an apparition rising from the darkness, sailboats, houseboats, docks, and dinghies. I asked again the question I probably should have been asking more insistently. What was he doing here, with us? A few tarnished old memories weren't really enough to hold his interest, and I knew it. I knew it but I didn't want it to be true.

What do you want with us, Cole Anthony?

When it was light, I dressed quietly and left the house, so I would avoid talking to either Cole or Lucas. I felt anxious, unmoored. And worse than that, I felt like a fool. I wasn't any freer now than I'd been. I certainly wasn't going to leave

Lucas, not now that a mistrust of Cole had sprung up over-night. I was still stuck on the island, and maybe more alone than ever, watching Lucas and Cole growing closer and closer in a dangerous brotherhood that excluded me and everyone else.

The waves were frothy on top, and they tossed the boats. I sat in the booth holding my hair to keep the wind from whipping my eyes. I bit my fingernails even though I'd recently kicked that habit. I felt cross with the tourists. *Yes, no, over there, here's a brochure.* An old Lab walked past, grinning the way some dogs can. A little boy ran by barefoot, holding a dead fish.

I was restless, tired.

I refused the doughnuts Eddie offered.

"Not worried about getting fat, are you?" Ed said. He stood in front of me, blotting out the light.

"I'm just not hungry for doughnuts."

"Because you have nothing to worry about," he said.

"Thank you. I just don't like doughnuts."

"That's a mystery I guess I'll never understand," he said.

"It takes all kinds," I agreed.

Eddie played with the zipper of his Jack's hoodie. The logo for One Eyed Jack's was a mean-looking pirate with an eye patch and a parrot on his shoulder and the words *yo ho ho* floating out of the parrot's mouth.

"How's old Returned-from-the-Dead?" Eddie asked.

I thought about Cole, sitting cross-legged in the sunlight, his unapologetic paleness. *Perpetual vacation*, he kept saying about the island. I remembered the warmth of his hand as he touched my foot. *Now he has me.* I pictured his bare chest and confused expression when we'd looked at each other in my mother's room in the night.

"He's great," I said. "Just fantastic."

"He's certainly making himself at home."

"That he is."

Eddie shook his head. "What are you doing, Lyd?" he said.

"What do you mean?"

"I've seen you with him. He's not a good guy. This whole story he and Lucas are telling each other. Are you buying it now, too?"

"Of course not. It's not that simple."

"I think it *is* that simple. I think there's something else going on."

I felt a swell of anger. "What are you trying to say? That I like him being here? That I want him to stay forever? You know what, Ed Frank? You don't get to give me advice. Not anymore."

He looked hurt and surprised. But I turned away, stared furiously at the brochures until he walked off. I wouldn't let myself regret snapping at him. What right did he have? If he hadn't married Kim, if things had been different—but things were the way they were.

Before lunch, Cole appeared at the booth.

"I'm sorry about last night," he said. "That must have scared you."

"It did."

"I shouldn't have stayed over," he said. "Or at least I should have warned you about my sleepwalking."

"That would have been a good idea."

Lucas came around the corner and joined us.

"Wait, what's going on?" I asked. "Why aren't you at work?"

Lucas shrugged. "Taking the day off. Cole and I are going to the Cape."

"The Cape? For what?"

"Just to look around."

"Come with us," Cole offered.

"I'm working."

"Take the afternoon off."

I grabbed a stack of brochures, shuffling them like playing cards. "I can't take the afternoon off," I said. "There's no one to fill in for me."

"There's no one here," Cole said, looking around. "No one needs you."

He leaned against the booth. He had good posture, straight teeth. His features were symmetrical, his jaw strong and square. He was handsome, but it was a closed-off kind of handsomeness. It was impossible to learn anything from looking at him. He breathed in luxuriously. I pictured the world around him sucked into his powerful lungs: air, buildings, boats, booth, water, sand, flora, fauna.

"Oz is waiting," Lucas said, looking at me shyly. I raised my eyebrows. It was strange to hear the teasing in his voice, see his shy, proud smile. He was trying out a new identity: ordinary person, normal brother, little devil, dangler of spiders, snapper of bras.

"Oz?" Cole said.

"The guy who works at the information booth on the Cape looks lionlike, like the lion from *The Wizard of Oz*," Lucas said.

"He just has this mane," I said.

"And Lydia likes him."

"No," I said. "Lydia does not like him. Lydia doesn't know him. I just see him sometimes at the Ferry-All meetings, and I don't know, I like the mane. Anyway, I'm not going. So it doesn't matter."

"That's okay, Lyd," Lucas said. "You don't have to come." He walked toward the Ferry-All office with Cole. "She can't really leave the island," Lucas said.

"I can leave the island," I called. "I can't believe you just said that."

Cole looked over his shoulder. He didn't say anything but I could see some realization crossing his face. Then he turned and said something to Lucas, too quietly for me to hear.

10

It was hard for me to leave the island.

That was true.

It was *physically difficult* to leave the island. Everything just seemed to speed up off island, everything in me: my pulse, my breathing, my racing thoughts. I don't even know when it started. After my mother died, I guess.

It *was* hard for me to leave the island, but it made me angry to hear Lucas say it like that, in that tone of voice. As if *I* were the one crippled by anxiety issues. As if he were the one who had to look after me.

After the 12:30 boat lumbered away, a front swept in, and the air turned soft, cool, and gray, and the sudden change in weather changed my mood as well. I settled down, quieted.

It started to rain, and you should have seen how sad the tourists were. They wanted sunshine! They walked around wearing clear rain ponchos and blank expressions.

All afternoon the rain drummed on the roof of the information booth. When I ran into the post office for the mail, inside there were five buckets set up to catch the drips coming through the roof, and they, too, made a cacophonous drumming. The postmaster was also the leader of a bagpipe band. They sometimes practiced behind the post office, as they were doing now, crammed together under a little back awning, the melodies of the bagpipes flocking over the water.

The sound of the instruments seemed to tug at my memory, nostalgia rolling through me like the fog over the water. I felt closed in, claustrophobic. I was wearing a big plastic poncho I got from Jim Cardoza, but by the time I got back to the office, my legs were soaked. Jim handed me a towel and I handed him the mail.

"I can't stand the feeling of wet jeans," I said.

Jim nodded sympathetically.

"Do you have a blow-dryer?" I asked.

He didn't, but he looked around anyway, as if one could materialize from looking. I sat in a chair by the window and patted my legs with the towel. The sound of the rain overwhelmed all the other sounds, so the few people I saw outside seemed to be in a silent movie.

"Forget the blow-dryer," I said. "I might run home early today, if that's okay with you, Jim."

"In the rain?" he said. "Better wait until it dries out."

But I was out the door already. I was running through the wet sand, out of breath. I didn't stop until I reached the Island Inn.

The girl at the desk had long dark hair pulled into a ponytail. On weekends she lifeguarded all day, and worked here at night. She was saving money to leave the island, but I could already tell that it would never happen. Soon enough, she'd fall in love, or get pregnant, or her parents would get sick, or she'd just learn to be scared of anywhere else. She was a lifer, I was certain. What mattered to me now was that she was scared of ghosts.

"Can you do me a really big favor?" I asked. "My friend left his ferry ticket in his room, and they won't let him cross if I don't show it to Jim by four. He said it's in his jacket pocket— do you mind grabbing it for him? He's in room eleven."

"Eleven?" she said. She tapped her nails on the counter. They were painted, but chipped, lavender, dusk colored.

"Or, I'm happy to run in myself," I said.

"Would you?" she said. "We're just having a really busy day." And she handed me the key, relieved to have avoided the haunted room.

I stood outside room eleven for several seconds. I put my hand on the doorknob and waited to feel something, but the knob was only old, cold metal.

I pushed the door open slowly and stood looking in, feeling the silence more than hearing it, the complete emptiness of the room. Cole had unpacked his duffel bag. It was empty on the chair like the skin of the bear when the enchanted prince has crawled out. A pair of shoes were lined up at the foot of the bed.

What was I hoping to find? I wasn't entirely sure. I knew what I didn't want to find: a diary documenting a scam of some kind, a newspaper article revealing Cole as an escaped convict, suspicious artifacts, evidence of hypnotism.

What did I find? Mostly just clothing in sharp, efficient folds, stacked in the dresser. There was a creased *New York Times* beneath the bed. I looked at the date. Yesterday's. On the nightstand was a stack of books, popular literary novels. When did he read? While we were at work, I guessed. Inside the nightstand drawer, I found a spiral notebook. The first several pages were ripped out, a few clinging shreds of paper left behind on the spiral binding. The next three pages were covered with Cole's neat handwriting. Our phone number was there among other numbers I didn't recognize, although I could see they were island numbers. I saw our birthday listed, month and day, the name of two plumbers, the address of a store on the cape that sold guitars.

Seeing his notes and lists gave me a strange feeling. He had drawn little pictures in the margins, boats and houses, all with dark firm pen strokes. He'd written sideways on the third page, *She Is Alive.*

I looked at the words, and felt my face flush, felt something shift inside, tiny fault lines. Who was *she*? I wanted it to be me, although I hardly understood why. I wanted, I guess, for those words to be mine, to act as an incantation, bewitching me into some higher level of existence. *She is alive. She is alive.*

I closed the notebook, placed it back on the nightstand, and continued my examination of the room. His empty duffel bag on the chair. The smell of the room—dusty, hot. I touched the blanket on the neatly made bed. I touched the pillow. I kneeled down beside the bed and examined it. There was no indent from a sleeping head, no stray hairs.

I remember my mother once told me you could tell a lot about a man by looking in his pockets. To demonstrate, she went to my father's old camel hair coat hanging by the door and reached into the side pocket. She pulled out a matchbook, a handful of coins that clinked together in her hand, and a bird's nest.

"I rest my case," she said.

"Found it on the path behind the school," my father had said. "Maybe wren."

In the closet, Cole had hung a jacket, and I reached in both pockets. A quarter. A receipt for coffee beans. I knew just when he'd bought them—one morning early after we'd discovered we were out of coffee entirely.

I returned to the duffel bag. I checked the outside pocket first and found it empty. On the interior, though, was a slim little pocket, which I unzipped, and inside was another zipper. A pocket within a pocket. When I unzipped that, I found a piece of paper, stationary size, folded into quarters. I almost didn't open it, sure it was another receipt, because it was that kind of thin, faded paper. But I did unfold it, and when I did, I felt a shock, a seismic shift, my feet no longer on solid ground. My heart pounded in my temples.

It was her pointy, calculated letters, my mother's handwriting. I turned it over to see the signature. Cecily, my mother's name. I shook as I read it.

Dearest C,

This is the time of year I think about you most, surprisingly. Not at your birthday, not the time of year when you died. This time of year feels like it should be your time because of the colors, because it's hot and cold both at the same time. Because the whole fucking season is about death, and I think about you when I think about Persephone and her new, dark world away from her mother, away from the sun, in the rocky palace under the earth.

That was what we chose for you, wasn't it, in the end?

I know it wasn't better for you that way; it wasn't better for Persephone either. But the earth needed seasons, and Persephone was sacrificed. And you were also sacrificed, for the good of the others, or maybe for the whole world. Who knows? Sometimes that's how I have to look at it.

But I'm sorry, my love, to digress. Actually, I should get right to it. Things are not looking good, and time is running out. Please come home. Please visit. Not to put too fine a point on it, but I will soon be dead, and then there will not be another chance, unless we meet in the underworld. You should know your family. I want to feel your hands. I've stopped punishing myself, and you should, too.

I'm sure someone else can do the work. I'm sure someone else can feed your dog. Leave that behind and come to the island. We all want you.

My love,
Cecily

I felt a shock of emotion, a thundering in my ears. I clutched the letter. I backed slowly out of the room, closed the door behind me.

"Find it?" the girl at the counter asked me. I nodded and slid the key toward her. "Are you okay?" she asked. "You look pale. Did you—did you see something in there?" She nodded sympathetically, but she had no idea.

I walked home in the rain, the letter tucked under my shirt, next to my skin, to keep it dry and safe. In my own room, I stood, wet and dripping, looking around like someone in a dream. T-shirts piled in the rocking chair. Discarded pants on the floor. Lotions and sunscreens. A towel hanging from the door, a bathing suit hooked on the corner of the mirror.

I thought, *She is alive.* Did he mean my mother after all? The letter had been written in September, in that last year of her life. *Dearest C.* Had she meant Colin or Cole? Or both? There was something strangely specific about the letter. What had she said? *Someone else can feed your dog.* As if she knew all about his dog, as if a dog were the thing keeping him from visiting her in those last months of her life. The intimacy between them was palpable in the letter, as if they'd talked dozens of times.

I looked around my room and felt a rush of tenderness, almost nostalgia, for my old things, as if a new life was nudging its way in. Already everything we did was affected by Cole. He had something to do with our breakfast, our lunch, our dinner, and he had something to do with our walks on the beach, and the way we took care of our house, and the magazine articles we read, and the conversations we had, and our thoughts and our dreams.

I felt a sudden stab of desire to go back to a time before he came. I imagined walking home on the beach in the late afternoon, the long shadows making a path in front of me, a path toward home, always knowing, all those years, what I would find at home. The predictability like the sound of the bay, always there.

I wondered and wondered what my mother had meant, and how they had met, and why she'd never told me about him. I thought about what Eddie had said about my dad being a Scout leader, how everyone had loved him. What else did I not know about my parents?

It continued to rain, the scent of electricity in the air. Normally I liked a gray day, but because of the letter from my mother, the gray seemed startling, ominous.

I held the letter. I read it over and over again. I put the letter in my pocket. Then I sat on the couch on the screened-in porch and watched the red houseboat rocking, until it was too dark to see it.

Soon after the nine o'clock boat came in, their voices floated toward me from the beach.

"Lydia?" Lucas said, peeking onto the dark porch.

"Hey," I said. "I was waiting up for you."

"Are you okay?" Lucas asked.

Cole appeared behind him.

"I'm fine," I said. "Just having a quiet minute out here."

"Mind?" Cole said, walking past Lucas and standing above me.

I moved to one side of the couch. "Go ahead."

"We saw your lion-boy," Cole said, sinking down beside me. I was aware of his warmth, the smell of his skin, something more than heat and dust. I reached into my pocket and felt the edges of the letter.

"We told him you said hello," Cole said, laughing, but he didn't sound amused. "How old is that kid?"

"I have no idea," I said. "I don't know him. As I told you."

We listened to the waves, the small splashes on the sand. Then a larger splash, as if a seal had surfaced and crashed back under the water.

"I'm surprised you're still up," Lucas said. "I'm going to bed."

"Let's stay up," Cole said quietly to me. "I have something to tell you."

We listened to Lucas climb the stairs, listened to water

rushing through the pipes—a soft, high-pitched keening—as Lucas brushed his teeth. What was Cole going to tell me? Was it about my mother? He seemed in no hurry to speak. He leaned back and stared straight into the darkness on the other side of the porch. His breathing was quiet and even.

"I have something to tell you, too," I said.

He reached down and touched my leg, just below the knee, below the ragged hem of my shorts. My legs were brown and scratched, dotted with mosquito bites. Cole ran two fingers from my knee to my ankle. My heart seemed to beat everywhere all at once, in my fingertips, my skull. I felt dizzy.

"You're not a child," Cole said. "That's what you don't realize. You're a woman. And you're beautiful."

This was not how I'd expected this conversation to go. I stood up, my heart racing, and he held out a hand to stop me. "You're wasting your time with that kid in the information booth in Carson Cove. You're wasting your time with Ed Frank." His voice slowed, and he enunciated every word. "You," he said, "have so much more to give than Ed Frank could ever ask you for. You have things to give that he doesn't even know exist."

"Why are you telling me this?" I said. My heartbeat filled my ears. The wailing of water started in the pipes again.

He said, "I thought maybe no one had ever told you."

I swallowed. "No one has," I said.

II

When we were thirteen, Lucas made friends with a summer girl named Katrina. Or rather, she made friends with him. Lucas didn't make friends, but if someone bossed him skillfully enough, he'd do what they said. We'd known Katrina for years; she came every summer, but she was a year older and while we were still digging for baby clams in the black sand around the rocks or making drip castles on the sandbar, she was enisled on the clean blue of her beach towel in a pink bikini.

When we were thirteen, she developed an interest in Lucas and started toting him around like a beach bag.

"Do you like her?" I'd asked Lucas that summer.

"She's nice to me," he said, although he looked terrified.

"Her hair is like plastic."

"I know," he said. "It's hair spray."

She smelled like flowers. Her legs were smooth and slick

with baby oil. She had blondish hair that always seemed damp, and intoxicating whiffs of floral chemical clean issued from her when she ran her fingers through it.

Lucas sat beside her on the beach, while I crouched jealously in the shallow water, grasping fistfuls of sand and squeezing so the sand squirted out. Lucas could hardly look at her but I did. She liked to sit with her arms behind her for support, her head thrown back, and her eyes closed, offering up the defenseless hollow of her throat and the perfect scoops of her breasts.

Once I saw her with Lucas in the bathhouse at Tame Jaw Beach. The door was locked, but I climbed up on the seat of a bicycle parked nearby and looked through the tiny screened window. They were sitting side by side on the bench, Lucas's eyes were closed, while her hand moved inside his bathing suit.

He would be mortified if I brought this up with him now, even though it's the most normal thing in the world, for a thirteen-year-old boy to mess around with a pretty girl. It wasn't normal for him, though. It wasn't normal for us. A funny thing happened to me as I watched them that afternoon in the bathhouse. I can't even say what it was exactly— a kind of disassociation. As if I were floating. I went back to the water, I remember, and poked blue crabs, which moved sideways, suspicious, through the sand and into the water as if to drown themselves. But even though I was in the hot sand, in the shallow water, I could hardly feel the sun, the water. Part of me was back in the bathhouse perched on the window like a spider, watching Katrina's awful hand moving.

Now, I stood with my back against the closed door of my bedroom, wondering why I was thinking of Katrina at a time like this. But I knew. It was because that was the first summer that desire confused things for us. And desire can be such a heavy, unwieldly thing, too big to conceal, the thing that makes you visible, public, as the poem goes, like a frog. And yet, it's also the thing that makes you *somebody*.

Fuck this, I thought. And I meant fingernails on skin. I meant the warm hand around my foot on the couch. I meant crows and train whistle. I meant mother. Brother. Stranger. I was angry that my mother had kept secrets from me, and that Cole had secrets, too. I was angry that Cole had distracted me from finding the answers I needed. But most of all, I was angry at myself—because alongside the anger, I felt something else blooming—a longing as terrible as thirst, but tender also.

My heart beat ferociously. The old life receded into darkness. The new life raced toward me. I couldn't stop thinking about him. As if thinking about him could prevent the new life from gathering speed. The letter was still in my pocket. I hadn't said a word about it when I'd had the chance, just fled to my bedroom like some frightened child. And why? Because he'd touched my leg and said I was beautiful. It was different when he was a stranger. The things you want from strangers are tiny things, disposable.

I'd thought that the attraction I'd felt when I saw him that first night had disappeared the moment we began to pretend he might be our lost—and returned—brother. But the desire was still there; I felt it when he touched me, felt its delicate leaves and roots, alive and growing somewhere in my rib cage. Now the things I wanted from him were complex and frightening, a whole jungle. I wanted the secrets he held. The past, the future. I took the letter out and smoothed it against the dark window. I read the words again and again.

When I finally slept, I dreamed of my mother.

"What do you want?" I asked.

She led me into the hallway. She had lit a hundred candles. Incense burned in a little clay pot she kept on her bedside table, with markings around the rim like bird tracks, something small, a wren. I could hardly see her through the smoke of the incense, with the candles winking everywhere.

"Where are you?" I said.

She was young again, younger than I'd ever known her. Beautiful, animated, alive.

"You're worrying for nothing," she said bitterly. "She is still alive."

And I woke up.

Graininess of dawn. Milky fragrance. A door closing downstairs. Footsteps in the hallway. A shadow in the doorway.

"Where is it?" Cole said. I scrambled out of bed, disoriented. I wasn't dreaming this time. Cole was standing furiously in the doorway, his eyes black, shining with rage, or tears.

His shirt was buttoned wrong, as if he'd dressed in a hurry. Somehow this fact, the buttons askew, the small white flash of skin showing where they failed to line up, compounded my sense of disorientation, the feeling that I was spinning, that all around me the world was blurred beyond recognition. There was something so starkly beautiful about his face. I thought with profound sadness of the bones of his skull, right there, just under the surface.

"Were you in my room?" he demanded. "Did you take a letter? I want my letter back."

"It's from my mother," I said. "So it's not yours. It's mine."

"Give it to me," he said.

"What does it mean?" I demanded. "How did you know her?"

"Show me the letter," he said.

It felt as though everything inside me were speeding up, blood racing through veins. I stood on the edge of a cliff, about to fall. I took the letter out of the pocket of my sweatshirt and opened it. Saw again her handwriting.

"What does it mean she stopped punishing herself?" I asked. "What does she mean about sacrifice?"

In one swift, furious motion, he crossed the room and took the letter from my hand. He held it crumpled, looking at me with an expression of deep rage, maybe worse. I wondered for a moment if he was going to hit me. His jaw seemed to grow larger. His eyes looked pure black. I was watching a transformation, a strange and terrifying metamorphosis. He was changing, becoming something fanged and brutal, a hungry beast, a wolf.

"Give it back," I said. "That isn't yours."

"It's all mine," he said and walked out. I was frightened and angry. My heart was a frenzy of wings and feathers, too heavy but trying, trying to fly.

12

Cole didn't return to the house that morning for breakfast. Lucas went off to work, but I waited at home for Cole. I was sure he would come, and I waited for him, practically vibrating with fear and anticipation—but he didn't show up. Then I began to worry. What if he was gone for good? What if the 9:30 ferry had carried him away? What if he'd taken the letter? I would never know the answers to the questions that now haunted me like little ghosts, little voices in my ear: Who was he? How did he know my mother?

I needed to find him and ask for the truth.

At the inn, the girl at the counter eyed me nervously. "Actually, I'm not supposed to let anyone in there," she said.

"I just want to know if he's here."

"I saw him this morning," he said. "He was pretty mad about someone being in his room. I didn't tell him it was you."

"Thank you," I said. She nodded.

"You can knock, I guess," she said. "I'm just saying, he seemed really mad."

But when he answered the door, he didn't look mad at all. He smiled serenely. His shirt was buttoned, hair combed. He had shaved. I had the distinct feeling that I was looking at someone wearing a mask—only this mask looked almost exactly like the real face underneath. His expression now was gentle and earnest. And when I asked if we could talk about the letter, he nodded and followed me out of the room, locking the door behind him.

Standing just outside the diner was a man everyone on the island called the-man-with-the-cat. He was middle-aged, tired-looking and bony. His particular craziness had to do with his cat, who he draped over his shoulders and took with him everywhere: down the aisle of the supermarket, into the post office, on his bike. Once I saw him teaching her to swim. Also, he introduced the cat as his wife.

Now he was sipping coffee from a paper cup, and his cat was wrapped around his neck like a fox fur collar. He looked me over as I approached, and I nodded.

"I see you found your child," he said.

"What?"

"You've got your child," he said, enunciating as if I were stupid.

"I don't have a child."

"You think I can't see her? She looks just like you!"

"This is Cole," I said.

"Have you met my wife?" he said. Then he bowed his head gravely and said, "Good day," while the cat scrambled to stay aboard. He walked away with stiff precision, as if he were on a balance beam.

"Holy shit," Cole said. "That guy is crazy."

"Right," I said. "You're our dead brother, but he's the crazy one."

The diner was full of the same fishermen that hung out at One Eyed Jack's every night. I saw Sebastian, who was my favorite of the old fishermen, because he seemed whole-heartedly sad about something, but he was also kind, and his sadness made him familiar to me. They hunched over their coffee the way they hunched over their beers. Today it was quiet. No laughing and clinking bottles. No talking. Maybe everyone was sleepy, or maybe without alcohol they couldn't think of anything to say.

We sat at a table in the back of the room. The waitress, Diane, brought us coffee and pancakes. She was another is-lander I'd known my whole life. She used to be young and pretty. Now she was old and pretty. The fishermen looked at her gratefully when she refilled their mugs. No one looked at Cole or me, and I felt chastened. This breakfast ritual had existed for a long time and I hadn't been part of it. How many other secrets had been kept from me on the island?

Cole shook a packet of sugar into his coffee. He kept shak-ing it long after the last of the sugar crystals had dived into the mug.

"Now will you tell me about my mother?" I asked.

"This is what I'll tell you," he said. "And when I'm done talking, you can stop asking, because I won't say another word. I don't like to be badgered. I did know your mother. Okay? We met because—we'd both suffered a loss. And she recognized something in me—or we recognized something in each other. We felt we belonged together."

"I don't understand," I said. "Did you meet on the island?"

"Not exactly, no."

"So—like a grief group or something?"

"Yes," he said. "Or something."

"This is maddening. Can you give me a straight answer?"

"What exactly do you want to know, Lydia?" He sounded tired, bored of me.

"I don't know where to start. I mean, is Cole even your real name?" The idea occurred to me so suddenly, I felt slapped by it, out of breath. I saw something on his face that wasn't there before, as if surprise had opened a back door and let in what he was trying so hard to keep out. Then he carefully shut that door, and smiled at me, but it was too late. I'd seen the shadow falling over him.

"Not exactly," he said. "You're right about that."

"Not exactly? What *is* your name?"

"I'd rather not tell you."

"Why?"

"I'm starting over," he said firmly. "The name, it represents everything I left behind. New name, new person, new life. I hope you don't mind. There are just—things I want to forget."

"No," I said. "Don't look at me like I'm supposed to just accept this. Everything has been a lie with you. You knew who I was all along. You targeted us."

"I didn't know who you were," he said. "I had no idea. *You* chose *me*. Out of all the men that step off that boat every day, you chose me. You saw something in me. I didn't know until Lucas started talking."

"But you recognized the house. I remember now. You stopped on the beach and stared at it like you knew who lived there."

"I *wondered* when I saw the house. I did wonder if it was the same house, that's very perceptive of you. But I didn't know until Lucas started talking about Baby B. And then it was like the universe had lined everything up. Led me here. Led me to you. Or led you to me. It's so perfect how things line up sometimes, like a machine. Like a set of intricate gears. You turn one lever and the whole thing cranks to life."

"You got the tattoo because of my mother? The lady's slipper?"

"Yes."

"Did she think you were Colin?"

He wrapped his hands around the coffee mug. "Yes."

I took a drink of water, suddenly thirsty. I wished we could swim. I wanted to feel surrounded by cool water. "Why didn't you tell us right away?"

"She didn't want you to know."

"But she's dead. She's been dead a long time. What she wants doesn't matter."

"It does to me."

"So why are you here? I mean why now?"

"Because that's also what she wanted. She wanted us to be together. All of us. She wanted that before she died, but I couldn't. Not then. But now that I've met you I feel...compelled...to respect her wishes."

"But—what do you want from us?"

A shadow passed the window. The new librarian, Elijah West, was setting up a tripod in the street and aiming a square, old-fashioned camera in the window of Mady's. He moved as if he were spring-loaded, hopping from place to place. He fiddled with the camera, then hunched over and pulled a black cloth over his own head and the camera. In his right arm he held a small black box, which was attached to the camera by a cord. It was the clicker for the camera, and, headless, he held it extended from his body and then clicked. He would develop the picture, and there I'd be, at the table in the back with my cracked white mug lifted in both hands, and my elbows leaning on the table, and my hair in two braids, Cole and I drinking coffee together, surrounded by fishermen, as if we did this all the time, as if we liked each other tremendously, as if we *loved* each other. And Cole was barely even real! He was a ghost. He was here for my mother, not me.

"I just want to be with you," he said. "I want us to be together."

"I know that isn't true," I said.

"Why are you so sure?"

"Because no one wants to be with me," I snapped. "My own mother didn't want to be with me. Nobody does."

I stood up so quickly my chair tipped backward and I had to catch it before it crashed to the ground.

Outside, the air was sweet with the smell of warm earth, browning leaves, the metallic tang of seaweed washed up on the sand. Cole tried to catch up with me but gave up when I kept walking. I tried to take deep breaths.

I felt ridiculous—acting like a baby. I thought about my mother, pulled up a series of memories I liked to go over when I had a chance. It went like this, in this order, as if the memories were one of those children's stacking games that could only fit in one particular way: me swimming from the end of the dock to the shore, my mother, resplendent in a red bathing suit applauding above me. My mother laughing at something I'd said, a joke, her laughter like a prize I'd won, a reward. A viola concert in sixth grade. My acceptance letter from Brown. It occurred to me now that the memories were all times she'd been proud of me.

Then I remembered what it was like to come home to take care of her. It was never pride I saw in her eyes all those months she was sick. It was something else: fear, resentment. I sometimes had the sense she was about to tell me something, divulge some great truth or secret. But she would always grow silent, turn away from me. Whatever she knew about life, whatever message she had for me then, I needed it now more than ever. I didn't need obscure dream sequences with candles.

By the time I reached the information booth, I felt a great swelling in my throat, and it seemed to belong to many different emotions, pushing and shoving for real estate in my body. I felt confused, with formidable questions rearing up again and again. Why hadn't she told us about Cole if she believed he was Colin? Where had she met him? And why did he suddenly want to be with us so badly, after all this time? Did he actually think he was Colin, too?

At lunchtime I went to the Day Estate where Lucas worked. He was raking the paths. Scooping up the twigs and leaves into a garden cart. There were smudges of dirt on his face, his bare arms.

"I have to talk to you," I said. "It's about Cole."

I told him that Cole wasn't his real name. I told him about the letter. He listened in stillness. Afterward, he asked to see the letter, but of course I didn't have it anymore. We sat down on a bench overlooking the water and the four sharp rock jetties stretching into the turbulent waves. Everyone called them the Claws.

"You see?" he said, his eyes bright and glassy, but I wasn't sure what I was supposed to be seeing.

"He's hiding things from us," I said.

"She told me once that she'd found Colin. She told me she knew who he was and where he was. She said he was coming here. But this was when she was really sick, and her mind was wandering. I didn't believe her."

The water before us churned rhythmically, beating on the rocks.

"I should have believed her," he said.

I felt a sweet familiar ache, what it felt like to take care of him. What is it about brothers? We take care of them, protect them, and feel grateful to have that important job—but under all of it runs a current of resentment. Because why aren't they taking better care of us?

That evening when I got home, Lucas and Cole were huddled at the kitchen table. Lucas's eyes were wet, bright. I sat down with them, the three of us around the tiny table. It was warm in the kitchen, that familiar hum coming from the refrigerator.

"I can't believe she knew," Lucas said. "She knew he was Colin. She sent him to us."

It felt as if something had changed inexorably. Something was...*decided*. I felt it in the air, as inevitable as weather.

"Wait, wait," I said, holding up my hands, as if that action could suddenly turn back time. They waited patiently for me to go on but I wasn't sure what I could possibly say. I felt a terrible rushing, my blood, my breath, my circulatory system on overdrive. A shift had taken place, and I had no power now. I clapped my hands together just to feel in control of something, one small action, one small noise.

"So—what?" I said to Cole. "Now you just live here. You're part of the family. I mean, don't you have a life some-where else? Don't you have to work at some point?"

"He doesn't have to work," Lucas said. "We have plenty of money."

"We don't have plenty of money."

"But enough," Lucas said.

I shook my head. The house was paid off now, but between taxes and insurance and repairs, there wasn't much extra.

"He's going to help us take care of the house," Lucas said, as if he'd read my mind. He was quietly crying, his cheeks wet. I felt for one vertiginous moment that I was occupying the same space as him, existing inside his body, feeling his chest bursting with emotion, the great swelling sadness, desire like a tidal pull. "The shingles, the side porch, the plumbing in the upstairs bathroom, the *foundation*. We probably should have done more to keep it in good shape all these years..."

"We did our best."

"But now Cole is here to help us. We're going to get a home equity loan. It's where you—"

"I know what a home equity loan is," I said, stiffening. "It's basically turning the house over to the bank. I mean, at least now we have the house. That's the one thing we have, whatever else happens. And anyway, there's no way we can afford it."

"But, see, if we go in on it with Cole..."

"Like put his name on the loan? Are you kidding me?" I looked at Cole, where he sat impassive. "If his name goes on the mortgage, then he would own part of the house. You see?"

"Well, in a way? He has a right to it. They bought it for all of us."

Suddenly I was crying, too, my face damp, my nose running. They were tears of anger, the tears of the powerless. It had something to do with my mother loving another boy, a stranger. The old fears. She was so desperate to love someone who wasn't us, even a ghost was better than her imperfect living children.

I shook my head, embarrassed to be crying, embarrassed by everything I was feeling. "The answer is no."

"We don't need you," Lucas said to me. When he was angry, his mouth parted to show his white teeth, like a small angry animal. I always thought of Peter Pan, wild irresistible boy-beast, how he still had all his baby teeth. "There are things about me that you don't know," Lucas said. "You think you know who I am, but you don't."

I didn't want to think about not knowing him. It reminded me of the conversation with Ed Frank about my father being a Scout leader, filled me with an uncomfortable sensation, as if I were looking in a mirror but didn't recognize the face staring back at me. There were too many things about my family I didn't know already.

"Don't do this," Lucas said in a different voice altogether.

"What now?" I said. "What exactly have I done to you this time?"

"Don't make me choose between you two."

I shivered all night and didn't sleep well. I dreamed about secret chambers, about letters. In the morning, very early, unable to sleep, I took my blanket and went down to the porch where I sat filling in a crossword puzzle with one small lamp on. Maybe the words were clues. *Adhere. Ode. Derail. Lament.* Dawn broke. The water was silver, placid, but I felt raw and edgy. I jumped when I heard a door open and close in the house. Feet on the stairs. Cole settled quietly beside me on the wicker couch, still in pajamas. I pulled the chenille blanket over my chest.

"What's wrong?" Cole said. "Can't sleep?"

"Did you stay here last night?"

He nodded. His face was composed, his gaze straight ahead at the bay. The little red houseboat swung on the placid surface, and we both looked at it, not at each other.

"You're scared of me again," he said.

"Yes," I said.

"We want the same thing," he said.

"Please don't tell me what I want." What I wanted was a mystery as unfathomable as everything else. I wanted to strike him. To bite him. Thank him. Shake him. I wanted to leave and to stay. I wanted my mother. "What I want is up to me," I said. "And my memories are mine alone, and you know what else? My mother is mine. And so is my brother, and you—"

"Shut up," he said.

I looked at him in surprise. He was angry, a faint red glow was climbing up his neck, his mouth parted. But then, just as quickly as it appeared, the anger disappeared. It was like watching a sheet smoothed on a bed. The crease disappeared from his forehead. The redness drained from his face. I felt startled by this kind of emotional discipline.

He leaned back on the wicker couch and stretched his legs out in front of us. I thought about running my fingers from his knee to his ankle. I felt my face blazing with frustration, embarrassment.

The sun bathed our porch in light. The boats in the harbor had all become visible in the morning light, the white sails, the wooden hulls, the tall masts with seagulls perched atop. The little red houseboat, the other little houseboats. Across the water on the cape, morning began. The citizens of that real place woke up and went out for jogs. On our island, morning began. Footsteps up above. Shower water.

"Lucas is awake," I said. I stood up, but Cole caught my hand before I could walk away. My breath of surprise was so fast and sharp, so loud in that quiet intimacy of dawn, so like the breath of arousal that I flushed.

He pulled me onto the couch, onto his lap, onto his warm body, held me there for a minute as the sun came up entirely and the smell of salt rose off the bay into the brittle air, and the warm and dusty smell of his skin made me dizzy. We sat together breathing and being quiet. I felt the life that pulsed in him. Inside our clothes, inside our pockets, our bodies strained toward one another, and we heard Lucas's footsteps on the stairs, and I stood up, blushing and confused.

13

Anxiety beat in me all morning. A feverish pulse. I couldn't stop thinking about his skin, so much heat just beneath the surface. My head ached. My throat felt dry. I could feel the shape of things between us, a specter rising in that lonely space, something that wasn't him and wasn't me but was a third entity, strong and cruel and radiant. Another front was moving in, and the air felt thick and still and heavy.

At lunchtime I sat in Jack's with a notebook and made some lists. The first one was titled What To Do Now, but the only items on it were 1) find out more about Cole and 2) find out more about my mother.

Eddie was sitting at the bar, filling out a time sheet. I waved him over.

"I'm really sorry for snapping at you," I said.

He sat down across from me. "I already told you. Think nothing of it," he said. Then he looked at me in surprise.

"Did something happen?" he said. "Why are you so—you look like you're going to cry."

"You know what I was remembering?" I said. "That time in fifth grade when the fire alarm went off at school, and we lined up outside and then just decided to go home. All of us, remember? We just walked home. The teachers and principal were so mad. No one thought to look for us at home."

"Actually, I didn't go home. I went to Kenny Costa's house because he had cable."

"Well, I went home. That's what I always do, I guess. My mom was home, but it never occurred to her I was supposed to be at school."

"You bring up shit I haven't thought about in years. You always do that! You remember everything."

Those memories were like anchors tethering me in place, keeping me from floating into an increasingly turbulent sea. I didn't understand if the turbulence I felt was inside me, or out there in the world. But I felt it, that storminess, every minute.

I reached for his hand, flipped it over on the table, and ran my fingers over his wrist, the bones and tendons, the blue-green veins, the skin as soft as water. The only place on his great body leftover from childhood, hairless and tender.

I heard his breath accelerate. He leaned toward me. "Let's go somewhere," he said. I dug my fingernail into the soft flesh of his wrist, just a little, heard his breath respond. I remembered how powerful it felt to have so much control over his body. "Come on," he said. "It's been too long."

I shook my head, and he pulled his wrist away from me.

"I'm trying to remember stuff about my mom," I said. "I think maybe I didn't know her as well as I thought."

"Everyone feels that way," Eddie said, a little terse. He stood to leave. "We all feel bad about the dead."

I added to the list: 3) stop feeling bad about the dead.

Jim Cardoza came out of the Ferry-All office when he saw me return to the booth. "You've been looking pale," Jim said to me. He noticed these things.

"Don't worry about me, Jim. I'm fine."

I wrote on the list: 4) find more letters.

"You seem awfully dependent on this job, that's all," Jim said, when I lifted my head.

"What's wrong with that?"

"It ends in a couple weeks, that's what's wrong. You've had your head in a cloud."

In the winter, no one needed information. The tourists disappeared, the booth closed down, and starting in October, I collected unemployment for six months, like the waitresses, cooks, dishwashers, and housecleaners. Usually I liked this time. Lucas and I did projects around the house. We built fires in the fireplace and curled up in front of it and read the novels Elijah West recommended. We slept long, ten-hour nights. But now I couldn't imagine being home all day with the two of them—Lucas and Cole. The house, big as it was, would feel miserably claustrophobic. I would forever be brushing past Cole in hallways, sitting next to him on the wicker couch on the porch. I was instantly dizzy, just thinking about it.

The worst part was that Cole was right. He hadn't targeted us. I'd targeted him. I'd brought him home, introduced him to Lucas. If I'd been a different person, a better person, it never would have happened. If I hadn't been trying to forget about Eddie, maybe I would never have noticed the stranger. If I'd long ago gotten married to some nice island boy, I wouldn't be thinking about fucking strangers in the first place, right? If I hadn't been so selfishly sure he was going to take Lucas off my hands and set me free, I wouldn't have let him enter our lives.

But now? Was it too late? Did I want him to go? Did I trust him to be in our lives?

I stared at the list in my hands. The truth was I wanted him to stay. I wanted answers. I wanted to know what he knew about my family.

The wind came off the harbor and got into my bones, a chill that stayed with me, penetrating deeper and deeper as the day wore on. The tourists turned their collars up, and dug their hands into their pockets.

I wanted him to stay because he had something to show me, about the past, or maybe about myself.

Everyone was searching. I was not alone in this. All the islanders, all the tourists, scouring the beaches, scouring the streets, scouring the woods and the rocks and the lawns and the restaurants and the shops and the movie theater and the bathrooms at bars, looking for what they'd lost.

This island was only seven miles long. How could so many lost things be crowded into such a small space? I thought of my mother's lost part of her soul in the dressing room, not taking up any space all those years. Lost things don't always take up space outside of us. What exactly had I lost, I wondered, and when? An image of dark water came to me then, and something like a face beneath the surface looking up toward the light.

And then I thought, without meaning to, of my mother on the ferry that night when Baby B died. Who cared about the part of her soul in the dressing room? The real loss was that baby. I imagined her taking great greedy breaths of air, trying to breathe for him. No wonder she wanted to believe he was still alive somehow or reborn. *Stop feeling bad about the dead*, I told her, and I was also saying it to myself.

14

I left work early. I walked quickly as if chased. I wasn't sure what I was running from, or to. All I knew was that I couldn't go home. It hurt my chest in a complicated way to think that somewhere in the house I loved so much was the stranger. I felt a knot of fear inside my ribs, a tough bud threatening to blossom open. Instead of going home, I went to Island Pie and ate two slices with tomatoes and broccoli. It began to rain and I stood under an awning on the street. The drops started fat and distinct, making satisfying plunking sounds on the gutters, drumming on the leaves. Then more rain, and more, one long blur, a murmur. The nails holding shingles in place gleamed. The masts of boats flashed out in the harbor.

Eddie, a kind of blur through the rain, waved me over to One Eyed Jack's.

"Get out of the rain!" he said. "I think I just heard thunder."

"I guess I'll have one drink," I told him.

"Totally on me," he said.

"You're a real gentleman."

"Where are the two musketeers?" he said.

"Home." I felt the muscles of my jaw tighten as I said the word, imagining Cole and Lucas, eating dinner together in a circle of light at the kitchen table, maybe drinking wine out of mason jars. *Home* certainly didn't feel like the haven it had always been for me; I was putting off returning to all that was waiting for me there.

Eliot Moniz brought me a scotch and soda. Beside me were the old fishermen. I couldn't hear their conversation, just comforting cackles of laughter. Over near the back porch, Elijah West was having a beer with his dad and brother. At nine, a band called Gin and Soda started strumming guitars in the corner near the porch. Eddie helped plug in their amp and microphone. Gin was the name of the bass player, an angular girl with thick dark hair. She'd grown up on the Vineyard and she still lived there, but she had a sense of otherness about her somehow.

The whole place was full of people I knew, plus the heartiest of the lingering tourists, artists probably. I liked the late lingering tourists. They typically had a we're-in-this-together attitude. At the table next to me, the tourists were yelling out the names of towns in New York. New Paltz! Ossining! Poughkeepsie! Redding!

I was lonely. I was envious of the people talking about New York towns. "Saratoga. Ticonderoga. Utica!" They all cheered. The band was playing weepy songs, drawing out the guitar.

Elijah West stopped to say hello on his way out. Elijah had grown up on Wolf Island, but after high school he'd stayed away for fifteen years. He'd become an art photographer. He'd published a book of photographs of bridges that half the islanders now had on their coffee tables.

"You've been busy lately," I said. "I've seen you everywhere, snapping away."

"You saw me, huh? I'm doing another book. On islands. The islands of the world, the charming, forgotten, undiscovered islands. The best islands."

"Are we one of the best islands in the world?" I asked.

"I think so," he said. "But I don't know which ones my editor will pick."

"What other islands have you done?"

"Remember when I went to Europe last year? There are a lot out there. One of my favorites is St. Michael's Mount in England. It's—"

"Oh, I know that one," I said, "with the little causeway, at low tide."

"And how it rises out of the, you know, stone. The castle. You've been there?"

"I've seen pictures."

"An island is the best place on earth," Sebastian, the old fisherman, said from nearby. I looked up at him, and he took off his hat. His hair was thick and wavy and white as the dawn.

"I agree," I said.

"I've been all over this earth," he said, "and no place feels like an island. It's where you leave your heart. Every time."

"That's exactly what I'm trying to capture in this book," Elijah said.

I beamed at them both. They understood. I loved the island so much I wished I could find some means of expression for my love, but I couldn't. I was envious of Elijah and his camera, trying to understand the island that way. If I'd been an artist, I would have painted it. If I could have eaten pieces of the island I would have, slabs of rock and sand. If I could have had sex with it, I would definitely have had sex with it. I felt a sudden conviction that the island was in danger, that Cole would do it harm, and it was up to me to protect it.

"I've always lived here," I said.

"I know," Elijah said. "Me, too."

"No," I said. "You left."

"I came back," Elijah said, offended. "Same as you."

Elijah walked out, and I was alone again, listening to the music: sad, dreamy stuff. I felt displaced, floating, as if my vision and sense of direction were suddenly impaired. I thought, *I don't understand anything.* Only what existed in that room. The sounds of the band. The sounds of bottles. The sounds of New York towns being spoken aloud like spells. The smell of salt, beer, and fried fish. The smell of damp wood. The dim light. The sense of companionship between me and Gin and Soda and the bartender and the tourists from New York and Sebastian and the other fishermen.

The scotch went straight to my hands, weighed them down, turned them heavy and tingly. I felt out of touch with them, with my whole real corporeal self.

"There are three types of people in this world," I told Eliot Moniz when he brought me one more Glenmorangie. "The ones who are dangerous. The ones who love the ones who are dangerous. And the ones who protect the ones who love the ones who are dangerous."

"True enough," Eliot said.

I was a little drunk.

"But which one am I?" I asked.

"I guess that's the question," Eliot said.

I went into the bathroom. It was a tiny room with a sink, a stall, and one open window letting in the smell of the ocean. In the bathroom mirror, my lips were swollen and my pupils enlarged. I recognized something I'd seen in other faces, usually at the bar after midnight when people began to look like their doppelgängers. It was as if something I was used to seeing on my face had been lifted, some subtle shading of constraint. Underneath was another self, someone I didn't know at all.

When I flushed the toilet, I heard my name, but it was immediately swallowed by the sound of the water rushing through pipes. I ran my hands under hot water and looked at myself again in the mirror above the sink. I listened, but I didn't hear anything except the faint thump of the music.

Someone knocked and I jumped. "Someone's in here," I said.

"Lydia," I heard.

It was Cole. I looked at my reflection, looked hard into the eyes of that twin. Asked her what we were going to do exactly, although on some level I already knew. We were going to be in control, for fuck's sake, we were going to take the reins. We were going to protect all that was ours.

I unlocked the door and he came in. We looked at each other.

"It's almost midnight," he said.

"I know that."

"We didn't know where you were."

I shook my head. "What? Did I miss my curfew again?"

"Funny," he said. "But really. I can't sleep when I don't know where you are."

"Aha," I said. "But you don't sleep."

"Okay, okay," he said. "No need for sarcasm."

"I don't need your permission to stay out late. I'm a grown-up," I said. "Aren't I?"

"It doesn't matter how old you are, you have to treat your family with respect. That's one thing I know."

I knew that on the other side of the bathroom door, Eliot Moniz was ringing the bell for highest tipper of the night, and there was beer in bright bottles, and rows of liquor, and seats made of old barrels, and lobster nets on the walls. All manner of comforting things on the other side of the door. Familiar streets running down to the ferry landing. The information booth, a little nut in the center of the island. One gull asleep on a streetlamp. A seal on a rock. Dinghies and dories wobbling in the cold water, their reflections like twins just beneath the surface.

"The thing is," I said to Cole, "we aren't family."

I looked up at the small, high bathroom window for a glimpse of the night outside, but instead of dark sky or stars or any other comfort, I saw a sleek dark head, the flash of a face. Floating for a moment, then gone.

"Did you see him?" I said, and Cole looked at me strangely.

"Who?" he said. "How much have you had to drink?"

"This has nothing to do with drinking."

I reached out and touched Cole's arm, felt the muscles. Tried to circle his wrist with my fingers. The skin inside his wrist was the same baby-skin as Eddie's, soft as milk. I lay my fingers in his palm, and his hand closed reflexively around them.

"Let's go," he said, and led me out into the bar and then outside.

The rain had stopped, but the beach air was charged with electricity, as if the storm were pausing to gather strength. I got the feeling someone was behind us. When I looked there was no one, but I felt a presence. I heard breath.

"Don't you hear that?" I said.

I held my jacket closed around my throat. Then there was a sudden absence of noise, as if whoever—whatever—had frozen, stopped moving, stopped breathing.

I imagined my mother stepping out of the shadows, see-through but comforting.

"Yes," she'd say. "It's me." And then what would she tell me? *Take care of your brother. Take care of the house. Don't forget Baby B. Don't forsake him.*

What about the letter? I wanted to shout at her.

But no one stepped out of the shadows. No one was there. Only Cole.

I moved toward the water. The air smelled like rain. I heard far off a low rumble. I loved a storm. A storm brought wondrous things to shore, and the morning after a storm was always a morning of discovery. I kicked off my shoes and stepped into the sea.

"Not really a good time for swimming," Cole called to me.

The water bit my ankles, shockingly cold. Ahead of me I saw something moving. What was it? People? Children? No, seals. I could make out their smooth heads. They rose off the rock so I could see their full beautiful silhouettes.

Cole had kicked off his shoes and was wading toward me.

"Seals," I told him, pointing. But when we both looked, they'd gone.

Cole steered me back to shore. We stood on the sand and waited for our feet to dry. We waited for that and the storm, if it was coming. My brain was busy cataloging. Sand. Stars. Drops of water. The scotch was still shimmering in my bloodstream. It made everything beautiful. Sailboats. Houseboats. Seagulls. Minnows. Hermit crabs. Jellyfish. Mother. Father. Brother. Lover. We were chilly from wading, but the heat from Cole's body warmed us both.

"Tell me more about the letter," I said.

"I'll tell you a story," Cole said firmly. "Okay? When you and Lucas were in high school, your friends had parties at the golf course, right?"

"They weren't exactly our friends."

"The point is you had a golf course. We had a bridge."

"You had parties on a bridge."

"On it. Under it. Not parties exactly. We went there all the time. On dates. With buddies. Alone. It's like we were drawn back there again and again."

"Like moths."

"The attraction," he said, "was that the bridge was haunted."

Then he told me the story: a long time ago, there was a beautiful girl. Her parents were wealthy, and she was their only child, and they doted on her. She fell in love with a local boy, handsome, kind, salt-of-the-earth. Her parents thought he wasn't good enough for her and told her she couldn't see him, but forbidding her only made her love grow stronger, and she and the boy made secret plans to elope. They planned to meet at midnight on the bridge.

"Can you guess what happens?" Cole said. "This is an old story."

Her parents discovered the plan and paid someone to kidnap the boy, and when the girl arrived at the bridge in the middle of the night, no one was there. She waited in the dark, getting chillier and chillier, but her lover never showed up. The first light came up softly, and she knew she'd been forgotten, or jilted. When her parents found her later that morning, she was swinging from the bridge with a rope around her neck. They saw her shadow swaying on the water.

Cole said, "Her name was Emily. *Emily.* Say it."

"Emily," I said.

He looked furious for a moment. Then he turned away from me and went on with his story. Emily haunted the bridge. She was still waiting for her lover to show up. All the kids in Cole's town went in the middle of the night to catch a glimpse of her shadow on the water, swinging from her rope. Or to hear her crying. The bridge shook, cars parked on it overnight rolled back and forth, even with the emergency brake on; cars came off the bridge with long scratches through the paint; kids came off the bridge with long scratches down their backs, their T-shirts ripped.

"So what does it mean?" I asked.

We picked up our shoes and began to walk home.

"Doesn't it mean anything to you?"

My shoulder bumped against his. I reached out and stopped him walking. "Some things last past death," I said.

"Right," he said. "Some things continue on."

I pulled him toward me. I pressed my cheek against his shoulder. I saw the threads of his jacket, each stitch. A strong wind blew my hair off my face, my clothes against my body. The sand hit my ankles, a little shower of artillery.

I wanted to know the things he knew, to have the things he had. I wanted what he had with Lucas, that effortless ease. I wanted the intimacy he'd somehow forged with my mother. My consciousness zinged around to each part of me that was touching a part of him. His fingers, my arm. His shoulder, my cheek. His hip, my waist—

Then the rain came. It happened in an instant. The sky went black. Cole put his arms around me. "Fuck," he said into the roar of the rain. I leaned my face against his rain-soaked chest. Water so near us, sand all around, air full of rain, clothes and skin soaked. The wind was rising, blowing birds out of trees. I put one hand on his neck, one on his chest as if listening for a heartbeat. We fell to our knees in the wet sand. Then we lay down in the wet sand. He reached into my clothes, peeled them off so there was nothing between me and the sand—between my skin and his. The rain crashed around us, and he pressed against me, and into me, and all my thoughts exploded into a million fragments, and then came together, floated together, like so many drops of water converging into one bright ocean. I had just this one thought with hard, impenetrable edges, just this: *now you are ours.*

15

"Wake up," I said.

"What is it?"

"I want to talk."

"Nightmare?" Lucas said. I sat on the edge of his bed.

"I dreamed you were so mad you stopped talking to me," I said.

Lucas sat up in bed. Something struck me as strange, but I couldn't tell what. Then I realized: it was a proportion problem. Lucas, with his broad shoulders, looked ridiculous in this twin bed. I didn't know why I'd never noticed before. His feet and hands were enormous. His chest seemed to take up the entire width of the bed. He looked like what he was: a grown-up in a child's bed.

I saw he hadn't put an extra blanket on his bed even though the nights were cold now. I went over to his closet and grabbed an old down comforter.

"I didn't mean it," he said sleepily, and at first I couldn't remember what he was talking about. Then I remembered how he'd said *we don't need you*. "I just don't want you to say no without considering the house—"

"It's not that. Listen, something happened tonight," I began. He had to hear it, he had to. I was resolved. If anything could help him see Cole clearly, it was this. And I needed Lucas on my side again, needed him as an ally helping me figure out what the fuck was going on. This would be hard, but it would shift the balance of power still further—hopefully in my direction. "There's something you should know about Cole."

After I told him, he looked out the window. Maybe he could see in the dark. I waited for some burst of emotion from him, something to match what I was feeling.

"You realize," he said, finally, "that this is it for me. This life?"

I looked around the room. "Me, too."

"No, it's different for me. I'm stuck here. It's not like I'm going to grow up and get married someday. I'm not going to have children or a career. Don't look at me like that, Lyd. You know it's true. I'm not good that way. I'm only good here, in this house, with the family I already have."

"Well, I'm not exactly heading toward marriage or any of that either."

"But for you it's a choice. I don't have a choice."

"Of course you do."

"No, it's not worth it, it's not worth it." He looked determined, sad. "You and Cole are the only family I'll ever have. It's all I have. Why are you trying to take it from me?"

I shook my head. "Me? I'm not—it's him. He's the one who showed up and changed everything—"

"You could have someone else. If that's what you're look-ing for, you could find someone else. He's my *brother*. Do you understand what a beautiful thing it is to have a brother?"

"Yes," I said. "I do."

"You can't take everything. You can't have everything. You can't have anything. You can't have him. You can't take it all away from me."

I heard a rush of static, felt humidity and pressure rise up into my throat and into the back of my head. For a moment I couldn't orient myself in the room. Which way was up, which was down, which direction led into the hallway, and which led out into the raw night?

"He's not our brother," I said, my voice rising. "Just stop with that."

A light came on in the hall. We felt a shadow in the door-way. Lucas sprang out of bed and stood facing Cole across the threshold.

"I don't want to see you," Lucas said, pushing past him. We heard his feet on the stairs, we heard the kitchen door. He didn't come back all night.

16

Rain continued, a fierce low rumble. Rain crashed against the windows. I wasn't worried for Lucas's safety, not at first. He had disappeared before and always returned home safe. Disappearing was a coping mechanism for Lucas. He knew how to hide, and he knew when to reappear. But as the hours passed, I began to feel scared. The night was cold, wet, and unrelenting, the wind off the water vicious. Around dawn, George Samson at the police station sent out search-and-rescue to check the woods and the shallow water, but there was no sign of Lucas.

Cole and I sat awake all night and into the morning. Cole's mood seemed to blow in and out like changing winds. "What were you thinking?" he asked me bitterly. "Why would you tell him?" Then he seemed to grow sentimental. He said, "Love scares him. That's the problem for Lucas."

I felt wretched. On the beach the night before, out of

breath, the rain on our faces, Cole's chest rising and falling, he'd looked at me and I knew what he saw: my eyes black, the pupils dilated into inky pools, cheeks flushed and hot. I had a birthmark on my cheek, a faint mark, like a brush of pale ink. When I blushed, it darkened, brightened. I sat up in the rain. I kissed his mouth, which tasted of rain and sand and sex. I remembered the notebook in his room and what he'd written. *She is alive.* I was, I was. I felt powerful, in control.

"The three of us are meant to be together," Cole had said. "Look at this." He scratched a deep line in the wet sand, then two more: a triangle. "We're the three arms of this triangle. You, me, Lucas. We're this solid thing, this shape."

Now I felt anything but powerful. With Lucas out there in the cold, I didn't feel like a solid shape. I felt adrift, alone.

He didn't come home all day. In the evening I walked to the old lighthouse and looked up, imagining what it was like on the top. Nothing stirred at the lighthouse, but still I waited below for a long time. I sat on the nearby rocks watching for its light to strobe on the water, a dull, lonely light that I couldn't imagine did much good in warning boats or attracting ghosts.

I was lonelier than I'd ever been.

I thought about going home, turning off all the lights, leading Cole to my bedroom, my narrow bed. I imagined the heat of his body, his beautiful ribs. I imagined how every thought and feeling would fade to nothing, leaving behind only that dense, bright, black hole into which all other feelings disappear—desire.

Instead I went to Jack's and sat at the bar with Gordon and Sebastian and all the old fishermen. I was as lonely as they were. I found myself telling them about Baby B, about Cole showing up and claiming to be my brother. I told them Cole wasn't his real name. I told them that he wouldn't tell us where he came from or what he left behind. I couldn't stop talking. I didn't mention his skin or the feeling of his feverish hands on my waist, although I thought about it the whole time. I didn't tell them how I felt caught in a fierce current, my head barely above the surface, being swept farther and farther away from the things I loved. I didn't tell them that every time I was near him I felt myself traveling miles away from any familiar shore. They listened attentively, nodding. Sebastian kept his eyes closed. When I was done with the story, he opened his eyes and whistled.

"Yes, indeed," he said.

"Sometimes I feel like nothing's mine anymore," I said. "He's taking everything. Lucas is *my* brother."

"Sure," Sebastian said.

"And it's *my* island."

"Wait a minute, now," Sebastian said, looking surprised. "This isn't your island."

"I was born here," I said.

"That don't make it yours," he said. "My granddaddy lived on this island. He came over from the Azores, little girl. You just showed up yesterday."

The fishermen looked at me with sympathy. My eyes welled up, and I felt embarrassed. They were right of course. People had lived here longer than I had. Families had passed down land over generations. Yet I felt deeply that it was mine, that I had some special ownership of the island because I loved it so much. Or because it was all I had.

Grow up, I told myself. *Stop agonizing over everything. So you made a mistake, miscalculated. You can fix this.*

★ ★ ★

The next day, I went to Eddie and Kim's place, a tiny apartment over Reeni's Salon. There was no actual Reeni, but the owners, two friends, both named Jennifer, thought it sounded more authentic. Kim cut hair there, and the smell of the place permeated the apartment as well, a clean, chlorinated scent. The hallway was full of it. I stood there knocking on the door, inhaling the fragrance of perms.

"Lydia," Eddie said, when he opened the door.

"Can I come in?"

"Um, yeah," he said. "Of course. Come on in."

I'd only been inside the apartment once before and I had the same reaction then that I did now, that while the furniture matched the curtains, and the curtains matched the pictures on the wall, none of it matched Eddie. It wasn't that Kim had bad taste, it was just a taste all her own. She liked ferns, that much was clear. Eddie and I sat across from each other at a table draped with a fern-print tablecloth. Hanging by the window were both a framed picture of a fern and the actual plant itself. The window looked over Clara Day Street.

"You can see the information booth from here," I said.

"I know."

"It looks lonely this time of year."

We both looked out at the landing, the dark water, the empty booth. Did he watch me from here? I felt that buzz of tension between us, something that skidded back and forth, like the puck on an air hockey table. And even here, Cole was somehow part of the tension.

"I think you were right," I said. "About Cole. He's—not right. And I think I just made everything a hundred times worse."

"Uh-oh," he said. "What happened?"

"I don't even know where to start. He—well, he knew my mother. That's one. They had some sort of relationship, but I can't get any answers out of him. Oh—and Cole isn't his real name. But he won't tell me what his real name is."

"That's fucked up," Eddie said. "It's fucked up to lie about your name."

"And now with Lucas off hiding somewhere… What I need is a place to stay. Maybe just for a night or two."

Eddie scratched the back of his head and looked gloomily out the window. I looked at the empty harbor.

"Do you ever want to be a new person?" Eddie said. He shook his head. "I'm tired of being the same person I always was. I still feel like I'm fifteen. Nothing feels different. Nothing feels better."

"I think everyone feels that way sometimes. At least I do."

"It's just you and me. Other people grow up."

"We grew up," I insisted. "Look at us."

Eddie raised his eyes. "When I look at us, I see children," he said.

"I have gray hairs."

"I'm talking about inside."

"I know."

"I want to help you," he said. "I would do anything—but you can't stay here. Of course you can't."

"Oh," I said. "No, that's fine. It was a stupid idea. You don't have the room."

"It has nothing to do with the room, and you know it."

When I said goodbye, Eddie handed me fifteen dollars. "It's all I have at the moment," he said. "But maybe you could get a room or something for a night." He hugged me tightly.

"You know what you have to do, right? You have to learn his name. His real name. Names matter."

He sighed and I felt his breath on the top of my head. "I'm really sorry," he said. "Find his name," he said. "That's the only way to have any power over him."

I looked back once from the hallway, and Eddie was still standing there.

Lucas came home the next morning. Or, was brought home. George Samson stood, ill at ease, in the doorway and told me he'd found him on the lighthouse eventually. Lucas looked pale and puckered, cold. He wouldn't talk to me. Wouldn't look at me.

Cole showed up after lunch, and the two of them moved the woodpile from the backyard to the woodshed. They stacked wood in each other's arms. I felt sharp envy. All was forgiven apparently for Cole; I sat in the silence of the house, wondering when I would be forgiven.

It was October. How did it get to be October?

When I couldn't take the silent treatment anymore, I took off for the landing. But soon, Cole caught up with me. We walked together in silence until we reached Clara Day Street. The landing was empty, and it felt as though we were the only inhabitants as we strolled the sidewalks.

"I should have said this right away," I began.

There were bright orange pumpkins and dark red chrysanthemums in front of every store. Jack's had decorated its doorway with a string of orange and black lights. I was shivering from the wind, or maybe from the invisible exchange I felt between us, something dark and overripe. I thought of berries, of brambles. I stopped walking, turned to him.

"It can never happen again," I said. "That's what I'm trying to say. I thought—I don't really know what I was thinking. It was a onetime thing, a mistake."

I saw a look cross his face, a tiny shadow, as if somewhere above him a small winged thing had crossed in front of the light. His jaw tightened.

I waited for him to agree, or argue. But he did neither. Instead, he put both hands on my neck, gently stroked the hollow of my throat. I looked around to make sure no one was watching. I shivered. His fingers sought out the most vulnerable spot on my throat in a way that didn't feel tender or romantic, as it could have. It seemed calculated, the way he touched me, as if he were doing research. I took a step back.

"It's cute," he said.

"What's cute?"

"The way you think you have control over things. It's innocent. Like a child."

"What do you mean?"

He shrugged. His fingers explored the ridges of my clavicle, and electricity coursed outward from that place like a star, like a sun. "I mean it *will* happen again, because it's bigger than you, or me. It's bigger than your will, or my will."

"I don't think so," I said, uneasy, afraid. "I don't even think I like you. In the end."

"The thing between us has nothing to do with what you like or don't like," he said. "The thing between us is already decided. It's written in the stars."

"I don't believe in that."

"Really?" he said. "I don't see how you can be your mother's child and not believe that."

"Leave her out of it."

He moved closer to me. "You know what she believed? She believed in tides. She believed that forces push and pull all of us the way the sun and the moon pull the tides. Low tide has nothing to do with the desires of the ocean. You must agree with that? And the forces that control us have nothing to do with our desires, not really. As for me, I can't wait to see how this ends. I'm breathless."

My thoughts were muddy and roiled, my body tense as a spring: stomach, diaphragm clutched. I didn't believe that the sun and the moon and forces bigger than me were pulling this way and that on the tides of my body, but what else explained the warm effervescence in my belly, my thighs, that sea foam of sensation?

"I'll see you tonight," Cole said, backing away from me. "I'll make a nice dinner."

After he walked away, I went straight to the Martha Day Memorial Library. Cole seemed to be gaining power and speed like a weather front, and I wanted to arm myself with the only thing I knew how to gather: information.

The library was a squat building that smelled of paper and glue and something sweetly yeasty, like bread dough. It was one of my favorite places on the island, a safe, familiar spot. Most of the books were on the second floor, which had steeply slanted walls like an attic. You had to duck to get at the books. On the ground floor there was a cheerful reading room with armchairs and racks of magazines, a couple of computers, and two librarians.

One librarian was Martha Day. The library was named after her mother, who had died when Martha was born. It was amazing to think of her as an infant, because as long as I'd known her she'd been ancient, wrinkled, and scrawny, and often looking sharply in a direction where exactly nothing was happening. She wafted around the library with an air of secrecy. Today, her eyes landed on me sitting at the computer, and she seemed to snap into focus. She nodded at me, and I picked up my hand and waved. If she'd kept looking at me like that, like she *knew* something more than the rest of us, then I would have told her about Cole. But she looked away and hurried off to shelve books.

Elijah West had returned to the island to be the head librarian—and part of the job description was convincing Martha he wasn't there to replace her but to aide her, which he pulled off impressively.

I turned to the computer screen, typed Cole Anthony. A few people popped up, none of them him. I typed Baby B, which turned out to be a company that sold babyproofing paraphernalia. I typed Pastlives.com, and a silvery screen appeared, with bold dark letters in some sort of handwriting font. This was a website Lucas used to frequent, and I would tease him about it.

Welcome to pastlives.com. According to the ancient beliefs of the Hindus and many other religions of the world, we are not born once, but again and again. We live many lives and learn many lessons as we make our way toward nirvana, the final state of bliss. Although many of us don't remember people, places, and events from our past lives, a few do. On pastlives.com you can discuss your past life memories and reach out to people from past lives.

I skimmed some of the forum discussions. One woman wrote that she and Harrison Ford had been in love in another life. That means he's part of your soul group, the circle of people who remain together life after life, someone had responded.

But I can't reach him, she wrote. He won't answer my letters, and I can't get him on the phone.

I read their queries and comments. A sense of belonging was waiting for them somewhere out there, and they were simply in the wrong place, the wrong body, the wrong life. Queries ranged from curious to desperate. Some people had specific memories of previous lives: a hoop skirt covering a long scar shaped like the letter S. For some it was just a vague sense that they didn't fit where they were now. Some people were aggressive in their insistence that past lives were real. Some were embarrassed but "had to give it a try."

There was nothing to help me understand Cole.

Beside the computer was a round end table, with a glossy coffee table book—Elijah West's book, the one he'd left the island to make, all the most beautiful bridges of the world. The cover showed a long causeway, with an orange sun balancing on its highest point. I picked up the book and thumbed through.

"Can't you find something better than *that* to read in here?" Elijah said, appearing behind me. He looked at the pages as I turned them.

"I guess I'm desperate," I said.

"Take it home," Elijah said. "Share it with Lucas."

He was so proud of the book.

"It's beautiful," I told him, and I meant it. "Seriously. I've been wanting a chance to look through it and really take my time."

He beamed.

At home, I tried to show Lucas the book, but he still wasn't talking to me. It was a lonely night—a long bleak dusk and silence in the house. I was restless. After eating alone, I shut myself in my room. In my notebook, I started a new list: Ways to Make Things Better. I wrote, *wait, apologize, leave, stay.*

I began to flip through the pages of Elijah's bridge book. It started with a series of New York City bridges: the George Washington Bridge, the Brooklyn Bridge, the Queensboro Bridge, Hell Gate Bridge. They rose up into the sky like bones, like the rib cages of giant fish, wrecked on the beach. Rib after rib. I had the strange sensation that Elijah's book, like a bridge itself, was connecting me to the rest of the world.

I turned the pages and saw bridges over streams. Log bridges. Bridges made from planks. A bridge made from the bottom of a boat. A bridge made from window shutters. Firm little walkways from one bank to the next. Then longer bridges. The Lake Pontchartrain Causeway, the Seven Mile Bridge through the Florida Keys. Suspension bridges. Swaying bridges. The covered bridges of New England.

Stop.

I leaned closer to the book. The bridges of New England were all dark wood against bright red and yellow leaves. Pretty and charming, but that wasn't what caught my eye.

I put my finger on the page and skimmed the caption, which told the story: the girl who hanged herself on the bridge when her lover didn't show up for their planned elopement. No evidence that this is historically accurate, Elijah's book said. But the story was passed around, a legend.

Emily's Bridge.

A long time ago there was a beautiful girl. The story Cole had told me on the beach. The bridge was in Lindenberg, Vermont, the caption said. Maple trees, yellow leaves, red barns. A real, tangible place. Emily's Bridge, the place where Cole and his friends had thrown parties like the ones Lucas and I went to on the golf course. I could feel my face burning with something. Excitement. Fear. The ghost in my house *grew up somewhere*. And maybe this was where. Just thinking the name of the place gave me an electric surge. Lindenberg.

Learn his name, Eddie had said. *That's the only way to have any power over him.*

Cole had been a child, a teenager. I imagined him riding bikes on a cul-de-sac. I imagined him eating bologna sandwiches. I already felt more powerful. Names did have power. Even the name of the bridge had power. And the name of the town was uplifting as a song. It was as if Cole were coming into focus, a Polaroid photo.

17

The summer I was seventeen, when I was preparing to leave for college, I'd felt something in the air around me, in the treetops, in the waves. It was as if the island were breathing, as if the heart of the island were pumping powerfully. I felt it when the wind swayed the branches or pinned the gulls' wings in place as they flew. I felt it when the rhythm of the waves became so loud and insistent, my own heart began to beat in time. I felt it somewhere deeper and quieter, too, in buds and blossoms, in the undulations of jellyfish, in the air molecules that shimmered with heat. I felt all around me the powerful opening and closing, filling and emptying, inhaling and exhaling of a living being.

I started to wonder if the island's breath and heartbeat were specially aimed at pulling me firmly to earth. I became aware of my own gravity. I was afraid that I would, in the end, be unable to get off the island. At night I dreamed I was escaping in a paddleboat. I exhausted myself pedaling, then glanced back to see myself still on the sand.

The day I finally left, I stood on the upper deck of the ferry, surprised at how easy it was to go. The island was like a glowing light that dimmed when we rounded the four sharp jetties, the Claws. Dimmed when we entered Vineyard Sound. Dimmed except for one speck of light, which was bright and painfully hot and scorched as I waited for it to disappear, one scorching speck of light, which was Lucas, waving from the dock.

But then my mother got sick, and I came home, stayed home. It sometimes felt like it was the island that had brought me back. But I didn't care. I loved it. I had to. When my mother died, I loved it even more. It was my new mother. It was all I had.

Every time I got on the ferry, I felt it again, the spark of light—my connection to Lucas as bright and electric as any lighthouse strobe. Every year it seemed to grow larger and fiercer, a whole blaze. And now it wouldn't dim. It never dimmed. It stayed hot and lit, pulling at me with its heat and brightness. Who could blame me for not wanting to ignite that blaze?

But here I was on the uppermost deck of the ferry, watching Wolf Island grow smaller and smaller behind me. I had made a decision to pursue the one clue I had about Cole's life—I was on my way to Lindenberg, to Emily's Bridge. It wasn't much, but sometimes all you need is one thread, one quick pull, and everything unravels.

I clutched the railing. Birds rode alongside me on the gusts of wind. The people back at the landing were like miniature versions of themselves. The postmaster was playing the bagpipes, the instrument like some outsize heart he had to hold outside his body. And there was Eddie lumbering down the street. I felt an intense desire for him to look up and see me. I wanted him to know that I was leaving the island. I wanted someone to know. I saw Jack's. I saw Mady's Diner. The Island Inn. The information booth. I could almost see myself there. I was waving. Goodbye. Goodbye.

When we reached the landing in Carson Cove, I drove off the ferry into the brightness. The sound of my tires on the grooved plank sent blood pumping through my temples. Carson Cove had a bright sky. On the sand was the carcass of a huge fish, pecked over by birds.

I parked the car and went into the Carson Cove ferry terminal.

There were rows of benches, a snack cart, and a counter with three stations for selling tickets, the workers behind plexiglass like tellers in a bank. The walls were lined with maps and displays of brochures. In the corner opposite the snack cart was the information booth where a young guy sat leaning back in his chair, looking bored. His mane of golden hair was as glorious as ever. *Hello, Oz.* It seemed inconceivable that I had ever joked about this boy with Lucas, even with Cole. It seemed like years ago, but really only a few days had passed since Cole had touched my leg on the porch, running his fingers from knee to ankle. *You're not a child*, he'd said. *You're a woman. And you're beautiful.*

I went to the coffee cart, but it was closed.

"Coffee?" Oz said. "Over here." He had his feet on the counter near a coffeepot and a stack of Styrofoam cups.

I went toward him gratefully. He wasn't conventionally handsome, not in the way Cole was, but I liked the way he looked—hopeful, *buoyant* somehow, with wild hair and a too-big mouth.

"What happened to the coffee cart?" I asked.

"Closed until May, but—" He gestured toward the coffee-pot on the counter and handed me a cup. He watched me sip feverishly. "Did you run out of coffee at home or something?"

"I like to have coffee throughout the day."

"I used to love coffee. But I gave it up. Last year when I started eating macrobiotic."

"I'm sure that's much healthier," I said.

"So where are you going?" he said. He nodded out the window to the dreary October rain.

"Vermont," I said.

"Nice," he said. "I went to school in Vermont. And my family used to go skiing in Vermont every winter when I was little."

"I'm going to the mountains. Lindenberg."

"That's where we used to go," he said. "You're a skier?"

"No. I'm—I'm looking for someone."

He peered up at me. "Okay," he said when I stayed quiet. "Intriguing."

"Is it all right if I—" I indicated the coffeepot.

"Go right ahead."

"I've never been to Vermont, so I have no idea where I'm going," I said as I refilled my cup. He stood up so he could rummage around under the counter for a minute. He finally produced an old road atlas and spread it out on the counter.

"This is kind of an old map," he said. "But I think it will give you the right idea."

"Thanks," I said.

"Not a problem." He considered the map. He was wearing a faded pair of work pants, a yellow shirt, and a brown hoodie. He stood on one foot for a second while he itched his ankle with the other shoe. People came and went, buying ferry tickets, grabbing brochures, using the bathroom, taking the free coffee. It felt good to stay put while others had to get back in their cars and leave. It's amazing how quickly a place can start feeling like home base.

"Here's the route you want," he said. "I've been this way a dozen times. It only gets tricky here." He put his finger on the map. The roads were tiny capillaries crisscrossing. "Seems like you don't have GPS. Why don't you just take this with you? You can return it when you come back through. I'll just highlight the road."

"Maybe you should come with me," I said.

He considered me for a minute. He didn't laugh.

"I'm kidding," I said. "But thanks for the map. That's super nice."

"Yeah, well. I'm super nice," he said.

I took the atlas from him. I liked the line he'd drawn with a pink highlighter, like a river I could follow to an important source.

"Bye," I said. He smiled, pushed his hair off his forehead.

I went to the door of the ferry terminal. People were rushing down the chilly street with their hands in their pockets. I saw my car in the parking lot, and I imagined myself walking toward it, sitting in the driver's seat, closing the door. I imagined myself driving down the road, leaving Carson Cove behind, joining the great migration of cars crossing the Cape Cod Canal, flooding onto the highway, heading north, heading to a town that might have a name I needed.

But I couldn't go.

The sound of cars rushing past came at me, and my heart started to pound. *There's nothing wrong with tires on a cold street*, I told myself. But my heart thumped, and blood coursed beneath my skin. *There's nothing wrong with tires on a cold street*. I decided to walk out the door, to my car. I saw it there and I decided to walk to it and get in and close the door and drive. But I could hear through the open door the rush of cars and trucks, and the rush was like the rush of blood in the ears, the rush of a terrible wave, of everything being extinguished at once—

"Is something wrong?" Oz had come out of his information booth and was standing behind me.

"I just changed my mind."

He said something, but I could hardly hear him. His voice was lost in the roar.

"What?" I asked.

"Are you hyperventilating?"

"Everything's fine," I said, a little angrily.

"Shit," he said. "Can you just try to breathe a little?"

I did try to breathe. But it felt like every breath was the same breath, a used-up breath, never big enough.

A small group gathered. Normally I would have been mortified. But who cared who gathered and gawked now? They closed in, murmuring what sounded like *shame, shame*, or maybe *what a shame*; I wondered if I was dying.

"I can help," someone said, a young guy with a shaved head and a beard. "I mean I'm no doctor, but—"

"I think we need an actual doctor," Oz said. He had a phone against his face.

"Is it your heart?" someone said.

"It's my heart," I said.

My heart was a bird flung against a window, that terrible thump over and over. The man looked into my eyes. He held my wrist between his moist fingers.

"Has she eaten today?" he asked. The crowd of people waited to hear.

"Have you?" Oz said.

"Breakfast."

"Breakfast," Oz reported to everyone. "And lots of coffee."

"You're having a panic attack," the kid with the shaved head said with certainty. "My old girlfriend used to have these. You need some drugs. You need like Valium."

"I need to look in a mirror," I said. And then everything went gold, and someone led me away, blind.

When I could see again, I realized there was a little mirror in my hands. I found my reflection among some scratches and smears. There I was, the same person, the same face. I wasn't gone or altered in any way. I held the mirror tightly and looked around to see where I was. A quiet room, an office. I saw manila folders in stacks on a metal desk.

"We've got an ambulance coming," someone said. It was Oz, and he was sitting on a plastic chair near me.

"No," I said. "I'm not going anywhere in an ambulance."

"Well, you need to get some kind of medical treatment from someone."

"I'm totally fine," I said. "Look, watch."

I stood up. He stood up, too.

"I'm sorry about this," I said.

"Stop right there," he said, holding up his hand. "You have nothing to be sorry about."

"I'm still not going to the hospital," I said.

"I heard you the first time."

I raised the mirror to my face and focused on the tiny blurred reflection of myself. Tiny Lydia. Smear of a face. My heart was calm now. Everything was slow and quiet.

This was what I meant when I said it was hard to leave the island. I had never thought to call it a panic attack. I always just felt waves, crashing, racing, drowning. Looking back, I realize I hadn't tried to leave the island for years. Since my mother's death, time had slipped by, and I hadn't needed to go anywhere—not really—so I didn't know how fierce it had become, the force pulling me home.

But now, another, equally important force was pulling me away. I was looking for Cole. Not for the Cole who was probably still happily stacking wood with Lucas right now. The *past* Cole, the real Cole, the Cole who had a different name altogether. In other words, I was trying to understand his history, his identity—and I had one clue, only one: Lindenberg, Vermont.

I looked up from the mirror.

"Do you want to stay here for a while?" he said, this beautiful boy.

We sat there together, and we sat there together, and we sat a little longer.

So this is the story of how I met Tuck, because that's what his name actually was, not Oz of course. First Tuck sent the ambulance away. Then he went out onto the street somewhere and brought me back a little bowl of chowder and a bag of oyster crackers. We sat there in the back office.

"Don't you need to—what about the booth?"

"Who cares about the booth?" he said.

A few people drifted in and out of the back office where we were sitting, but mostly we were alone.

"Panic attack, huh?" Tuck said.

"I guess so."

"First time?"

"I've had them before. But I didn't know they were panic attacks."

"What did you think they were?"

"I'm not sure. I thought there was really something to be scared of."

He nodded. "Yeah. I know how that feels."

I doubted that. Everything about him—his posture, his legs, his open face—seemed to say *not afraid*. But I knew he was trying to be kind, so I smiled and kept on eating soup.

If I couldn't leave the ferry terminal without having another panic attack, then my only option was to go back home to Wolf Island. There was no room on the four o'clock ferry for my car, so I made a reservation for the nine o'clock boat. I migrated from the back office to the waiting area, so I could look out the windows at my car and the rippling water in the harbor. Tuck was back at the information booth, talking with tourists, chatting with locals. He was tall, smiling, friendly. People gravitated toward him. He was totally unselfconscious, throwing back his head to laugh, not caring who saw or heard.

During a lull, Tuck came over to me on a bench looking out over the harbor.

"I pretty much saved your life, right?" he said. "I figure you owe me."

"I don't know what to say to that."

"Kidding," he said. "Sort of. What I mean is I'm curious about you. And since you don't have anywhere to go, I think you should tell me your story. And I brought you gumballs."

He rolled six small green and red gumballs into my palm.

I looked at him. *It started in August. It was August, and you know August, how the smell of dead sea creatures is always in the air.*

"Okay," I said. "Why not?" I started slow. I told him about Baby B, about Lucas and the candles, I told him about the day Cole arrived, about Eddie's advice, and how Cole waved to all the islanders as if he'd known them forever, how he'd been helping the Grendles clean their gutters. How he had a tab at Hiram's Bounty, and at Jack's, and at Island Pie.

"Holy shit," Tuck said. "He's weaseling his way into your life."

"Exactly."

"That's so creepy."

"But see, he's also really charming. And…handsome. Everyone loves him."

I opened my mouth to tell him about Cole and me, that night on the beach, but I couldn't. My heart contracted unpleasantly. I shook my head. "I think he grew up in Lindenberg," I said. "Just based on some things he's said."

"Way to sleuth."

"And if I want to learn his name—I have to go there."

"Or just get in touch with the right people in Vermont. Email them pictures. You can do these things remotely. I'm getting the sense it might be hard for you to, you know, go *anywhere*."

But I wanted to go there. I wanted to see Emily's Bridge. I wanted to stand on it and know that Cole had been a teenager there, in that very spot. That somewhere nearby he had had a house, and a bed, and a mother. He'd done homework at the kitchen counter and eaten peanut butter crackers. He'd been a child.

But Tuck was right—that would have to wait, and until I could leave the island without falling to pieces, there were other ways to investigate.

The closer it got to nine o'clock the better I felt. I could breathe deeply again. I could think again. I thought about Tuck leading me into the office and placing the little scratched mirror in my hands, and I felt layers of embarrassment at this display of vulnerability. I wondered what Lucas and Cole were doing. I closed my eyes and tried to feel what the house felt like without me. I felt a chill, even though I wasn't cold.

Then, just as an exercise of thought, I imagined myself in Providence, where I went to college that one semester. I was wearing a blue hat and walking down a narrow street past a tea shop with a wooden sign hanging above its door. I saw the door of an apartment, and I knew it was where I lived, although it wasn't anything like the dorm I'd lived in when I was actually in Providence. Over the small sink in the kitchen was a window and through it were tall fir trees and beyond the fir trees tall buildings. And in the branches of the fir trees, crows. I heard the chaos of the crows' lonely voices. And then the train, its whistle.

No. I shook my head. The trains and the crows—that wasn't my life.

At six someone came in for the evening shift in the information booth, and Tuck came over to me.

"Should I go get dinner?" he said.

"Yes. You've been really, really nice today. Please don't feel like you have to stay any longer."

"No, I mean bring dinner back here."

"Oh no," I said. "I can eat when I get home."

"Please," he said. "You can't wait until eleven or whenever to eat."

He touched my shoulder and said, "Be right back."

He was nice. Nice. Nice. Nice. Unafraid and nice. What if he were my boyfriend, what if we were both twenty years old and neither one of us was afraid? What if I were someone else suddenly, someone like him, with his pretty childhood, and luck with the ladies, and that unselfconscious laugh. It was a relief to be someone else for a minute, even just in my imagination.

★ ★ ★

From our window, we could see most of Water Street, which was like Clara Day Street. Tuck pointed out the buildings, told me what they were and who worked there. There were several large scientific labs on Water Street, because Carson Cove had two big science institutes.

"Let's play a game," he said, "called local, tourist, or scientist."

"I'm really, really good at this game," I told him.

"*I'm* really good at this game."

While we ate fish and chips out of paper cartons, we eavesdropped on conversations of groups coming in to buy tickets or use the bathroom. When we heard bits of conversations about bones and neurons and cartilage, Tuck and I listened intently, as if the word *Dinoflagellata* held some sort of important clue.

Tuck smoothed the take-out bag and produced a pen from his pocket, which he used to draw a map of Carson Cove, the important parts of town we couldn't see from our window. A pathway along an icy pond. A bell tower rising up out of a garden where, Tuck told me, local kids went to *get it on*. He ran out again, for coffee, and came back holding two blue ceramic mugs, the liquid still steaming. "I'll bring the cups back when we're done," he said. "The last thing you need right now is a paper cup." We ate pastry, left over from the morning, so half price, and we sipped coffee and suddenly it was after eight and time for me to get in line for the ferry.

I felt strange leaving Tuck; we'd spent so many hours together. "Seven hours," I said out loud, and then blushed.

"I know," he said. "It's been an unusual day at the old Carson Cove Information Booth."

I thought of the information booths, his and mine, separated by a strip of cold, deep water.

"You know what would be fun?" he said. "To do this again, only leave the building."

I laughed.

"Or you know what?" he said. "I could come over to Wolf Island."

"Oh. Okay," I said.

"To meet this dude," he said.

"You'll probably love him. Everyone does."

Tuck walked with me to my car, staying close, like a bodyguard. When we reached the car, a seagull swooped near us, and Tuck lifted his arm, as if to shield me, but the bird hovered, staring at us with its black-bead eyes.

"This guy's the reincarnation of *my* long-lost brother," Tuck said.

"Learn his name."

"His name is *bird*."

"I'm beginning to think," I said, "that the only way to escape your family is to move far away."

"To another island?" Tuck said.

"Just far away, and never have kids and isolate yourself from everyone. That's the only way to really escape your family."

"Or just stop believing in this crap," he said. "Just leave all this crap behind and live your life."

I sat again on the upper deck of the ferry in the cold night wind. I couldn't stand being indoors: the stuffy enclosed space, the windows with their warped views. I sat in the frozen air, under the dark sky and let myself be pulled back home. Gulls zipped past. I watched them watching me.

Bird, I thought, relieved to be able to name something.

18

When I arrived at the house that night, headlights making a wide path of light across the dark lawn, I saw that the kitchen light was on, and had a flash of what I would find inside. Cole and Lucas at the kitchen table, drinking, waiting. And there they were, exactly as I'd envisioned it. Cole did all the talking, not asking where I'd been, or why I'd gone, but politely, coldly reminding me that the car wasn't mine to take. What if they'd needed it? What if there'd been an emergency?

"Don't do it again," Cole said.

"Don't tell me what to do," I said. But they ignored me, walked into the living room. I followed, watching in baffled silence as they climbed the stairs. I ran up behind them.

We all looked through the open door to Baby B's room, where Cole's duffel bag sat empty on the rug. I went into the room, opened the drawers, saw his clothes folded inside. In the closet, his shirts were hanging. Stacked on the dresser, his creased newspaper, his notebook with the torn pages, where I'd first seen his scribbled notes, the words *She Is Alive* traced and traced until they were darker than all the other writing.

"You're not welcome here," I said.

"I invited him," Lucas said. They were the first words he'd spoken to me since he'd run away.

"I'm uninviting him," I said.

"Too late," Lucas said. I didn't know if he meant the hour—nearing eleven—or if he meant something more permanent.

"What will you do?" Cole said to me, smiling. "I wonder. Will you carry my clothes out and throw them into the bay? Will you try to drag me down the stairs? I wouldn't if I were you, I'm far stronger. Will you call the police? I'd love to see that giant idiot who brought Lucas home trying to figure out whether I'm doing anything illegal or not. Hint? I'm not. No, you won't call the police. You know better than that. I'm wondering if maybe you aren't going to do anything."

His face had arranged itself into an expression of sympathy, but underneath, like some awful palimpsest, was suppressed glee glimmering through, and another layer, too, of smooth cruelty.

What could I do? He was right. George Samson wouldn't be able to help—Cole wasn't doing anything wrong on the surface; he was Lucas's invited guest.

But if he was staying here, then I wasn't.

I turned my back to them and walked down the stairs, through the kitchen, and out into the night. I left the fucking car. I didn't need it. I walked along the beach, toward the landing.

The girl at the front desk of the Island Inn, the one who was afraid of room eleven, looked surprised as I approached her.

"You want a room?" she said to me. "Uh-oh. Is everything okay?"

"What? Fine! I just want a vacation," I said. "For like one night."

"Here?" she said. "A mile from your house?"

I looked around at this world of big soft chairs. It wasn't like the rest of the island. It was rich and new. Clean and constructed. People came and went all year long leaving nothing behind. I felt like the opposite of that—burdened by all the trappings of my life, weighed down by the past, and not just my past! I was carrying all of it. Lucas's past. My mother's past.

"Room eleven," I said.

"Seriously?" she said.

The room had a huge, clean bed with white sheets, a velvety, rich-feeling bedspread. I sat on the bed and looked out at the harbor. If I stood right up against the window, I could see down Clara Day Street, see all the familiar roofs and windows, see the light spilling from windows out onto the street, all of which looked less and less familiar as the lights began to blink out and the night grew darker.

I got into the vast bed. I desperately missed the feeling of drifting off in my own bed, knowing what the morning would bring, knowing that things were good between Lucas and me. Knowing that we didn't have many people to love, but we had each other, and that was something to count on. I wanted to find my way into that world again. I wanted it so badly, I could taste the wanting, like blood on my tongue.

I woke in the dark with Cole beside me. I recognized his smell, felt his breath and his feverish heat against my back. I heard him whispering in the faintest paper breath of a voice. I was frozen, as if in a nightmare, but it wasn't a dream. My senses were sharp and raw. There was salt on the air, and on his skin. I heard gentle waves in the harbor outside.

"It was many, many a year ago, in a kingdom by the sea," he whispered, and the skin of my neck crawled. *"I was a child and she was a child, in this kingdom by the sea. But we loved with a love that was more than love."*

I couldn't catch every word, but I heard the rhymes, the incantation.

"Neither the angels in heaven above, nor the demons down under the sea, can ever dissever my soul from the soul of the beautiful Annabel Lee."

Then I recognized it completely. We'd learned the poem in high school, along with "Bells" and "The Raven." He recited into my ear, so I *felt* the poem as well as heard it, each breath a small hot gust—*"For the moon never beams without bringing me dreams. And the stars never rise but I feel her bright eyes."* His forceful breath over and over with every consonant. *"All the night-tide, I lie down by the side of my darling, my darling, my life and my bride, in her tomb by the sounding sea."*

Then his breath was the only thing I could hear.

I was frozen with fear, unable to move or even think.

"Cole?" I said finally—I hardly recognized my own voice, it was so quiet, muted with fear.

He pulled my hips against him, nuzzled his face into the back of my neck. "We belong together," he said. "Lucas will come around, I promise you. He knows the nature of tides as well as you do. Then we can all be together." I twisted to look over my shoulder at his face, which was defenseless and bare. I'd wanted to see vulnerability in him, sure it would make him more human, frail in some way. But it only made him desperate. It meant he would do anything. "You belong to me," he said in a low, raw voice. "Sleep," he said. "I'll watch over you."

He was soft, limp, quiet. But if I moved at all, his arms clamped over me, holding me in place. "Shh," he said. "You're safe."

An hour later the light changed subtly, the grainy sky showing over the harbor out the strange window. The room was so quiet, the sky outside dark and still and lovely, it seemed unbelievable that my thoughts could speed with such intensity. I told myself to keep still—I told myself when the sun flooded the room all would be different. He would click into the Cole I knew from daylight, the careful, controlled Cole. I told myself Lucas would feel that something was wrong and come looking for me, but I knew he wouldn't.

Then, just as dawn was about to break in earnest, he rose quietly from the bed, dressed, and left the room. When the latch of the door clicked into place, I sat up in bed. I looked around the dark, strange room.

My eyes were gritty, and my head ached. I felt cold, and I didn't get out of bed for a long time. Where would I go? I thought about the *kingdom by the sea*. I thought about his name. I thought about his warm body and felt a terrible rushing sense of loss. Whoever I'd thought he was, that person was slipping away from me, swept right out to sea. Whoever he really was, he was strong, and lawless, and undeterrable.

19

In the morning, I went to the police station, with a tiny desperate hope that they could help after all, although I had a hard time piecing together what I would say to them. How could I possibly explain how we'd arrived at this point? I imagined George Samson looking at me like I was crazy. I imagined what he'd say: so now tell me again—really slowly—*why* were you sleeping at a hotel? And *why* exactly did you think he might be your dead brother? And *what* exactly made him think he could climb in bed beside you?

The police station was homey in a way I did not expect. There were yellow-and-white-checkered curtains in the windows, and a kind of reading nook in one corner, with an old gray armchair and a bookshelf full of books and magazines, and one lamp giving off a warm glow. On the counter in front of George was a collection of Hummel figurines. It was warm and smelled like microwave popcorn.

"Can I help you?" someone said, and suddenly I understood the yellow curtains and collection of Hummel figurines. The receptionist was short and round and very sweet. Her sweetness was almost aggressive, the way she clasped her plump hands and leaned forward to listen to me.

"I'm Lydia Moore," I began. "I—I live here."

"Marlene Hart," she said. "I've been here—" she thumped her palm on the desk "—since 1972. Now I'm surprised I don't know you. I usually know all the kids on the island. They usually show up here at least once or twice."

"Well, I never got in trouble," I said.

"That explains it then."

"But my brother is Lucas Moore."

"Okay," she said, nodding. "Now, how is *he*?" She looked sympathetic, expecting the worst apparently.

"Well, I think we need help. Lucas and I both. It's hard to explain."

We were interrupted by the bells on the door as it swung open, and Stephanie Conn walked in with Eva Cardoza. Stephanie, of course, was married to Stephan, both of whom I knew from the island school. They were the ones I often saw together at Jack's late at night, looking into each other's eyes, still so lost in the romantic bubble of first love they could hardly hear when someone spoke directly to them. I'd envied them so often. I'd wanted that kind of love, that intensity of belonging.

Now Stephanie was sporting a puffy black eye and a long gash on her cheek. She was crying, noisily, like a little kid, an unabashed sound, guttural, indulgent. Eva Cardoza, who was leading her by the elbow, looked like the sound hurt her ears.

"Again?" Marlene said. "I don't know why you keep bringing her here. Honey, you have to go to the doctor. You might need stitches."

"What do I know?" Eva Cardoza said. "I don't know what to do. I'm just the neighbor. We try the clinic, no one answers. Dr. Lyle is sleeping in, because I happen to know he is drinking all night at the bar. So I bring her here, and now you can have her."

"But what happened?" I said, aghast.

"You shush," Marlene Hart said to me. She picked up the phone and dialed. "It's Marlene down at the police station," she said, in the same cheerful voice. "Yes, we need the clinic. Well, go next door and wake him up, would you, dear?" she said. "You know where the key is. If he doesn't answer, just go right in and shake him awake."

"Did Stephan do this?" I said.

"He does it once a week," Eva Cardoza said. "She cries and cries and then next day she's so in love again."

"He does this once a *week*? Oh my god. Why doesn't anyone stop him?"

"This is what their love looks like," Eva said, shrugging.

Marlene had found an ice pack in the back and was holding it to Stephanie's face.

"There you go. You hold this right here. I don't think this is going to need stitches after all, honey," Marlene said. "Isn't that good news?" She turned to me and gave me an accusing look as if I were somehow responsible. "No one's perfect. But I think you already know that."

I walked out into the weak sunlight, desperate to get away from Stephanie and her swollen eye, bloody cheek, her terrible crying. And worse still was Eva Cardoza's casual shrug. *He does it once a week.* I couldn't stand it. I didn't want to see below the surface if this was the kind of thing I would find. And—I was seeing something else that maybe I'd known all along—George Samson wasn't going to sweep in and save the day. He hadn't done anything for Stephanie, not in all these years. What could he possibly do for me?

No one was going to save me.

That was the truth, and it landed in my gut like a rock.

The rhythm of the poem was in my head all day. I thought of the notebook paper I'd found in Cole's room weeks ago. *She is alive.* That sentence marched along beside the poem, making a chaotic mess of the *tomb by the sounding sea.* A voice as clear as the autumn air called out to me: *Which do you want to be? Alive? Or in a tomb by the sea?* I wondered if it was my mom.

I walked down to the landing. The afternoon light turned the sand to gold. My face and fingertips burned. Clint had his bagpipe on the dock, and it sang and sang. I heard the lines from the poem as my own heart beat in rhythm. I imagined the *tomb by the sounding sea* but I didn't shiver. I felt a warm rebellion deep in my gut.

This wasn't me. I didn't lie still while a thief took all that was mine. I was someone who fought back. I was slowly filling up with something, a large, warm sensation. It was courage, coursing through my veins. I planted my feet in the sand and lifted my arms above my head, lifted them to the golden sun sagging in the west. Things were going to change, because I was different now. I felt the change like a turning tide. I was scared of Cole, yes, and I was sad about the past, but I was also brave. All this time I'd been waiting for someone to throw me a life buoy, but I didn't need the buoy. I was a strong swimmer, a fierce swimmer, and I knew how to fight against a current.

20

I made three changes when I returned home from the Inn, and I implemented them like they were my job.

First, I installed a lock on my door, a sliding lock I could secure from the inside, and I stashed a bottle of spray cleaner under my bed, which I could use to blind him, I thought, if I needed to. Even so, I had a hard time sleeping, and when I did my dreams woke me up.

Often I heard knocking, but when I went to the door no one was there.

Often I saw twin creatures running across the lawn, raccoons, or foxes, or stray dogs.

I dreamed Cole was telling me secrets.

"It's the same every time," he said. "It's you and me in a dark place—together. I'm inside you. Over and over."

"What are we talking about?"

"The dream. The most perfect dream I've ever had."

He touched me with one finger, letting it run along my throat, my collarbone, my breasts, first one, then the other, his fingernail as light as wind, on my rib cage, my stomach, my hip. I felt myself sinking, submerged.

"Can I ask you something?" I said. "What's your real name?"

He laughed. "Colin," he said.

"Is this a dream?" I asked, just to be sure.

The palm of his hand on the outside, then the inside, of my thigh. I was out of breath. I was slipping underwater.

The second change: I made an appointment with Dr. Brent, a psychologist whose office was at the small medical center inland, to talk about my panic attacks and how to manage them.

"I didn't realize what they even were," I told her, "until suddenly I was passed out in Carson Cove. I have to be able to get off the island. I mean, if I ever really needed to. Can you write me a prescription, something I can take to manage them?"

"Drugs are good. Drugs are fine," she said. "But there may be other ways. Meditation really helps some people. And you might want to sign up for a yoga class?"

"Oh god," I said. "You really do turn into your mother."

Dr. Brent said, "I knew your mother. I'm sorry you had to lose her. And you were just a teenager."

"I was twenty when she died."

"That's too young to be without a mother."

I wanted to cry, knowing someone had noticed what was happening to me back then. People had sent flowers and come to her funeral, but afterward, everyone had gone back to their lives, the business of cooking meals, and cleaning rooms, and fixing rain gutters, and bathing children—and Lucas and I had been forced to cobble together a life of cleaning and cooking and paying bills and caring for each other, without really knowing how to do it.

I shook my head, pressed my fingertips against my eyes. "I guess I'd like to be normal," I told Dr. Brent. "You were wondering about my goal. That's my goal. I want to live a normal life."

"I doubt that," she said. "I mean, what's normal? What is it you'd like to do that you think normal people do?"

"I don't know," I said, but I did know. I knew one thing I wanted to do. "I'd like to go to Carson Cove and walk around. Without, you know—"

"Perfect," she said. "Let's make an action plan."

Dr. Brent's action plan involved small, every other day trips to Carson Cove. The idea was to rewire my brain to associate Carson Cove with something other than fear. Once I'd experienced the town without panic, it would be easier and easier to step off the ferry, get into a car, drive toward the highway.

I was glad for the excuse to return to Carson Cove because I was anxious to be away from home, away from Cole with his smile, his muscles, arms, mouth, chest, ears, neck, the smell of his sweat. His fingernails. His breath in my ear. I'd begun to think of him as something other than human, but not a ghost. Something flesh and bones, but complicated by the heft and history of myth and fairy tale. A wolf. All teeth and hunger. All ripping, tearing, cunning trickery. It was as if the beast the island was named for had returned to claim all that was his. Names matter.

I was also glad to return to Carson Cove because I wanted to see Tuck again, his bright smile that had nothing to do with what was happening at home.

I wanted to give myself a few days, a chance to catch my

breath before I risked another panic attack in Carson Cove, so in the meantime I concentrated on the third change. In addition to the lock and my sessions with Dr. Brent, I rented a safety-deposit box at the Island Bank. I planned to systematically go through the various files in the house and make sure the important papers—the deed to the house, the copies of our parents' wills—were locked up where Cole couldn't find them.

I hadn't paid attention to these things before. The house was paid off. Once a year, a tax bill appeared, and we paid it. When the electric bill came, we wrote a check for that. I deposited my paycheck and Lucas's paycheck into our checking account at the island bank every two weeks. There was usually enough to pay our water and electricity, to buy groceries. When something came up, we went to our savings account—which our mother had left for us when she died. It was slowly getting smaller, but I had always assumed it would last until—until it ran out, and then we would figure something else out.

It was all stunningly simple. Bills came and we paid. Now things felt more complicated. I was aware suddenly of all we had to lose.

I started in my mother's room, looked once again in the drawers of her bureau. I went into the closet, where a few of her dresses were still hanging. The smell of sandalwood was still there, faintly, in the folds of her clothes, in a few sweaters still folded on the high shelf. I ran my hands over the dresses, felt their ghostly flutter. I put my hands into her pockets, but there was nothing there.

In the upstairs hallway, I stood for a moment smelling the

house's familiar scent: salt, dampness, bread, coffee. Cole and Lucas were out, and the house was quiet.

I pulled the attic ladder down silently and climbed through its trapdoor onto the dusty plywood floor.

"Hello?" I said, although I knew no one was there.

Then something moved in the corner, large and dark, and I caught my breath. For a moment I felt trapped, in danger. My nightmares. But it was my own reflection I'd seen moving in the old walnut-framed mirror my mother had brought back from her grandmother's funeral a long time ago. The glass, now under a thick layer of dust, had always been strange to look into—a kind of wavy, distorted reflection. I didn't know why she'd wanted it.

The attic reached the entire length of the house, and was built around the big brick fireplace, which stretched up from the living room. It was relatively bright for an attic, with big windows on either end, one looking over the side lawn, and one looking out on the driveway and street.

Boxes of Dad's stuff made a kind of wall on one end of the room. His clothes, the books from his office. Boxes of Mom's stuff created another wall on the other end of the room. Her clothes, her perfumes and lotions from the bathroom. We didn't want to throw it away. It was as if we thought she'd come back and want it again. We'd packed everything neatly and brought it up here.

Behind the chimney were old pieces of furniture: a futon, three ladder-back chairs with broken rungs, an armchair, a wicker patio set missing cushions. The furniture leaned all up against itself like pickup sticks, like kindling laid for a fire. Two boxes were open on the armchair. I peeked inside.

Photographs, paper, an old paperweight one of us had made in grade school.

In an old wooden filing cabinet, I searched for information about the house, the bank account. I discovered a file entitled COLIN. It was a thin little manila folder. There couldn't be much inside, but still, my heart began to pound as I opened it.

Inside I found three things. The first was a half-page program from Colin's memorial service. I hadn't known there'd been one. I envisioned my mother, tall and well dressed, greeting each mourner with regal finesse, the way she had at my father's service. Where had Lucas and I been during Colin's memorial service? Who had taken care of us? Who had attended the memorial service? My mother and father had only just moved to the island. They wouldn't have known very many people yet.

There was also a letter from my mother's mother, who had died twenty years ago. I'd met her only once. I opened the envelope and drew the letter out.

Dearest C, it said.

God doesn't give us more than we can handle, so I know you'll be all right. You may come home whenever you need to. You know they'll never forgive you. But we will.

Love and condolences,
Mother

At first I thought the letter must be meant for Colin, or for Cole, but I quickly realized C was also for Cecily, my mother. I imagined my stern grandmother, basically a stranger to me, and wondered what she meant when she said they will never forgive you. For what? The letter was so brief, I thought it might be the culmination of a longer correspondence. But if so, the rest of the letters were somewhere else.

The final document was Colin's death certificate. It was a strangely cheerful document, like the awards I used to win in school for good penmanship. There was even a gold seal at the bottom of the page. I read through it.

Name: Colin Matthew Moore. The middle name struck me suddenly. It wasn't that I'd forgotten his middle name; I just so rarely thought of it. Date of birth: that was our birthday of course. Date of death: less than three months later. Address at time of death: the same address we still used. Primary cause of death: drowning.

I held the paper closer to my face.

Primary cause of death *drowning*?

This made no sense. Colin had died of pneumonia, on his way to the hospital with my mother. I'd heard the story from my mother. I could picture it as clearly as if it had been me on the deck of the ferry so many years ago.

I shuffled through all the papers again, as if I might find an answer I missed.

"Lydia?" I heard my name faintly, someone calling from downstairs. I closed the folder and held it against my chest.

"I guess she's in the attic," Lucas said. And I heard their feet on the ladder coming up, Lucas first, his head, then shoulders, then the rest of him. "What are you looking for?" he asked suspiciously.

"I thought I heard something," I said. "I thought something was moving up here." I put the folder quickly behind my back.

Cole emerged next, and I felt both afraid and inexplicably

guilty. But they didn't look at me. Instead, they moved from thing to thing in the attic, touching what they saw: an old double stroller. Two tricycles. Four old suitcases with broken zippers. It's both sad and comforting to stand among the detritus of your life. Your mother's stuff, your father's stuff, the treasures that belonged to you as a baby, a child, a teenager. Except for the boxes that were open or out of place, the rest was thoughtfully organized and stacked, even labeled. We might not have gotten rid of stuff easily, but we knew how to put it away.

I watched Cole touch the roof of a broken dollhouse. I watched him run his fingers over my father's suits on the garment rack. For a minute I felt sorry for Cole. This whole room was about memories, the past. Maybe that was what the whole house was about. We could look through these old things anytime we wanted, we could gather the past around us, touch it all, count it all. And his past was somewhere else, inaccessible.

And then he looked at me, and I understood that he wasn't sad about what he saw. He was exhilarated. His eyes were black and shining. He was a collector, only he wasn't interested in collecting any of this old stuff. What he collected was much more complicated: our memories, our past. It was as if he wanted these things for himself.

"Here's what you heard," Lucas said from near the wall of Mom's stuff. I took the moment to stash the COLIN folder under the old futon. Then I turned to Lucas. He was poking something with the toe of his shoe. It was a bat. Tiny and curled into a ball, like a stone thrown through the window. "Dead," he said.

At the bottom of the attic stairs, Cole grabbed my arm.

"What is it you're looking for?" he asked. He tilted his head and waited for me to speak. When I didn't, he reached out and took a lock of my hair and held it between his thumb and finger, as if testing it for strength. He let it slip between his fingers. *Your name*, I thought, but I didn't say it. Fear and exhilaration seemed to inch higher, into my chest, my throat. I felt like a high striker at a carnival. Cole was holding the hammer, trying to send that marvelous little puck right up to the bell. I felt the bell in my throat, in my mouth, that fearful ringing.

That night I lay awake for hours. I was thinking about Colin and his cause of death. Maybe *drowning* was what they called it when your lungs drowned in fluid from pneumonia. I knew that couldn't be true even as I thought it. No, our parents must have lied to us about Baby B and how he'd died. Was this what my grandmother had thought my mother could never be forgiven for, this lie? He was seven weeks old. He was the size of my mother's forearm. She'd told me that once, that she could hold each of us on her forearm, our heads cradled in her palm, the rest of us fitting neatly between wrist and elbow. How had he drowned? I imagined him in the bathtub, and shivered.

At some point in the night I heard a sound above me, a creaking, a slow tapping. I sat up in bed, straining to hear. It was Cole, I felt sure, looking through files in the attic. I crept out of bed and into the hallway, but the trapdoor to the attic was closed, the ladder hidden away behind the door. Cole's bedroom door was closed and quiet. I went back to bed, but all night long I heard noises. I told myself they were the sounds of the house, the small adjustments and settling of a house a hundred years old. But so often in the night the noises sounded like small footsteps, like tiny fists knocking against a closed door.

21

On my first trip back to Carson Cove, Tuck met me at the boat.

"Hey," he said, grinning.

We walked to the coffee shop on the corner and sat so I could see the ferry and the expanse of water leading back home. That was as far as I was willing to go. Tuck picked up a pack of sugar and ripped the corner off, then shook the sugar into his coffee, leisurely, like he had all the time in the world.

"Well, I'm impressed," Tuck said. "Half a block from the ferry, and you're cool as a cucumber. I guess you've been working hard at this."

"Please," I said. "I'm shaking, I'm sweating. My knees almost buckled when I walked off the boat. I'm a mess."

"You're perfect," he said.

Later we sat on the shore, our coats buttoned up against the wind. In the sound of the waves, I heard the funeral march of

Annabel Lee, but I couldn't bring myself to tell Tuck about that. I would tell him later, when I could explain the whole story, all of it, when the nightmare had faded. Instead I told him what I'd found in the attic.

"The crazy thing is that they told us this detailed story about his death, how he had pneumonia, how he was struggling to breathe. They told us the same story a dozen times. And it wasn't true."

"That's wild," he said.

"I don't even know who to ask about it. It's embarrassing to admit I didn't know my mother at all. I didn't know anything about either of them. What else were they lying about?"

"People will remember drowning. That's not just sad, that's *news*," Tuck said.

We looked out at the water. It was funny to think that water was the thing that grounded me, but I was immediately calmed being near it, soothed by the movement of waves, its intricate systems for filling up space. And I liked the idea that in the midst of the rise and fall there was me, solid and still, the one who didn't go anywhere.

"I'll find out more before my next Carson Cove trip. I vow it."

"Solemnly?" he said.

He walked me to the ferry and waved as it slid away. I stood on the deck in the bitter wind, sad to be returning home, scared of what I'd find there. It was like that other time years ago when I stood on the deck of the ferry, returning to my sick mother, my lonely brother. Those old feelings were still there, the way old feelings are, dusty but alive, the layers of anger and sadness and fear. This time, though, it was Cole who had somehow brought it all about,

Cole who had stirred up the placid water until all that lay beneath rose to the surface, a roiled, cloudy mess.

George Samson groaned when I walked in.

"That's so impolite," I said.

"What has he done now?" he said. "Let me have it."

"This isn't about Lucas," I said. "It's—well, it's about my other brother, Colin." I took a deep breath. Why was it so painful to talk about him? I felt my face grow hot. I was embarrassed, afraid. George Samson looked confused, and I made myself keep talking. "Do you remember I had a brother who died when he was a baby? This was almost thirty years ago."

"I'm sorry to hear that," he said. And he seemed honestly sorry. I wondered if maybe I'd misjudged George Samson all this time. Maybe he had a kind heart underneath his bluntness.

"And I'm not really sure how to say this," I said, "but I'm confused about how he died exactly."

George dropped his head into his hands. "Of course you are," he said bitterly. "Why am I not surprised? Well, you're going to have to talk to Marlene. I've worked here eleven years, as you know. So I can't tell you anything about your brother from way back when."

Marlene appeared as if summoned from the back of the station. She moved with the same pugnacious cheer. She made me weary. I felt like she would cheer me to death.

"Look who it is!" she said. I found it strange that we didn't acknowledge that the last time I was here, Stephanie had been blubbering with a black eye. That was part of the code of islands, I guess. Nothing changes, stores are never renamed, children never grow up, and secrets are kept secret even after every last detail has been revealed. "Now, what can I help you with?"

"Okay, here goes," I said. I told her about Colin, the dead brother, the baby. "It looks like there are some conflicting stories about how he died," I said. "I guess I thought there might be a police report."

"Oh my goodness," Marlene said.

"We were always told our brother died of pneumonia," I said. "But his death certificate says drowning."

She leaned back in her chair, regarding me. "Honey, he didn't die of pneumonia," she said. "I remember it. That baby drowned."

"But—how?"

She nodded her head sympathetically, her ugly curls bobbing up and down. I hated her face, poor Marlene. "He went over. That's all we knew. It was a terrible accident."

"Oh shit," I said. "The ferry?" She nodded again. "When you say went *over*, you mean—the railing?" I pictured Baby B soaring through the dark night toward the water, and felt a kind of darkness moving over me, like a swarm of insects all around my head. "I better go outside," I said to Marlene. But outside I felt only a little better, the cold wet air as heavy as a blanket.

"You need me to get you some water?" Marlene said, from the doorway.

"No, thank you," I said. *I need to be* by *the water,* I told myself, and headed toward Tame Jaw Beach. When I got there I kept seeing seals by the rocks, their silver heads as smooth and round as infants.

Baby B hadn't died of pneumonia on his way to the hospital. He'd drowned in the harbor, in the channel, or the bay. I couldn't think of anything worse. It was the secret fear under every other secret fear. Whenever Lucas came home late or didn't come home at all, that was what I wasn't letting myself imagine. The dark water, all around. This was the worst kind when it came to my nightmares, the one I awoke from gasping.

I couldn't stop thinking about Colin, the ferry, the water. I tried to use Dr. Brent's meditation techniques, but it was no good. The thoughts wouldn't go away. How had it happened and why had they lied? And underneath those questions was Cole. Did he have something to do with it? How was that possible?

I saw the Grendles, our neighbors, in their driveway, both of them eightysomething and plump, always in jogging suits. We'd lived next door to each other all my life.

"Sorry!" I said. "Sorry to bother you, but I have a question about my family. It's about my brother who died. Remember?"

"Of course we remember," Mr. Grendle said.

"Do you remember *how* he died?"

"Do you think we're senile?" Mr. Grendle said.

"It's not that," I said. "*I* just found out how he died. I always thought he died of pneumonia."

"No," Mr. Grendle said. "That's not how it happened."

"Why didn't you tell us?" I said. "Do you know why our parents lied?"

"I don't know what your parents meant by it," Mrs. Grendle said. "But as for us, we don't make a habit of chasing other people's pain. Why would we bring it up? It's not our story."

"But how did it happen? I mean, how could he possibly go over the railing?" My throat felt like it was twisting shut. I made a little gasp.

"You're not doing yourself any favors worrying over it," Mrs. Grendle said.

"And my parents? Were they—they must have been—I mean did they blame themselves?"

"They went into the house and didn't come out," Mrs. Grendle said. "They just closed the doors. But by summer they were okay. Not the same, you understand, but they could live with themselves."

"Your mother lost her looks," Mr. Grendle said. "She came out of it ugly."

"It was the look of someone who's seen the shadow," Mrs. Grendle said. "I'm sure that's why they never told you. They were trying to protect you."

When I talked to Jim, he looked at me in surprise. "I assumed you knew," he said. "You never talked about it, so I thought it was too painful to bring up."

I asked Elijah West to help me find old copies of the *Island Sun* or the *Cape Cod Paper*, something that might talk about a ferry accident, a baby's death. He showed me how to use the microfiche in the basement.

"It's kind of old-fashioned," he said. "But we have every single issue cataloged. You won't miss anything."

"It would have been January," I said. "And really, I'm looking for an obituary, or any information about an investigation."

Elijah looked at me curiously. "About a baby? That's not the kind of thing you like to hear about, ever. Even in the past."

"My brother," I said.

"Oh Christ," he said. "I never knew."

"It seems like we're the only two people who didn't know. The whole island knows more about it than I do."

The first thing I found was an article about my father. Or not so much about him, but he was mentioned in it. It was about the college where he worked in Boston, about how he was resigning following the birth of triplets. There was something profound even about seeing this in print, the reality of the three of us. There it was in black and white. We had existed, all of us. Not that I had doubted reality—I mean how could I? Our lives had been tainted permanently by the birth and death of Baby B. But that reality had felt for so long like an internal thing, a legend, a story, a private truth.

The article ran a picture of my father, a small black-and-white photo. It was even a little blurry, the way he had been. Ill defined. Quiet. Muffled. What other man would have been the right match for my mother, with her habit of bright, loud insistency? There was no doubting her, no questioning her. She didn't just make the decisions in our lives; she defined our lives. We existed because she told us: exist. Things had names and meanings because she said it was okay. My father went along, the way we had. Agreeable. I felt a kind of haze of love as I looked at his tiny, blurry, colorless picture.

There was no mention of my mother in the article, not even her name. It seemed unbelievable. She was the creator of the world, wasn't she? I almost laughed. Maybe all little girls thought that about their mothers. But why would I still feel surprised that the world and all its journalists weren't forever writing articles about my mother?

Mother of Two Insists on Adding Nutritional Yeast to Orange Juice for Health Benefits. Mother of Two Allows Swimming in October. Mother of Two Fills Room with Candles Again.

She lit candles around the room on our birthday, and sometimes other days as well, the light like a beacon that Colin might see. Her own private lighthouse. She lit so many candles the quality of air in the room changed, grew dazzling, smelled sweet, mouthwatering. I could feel the wax between my teeth.

Once firemen came because neighbors saw the dancing light through the window. They stood in the kitchen, while she explained. She didn't mention Colin. She said, "I light candles." That was all. No apology, no explanation. And yet, when the firemen left, one of them looked back at her with pity. I could still see his expression, *feel* it like scar tissue still there after so many years. After they left, she was small and sad. It was a terrible sight. Stripped bare, that blurry vulnerable look of someone wiped clean of makeup, someone without their glasses, that terrible feeling that you can almost, but not quite, recognize someone who should be more familiar to you.

I don't know why I thought of this that day in the library. I wondered if memories were surfacing because I was approaching the truth. But as I read through those old papers from so many years ago, I felt further and further away from any truth.

But then I found it: Tragic Ferry Accident Leaves Infant Dead. It was front-page news, of course. I read it in a kind of panic, wanting to know more, but afraid to. The night had been stormy. The baby had been sick. The boat had pitched in some rough water, and baby and mother had tumbled over the side.

Baby and mother?

Both of them?

I looked up from the article, reimagining the night once again. Baby and mother. *That doesn't happen*, I thought. You'd have to climb onto the railing to tumble over.

My father was quoted in the article. "'We're devastated,' said William Moore, husband of Cecily. 'We've lost our son, but we're trying to count our blessings. I could have lost my wife as well, but she's still here today. She is alive.'"

She is alive. The last line chilled me. It had to be a coincidence that the quote matched what I'd seen written in Cole's notebook. Still, the hair on my neck stood on end. It seemed incredible that no one on the island had told me the story before. Hadn't any of the kids we'd gone to school with heard the story from their parents? How had we been protected from the truth for so long? The truth was beginning to seem like a strange and duplicitous thing. There were truths inside truths, many-headed truths, infinities of truths. Everything I knew to be true about my mother, for instance, might have come into being after we were born, after Colin died. She had lived forty years before we were alive. I had known her for only twenty years, I realized, less time than I'd known everyone else on the island.

At home, there was a fire in the fireplace. Cole was reading on the couch; Lucas was tying flies at his desk. I wanted to tell them the whole story. It was eating at me, a nightmare. And telling the nightmare is the best power over it. But when I saw them, cozy like that in the living room, something like déjà vu swept through me, and then a terrible tingling, the sensation of rain in my head. For a moment I couldn't tell *what* I was feeling, and then I knew it was anger, a thousand points of anger like the pinpricks of fast falling rain. The fire, the furniture, the room, the house, none of it felt like mine anymore.

How had he managed, after all, to take my home from me like this? Seeing him so at ease, sitting where I should be sitting, reading a book from our bookcase, I realized that bank or no bank, refinancing or not, the house was more his than mine now.

That night I dreamed of the seals standing sternly at the foot of my bed. They struck their flippers together.

"What do you want?" I asked them, afraid.

"You know," they said.

I woke with a start. My bedroom door opened and Cole stood there.

"What do you want?" I cried.

"You know," he said.

I woke with a thundering heart.

In Carson Cove later that week, Tuck and I sat on the sand again. His scarf flapped in the wind, and I took the edge and tucked it into the collar of his coat. Felt the warmth of his throat, the secret edges of his collarbone.

"So now there are two things to solve," I said. "What happened to Colin, and who Cole is."

"And how they're connected," Tuck said.

"Exactly. I feel like he has something to do with it. Like he's responsible for Colin drowning. But that's crazy, right? He was a baby then, too."

"So what's the plan now?" Tuck asked. "Back to Vermont?"

"This is like step one of phase one of even being a normal human being," I told him. "I can't go to Vermont, probably ever. I'm going to grow old and be an ancient recluse on the island, and kids are going to call me a witch and dare each other to knock on my door and run away. No, I can't go to Vermont. I don't know what I'm going to do."

He took up a handful of sand and let it trickle between his fingers. "Then we start the investigation here," Tuck said. "Get a picture of him and email it around. You know, *do you know this man?* That kind of thing."

"We? It's your investigation now, too?"

"Yeah!" he said. "I want to learn his name."

"You don't even know him."

"For you, though," he said.

We looked out across the water, and pretty soon the ferry rounded the corner, getting bigger and bigger as it slid into the harbor.

"Get a picture," Tuck said as I walked onto the ferry. "Email it to me. Then you don't have to worry about you-know-who finding it."

I did get a picture—on our birthday. Our birthday fell at the very beginning of November. It was the season of wind. Winds that met and tangled over the harbor, winds that whipped the bay into a frenzy of waves with little whitecaps, like invisible egg beaters, frothing up a meringue.

The night before our birthday, with wind moaning in the rafters, I took out the present I'd gotten for Lucas, wrapped it, and set it on the kitchen table. I stood alone for a minute, looking at the wrapped package, the color of the paper, so strange and sad in the darkness of the night. I looked at the package and listened to the wind and felt suddenly dizzy with sadness. What was happening to us? The life we loved?

When I came down in the morning, tired and on edge from the wind and my own uneasy thoughts, there was another, tiny package on the kitchen table, and Lucas was standing by the stove with a spatula and pancakes sizzling. I felt moved by the sight of him, grateful and heartbroken all at once.

I poured coffee. Lucas flipped pancakes. He was wearing the Kiss the Cook apron, and from the back he looked exactly like Dad. I hadn't noticed the resemblance in a long time.

Cole took his coffee out to the dock and stood in the cool air, looking at the sunrise over the water. He was wearing a navy sweater with a cable-knit pattern, and when he came back in, the sweater seemed full of the smell of outdoors. It reminded me of something, some elusive thread from way back. I felt dizzy, breathing in the smell of the woolen sweater, the scent held in its fibers—sun, salt, earth—and the smell of coffee and bacon, which were so familiar and wrapped up in *home* and *family*.

Cole's hair was longer than when he'd arrived, and it looked rich and healthy. Had he gained weight? Just a couple pounds, enough to fill out his face. He looked healthy and vibrant, as if now instead of simply emanating heat, he also emanated light.

Later I caught the reflection of my face in the old coffee-pot. It was distorted by the curve of the pot, but distorted or not, I saw my huge eyes, my pale skin. I hadn't had a good night's sleep in weeks, and that was probably why I looked the way I looked, but it occurred to me that Cole had been siphoning my well-being, stealing a vitality for himself that used to be mine.

After breakfast, Lucas unwrapped his present, carefully, without tearing the paper.

"Look at it," he said. It was a camel hair overcoat. He held it up. "Like Dad's," he said.

"It's like the one he wore when we were really little. I thought you would like it, even if you don't get a chance to wear it much."

"I love it," Lucas said. He tried it on, and it transformed him even more than the Kiss the Cook Apron. It wasn't even that he resembled Dad so much, I realized, as that he resembled *a dad*. We were grown up, or something like it. We were twenty-nine that birthday.

Lucas and Cole gave me a jewelry box, and inside was a silver bracelet.

"There's more," Lucas said, and held out his hand. Clasped there was a charm: a silver jellyfish. "You put that on the bracelet," he said.

"I get how it works. Jewelry isn't that foreign to me. I've seen it on TV."

"Very funny," Lucas said. Then Cole handed me a charm, a silver pyramid.

"Triangle," he said, reaching out to fasten the charm on the bracelet. His fingers on my wrist. Both of us thinking of the night on the beach when he'd drawn the triangle in the sand.

"And," Lucas said, taking out one more box from where he'd stashed it in the cupboard where we kept the cheese grater, "here's one more. For you." He handed it to Cole.

"It's not his birthday," I said and they both looked at me, offended.

Cole unwrapped it. It was something they sold at the little gift shop at the landing. A miniature island in a glass dome. When you shook it, sparkles rained down on the sand, the blue plastic waves, the trees in the center of the island, the houses, the shops, the tiny plastic seal on its tiny plastic rock.

"It's not much," Lucas said. "It's supposed to be Wolf Island."

I felt sick with envy. A stupid gift from a stupid tourist shop, a stupid snow globe. But I wanted it. I wanted it for myself.

"Okay, smile," I said, grabbing the camera. My voice was bitter as metal, and they looked at me, surprised, suspicious. But they obeyed, standing with their arms around each other awkwardly.

"Got it," I said. The envy seemed to change, mutate, grow spines, wings. It took off, great uneven breaststrokes through my own chest cavity. I was in charge now, I thought. I was telling the story. The next thing that was going to happen: I was going to find his name.

Tuck and I looked up email addresses and composed an email. We sent the photo as an attachment. We started with the secretary at the Lindenberg High School. "Secretaries are always helpful," Tuck said. We also emailed librarians, the police department, and the fire department. This was my fifth trip to Carson Cove, and it was getting easier—incrementally—every time.

There was a weird reversal happening with my visits. It was now on the island that I felt crazy. I felt it in me like something boiling on a fire. Faster and faster, hotter and still hotter. I felt things evaporating at alarming speeds. The only relief was to be in Carson Cove with Tuck. There, things quieted to a simmer. It was so organized, so planned, those excursions off the ferry. Each step felt premeditated. We were like children working on a school project, that soothing level of safety. I felt like someone's mom should appear at any moment with crackers and milk.

That afternoon Tuck waited with me for the ferry back to the island. Then he turned to me. "Why don't I just go with you?"

"What? To the island? Now?"

"Why not? I could meet Lucas and Cole, and see where you live."

I looked at him. The sun shone through his hair. His face was wide, happy. He was like a puppy wagging his tail. I thought he was beautiful. Every time I saw him I wanted to touch his hair. But there were other things, too. When I came over on the ferry, he would leave work to sit with me, walk right out, leaving the other employees staring after him. When I asked about his job, he shrugged. Didn't matter. Who cares. Once he was drunk when I arrived, and his coworkers raised their eyebrows in a way that meant as soon as we walked out they were going to talk about him. I liked him drunk. He was sweeter than ever, even sentimental. "You're so pretty," he said that day. His long arms and legs seemed longer. Once he told me he'd gotten some mushrooms and asked if I wanted to take them with him. I declined. More than once we passed women on the street who looked at him and then me with a kind of vicious chill.

"Old girlfriend?" I asked.

"Not exactly," he said. "Just a…friend."

I thought I understood why he enjoyed being part of the investigation, why he was curious about Cole and Lucas, how fun it must have been to be on the edge of something dark, something scary. Safe but thrilled. That was fine with me. I appreciated his company and his help. But when he asked about the island… Well, there were things I didn't want to share. Even my loneliness was private.

"Another time," I told Tuck, about the island. "Soon, okay?"

I stood on the deck of the boat in the wind, watching Carson Cove get tiny as we chugged toward the island. The boat was almost empty. I made myself stand on the deck and look down into the water. I don't know what I wanted to see or feel. Certainly, I thought about the baby. But I imagined it was me under that water.

22

November was gray and silver: water, sand, branches, sky. Tuck called to tell me that he'd heard back from the school, the police department, and the library of Lindenberg. No one recognized Cole.

"That can't be true," I said. "Are we at a dead end?"

"We have to keep trying," he said.

I went to the Grendles again, one afternoon when thunderclouds were gathering in blooming masses over the water. The weight of water in the air and quiet in the house made me feel like a spinning top, unable to be still. I stepped out into the chilly yard. I picked up a rake, then leaned it on the house again. I wanted to do something, to make a list, solve an equation, answer a question. Finally, I marched across our yard and into the Grendles'.

Mrs. Grendle was home alone. She waved me in without a word. Inside we drank bourbon at the kitchen counter, until her cheeks flushed, and blood vessels like rosy spiderwebs blossomed just above her cheekbones.

"I've been meaning to ask you something," I told her. "I've been trying to find out more about my mom. I don't know. I just thought maybe you—being neighbors for so long—"

I thought, but didn't say aloud, that I doubted how well she knew my parents even if she thought she knew them intimately. What we think we know about our neighbors is a veneer. Take Stephan and Stephanie, and the black eye, the cut cheek. Those were islanders I'd thought I knew pretty well, actually. But what I'd forgotten to account for was secrets, how secrets are as common as freckles. Perhaps to the rest of the island, Lucas and I looked happy.

No one saw that under the surface we were battling for control of our memories. No one imagined that I was haunted at night by dreams that alternated between drowning in black water and drowning in a kind of terrible desire. And that every time I walked to the landing along the bay, I felt again the wet sand, the fierce wind, his mouth—when what I really wanted was to forget that night. No one looking at me would know that I was trying to unravel the secrets of my mother's past, and what exactly had happened on the deck of the ferry twenty-nine years ago.

"Your mother was a memorable woman," Mrs. Grendle said. "Beautiful, and a talker. She was very proud of you kids. You know it's rare to have twins. It's special. And she loved being special."

That was an understatement. "Did she talk much about the baby?" I asked. "The third baby?"

"Oh sure, sometimes. It weighed on her." Mrs. Grendle herself was talkative now, more than I'd ever seen. She swirled the liquid in her glass and took a slow sip. "Losing a child changes you in unexpected ways, and I know this from experience, but it's not a story I like to tell. Your mother... One time I overheard her. I was at the table next to her at the Quahog Pit. I heard her telling a stranger, a tourist, that she had a third child, but he lived with another family."

My stomach seemed to swoop like some seabird on the wind. I felt nauseous. I stared at Mrs. Grendle. What did that mean? A third child who lived with another family. What family? What child?

"The only other child is Baby B, and he drowned."

"Grief makes us say strange things," Mrs. Grendle said.

"But that's not strange, that's crazy," I said. "Why would she lie? I don't understand."

Mrs. Grendle picked up her bourbon again and downed it. "Maybe she was protecting herself. It was easier to think the child had gone to live with someone else, better to believe a lie than to remember the real story every day of her life. Anyway, she's dead and gone now. And this was probably fifteen or twenty years ago."

I felt a whirling sensation. Yes, maybe in her grief she'd concocted an alternative story about Baby B. But maybe it was true. I was overcome with dizziness. He'd been dead all these years! His grave was by the fence in the cemetery, covered with lady's slippers. I remembered standing by Cole in the kitchen that first day, how Lucas had said so happily, *Lydia, it's Baby B.* And here he was resurrected again, in a new way. How many times could he come back to life?

The idea took hold of me with such force I couldn't think of anything else. What if Baby B hadn't drowned? What if he hadn't died at all? What if he had grown up somewhere else, with another family, and come back to find us later? The thought was too much to bear. When I saw Cole now I felt instantly queasy, overtaken by seasickness.

He was everywhere. In the kitchen when I wanted breakfast. In the living room when I wanted to sit on the couch. He was in the bathroom when I needed a shower. On the stairs coming down when I started to go up, and going up when I wanted to come down. We were passing each other in hallways constantly like figures from an Escher dream. I couldn't stand to think about him. But I couldn't stop thinking about him.

Finally, I went back to the police station. I almost cried when I saw Marlene's plump face.

"Why do you want to linger on something like this?" she said. Her curls bouncing on either side of her head felt sinister, like something out of a horror movie. Shirley Temple's hair on an old woman's body. Maybe this was how Marlene's past self met her future self, right here in this moment with a crash of curls. "This can't make you feel good," she said.

"All I want to know is which direction the ferry was going? Were they coming home, or going to the cape?"

"I don't remember, honey. I try not to think about it."

"Did they find him?" I said. "Or is he still out there?"

She blinked at me several times. "I don't know about his body," she said. "But *he* went to heaven and stayed there, honey, in the bosom of our Father."

"You don't understand," I said. "It's not that simple."

"You can decide how simple you want it to be," she said. "That's your choice."

She looked at me with a terrible expression. She was sorry for me. She was scared of me. Me!

I hated her, but then on Clara Day Street, I caught a glimpse of myself in the reflection of the T-shirt shop. I was hunched forward, my whole posture announcing to the world how afraid and anxious I felt. When I tried to stand up, I looked stiff and ridiculous. No wonder Marlene looked at me like that. I hadn't slept, hadn't eaten much of anything. All I'd done for days was think about my mother and the baby, and whether or not he was alive. It was the worst thing I could imagine.

I spent the following days looking for someone who remembered the accident, someone who had been involved in more than a marginal way. The fishermen, Sebastian and Gordon, remembered it, they said, but they hadn't been around that night, and they hadn't been at the funeral. I had lunch with my mom's old friend Peggy, who lived inland by Hiram's Bounty.

Her house was tiny and cramped, and she seemed that way, too—a bony woman, who lived alone, and seemed intent on taking up as little space as possible. She crouched in her seat as if there were low-flying birds above her. We ate a tiny lunch—apple slices, cheese, crackers, and pickles, arranged on a plate. When Peggy talked she moved her hands, but in such small ways it looked like she was knitting. No wonder my mom had liked her—Peggy left plenty of room for my mom to take up. She'd been at my father's funeral, and at my mother's funeral, but I hadn't seen her much since then. She hadn't been at Colin's funeral, she said, because she wasn't yet friends with my mom at that point. She hadn't even met her.

"Are you sure there was a funeral?" she said. "It might have been very small."

"I found a program from a memorial service. Did my mom ever say anything about it? About Colin?"

"Oh sure. All the time. She never stopped talking about it. Losing a child is the most traumatic event in a woman's life. It defines you."

"It defined all of us," I said. "Our whole family."

I thought about that as I walked away from Peggy's house. Being defined. What your meaning is, what your very existence means. All my life we had meant grief and sadness, we meant missing something that could never come back. We meant loneliness and isolation. We meant being stuck here. But we meant other things as well, I told myself, remembering sitting on the porch with Lucas, looking out at the bay night after night: love, intimacy, intensity of closeness. Passionate care.

I asked Jim over and over again about the night of the accident.

"I didn't own the place then," he said helplessly. "I don't have records. I know about it the same way you know about it, Lydia. Just heard about it. Linda cried when she found out, I do remember that. We were twenty-five. We weren't even married yet."

I found out that there was no medical examiner on the island, but someone from the cape handled all our deaths. When I called, though, it turned out that the medical examiner who would have been working at the time had died himself twenty years ago.

There was one funeral home on the island, and it doubled as a photography studio—specializing in passport photos. It was run by Jonathan Day, who I'd gone to school with. He'd taken over the place from his parents a year ago. He'd never been a likable guy, but things had gotten worse since I'd last seen him. His large face was expressionless. It was as though he were incapable of smiling. He stared at me morosely across a tiny desk in the corner of the room, showing no sign of recognition.

"Hey," I said. "I'm Lydia. Lydia Moore."

"I know who you are," he said. I looked at him and thought, *embalmed*. I wondered why he didn't get a bigger desk. His knees seemed to bump against this one. I remembered that his mother had been very small. Maybe it had never occurred to him that he could use a different desk, the way we didn't change the things our parents had arranged in our house.

I explained what I was looking for. Even when I said the words *brother*, and *baby*, and *dead*, the expression on his face didn't waver.

"You can buy the records," he said when I was done.

"Buy them? Like with money?"

"Yes, with money."

"Are you sure you can't just give them to me? I mean, my parents probably paid for the funeral arrangements in the first place. So."

"Five hundred dollars," he said.

"Are you kidding me?"

"No," he said.

"I literally want to know one thing—was there a body?"

"If we were involved there was probably a body. Otherwise why would we be involved? But who knows? If you want to know for sure, you can buy the records."

"You can go to hell," I said.

★ ★ ★

I found Cole in his bedroom. I stood in the doorway. He was in jeans and a gray T-shirt, barefoot, handsome. I remembered the sound of that terrible poem, the feeling of him holding me in place. I thought about the snow globe in his hands, and inside the transparent dome our house, and in the doorway a Lydia and a Lucas trapped under glass, forever. Tiny brother, tiny sister.

We looked at each other, and my heart raced. His expression softened. He waited, smiling. I wondered what he thought I was going to say. We hadn't spoken directly since the night at the inn. I'd avoided him, practically fled from the room when he arrived. I'd locked myself in my room at night and left the house as soon as possible every morning. He thought now I was going to—what?—ask him about that night at the inn? Tell him I was afraid? Tell him I missed him? His smile told me he was expecting to enjoy whatever it was I was going to say.

"I need money," I said.

His smile faded. "What for?"

"I'm trying to find out about Baby B. About his death—about his burial."

Cole looked at me now with an odd expression. I was never good at reading him—there was too much going on—and now there was definitely too much. A whole landscape of emotion. I heard a faint sound like a little horse galloping, and thought it was his heartbeat. Then I thought it might be mine. Then I saw his foot tapping.

We heard the kitchen door. We heard water from the kitchen tap. We both pictured Lucas, the way he sometimes put his entire head into the sink to drink straight from the tap.

Cole placed his hands on my shoulders and pushed me into his bedroom. I tensed and lifted my arms, ready to fight, but he shook his head and closed the door silently.

"Leave him out of this, that's all," he said, nodding toward the hallway. He meant Lucas.

I stood with my back against the door, and he stood close to me. I was aware of his body, so real, so close, so wolfish with its heat and scent and that notion of blood coursing just below the surface.

"Money has nothing to do with the past," he said.

"I found Baby B's death certificate," I said. "Cause of death? Drowning. Okay? He fell off the ferry in the night, he and my mom both. At least that's the story. But there's a piece of it that doesn't make sense. I want to buy the report from the funeral home, to understand more about what happened that day. Unless you know more than I do?"

Cole turned abruptly away from me, going to the window. He stared moodily toward the bay. I joined him at the window and looked where he was looking.

"Why are you always staring at that thing?" Cole snapped.

"The houseboat?" I said. "I don't know. Habit."

He snorted as if this were an outrageous thing to say.

"I just want to know for sure how he died—and *if* he died. What if—" I looked at Cole's face. "What if he didn't die? What if he grew up? And—"

"He died," Cole said stiffly. "He was buried in the earth. Trust me. You're worrying about the wrong things. Playing detective, digging up the past. And meanwhile your house is literally crumbling into the sea."

I heard the waves outside, the wind in the trees. I heard the sounds of the house all around me, the creaking and settling.

"Don't change the subject," I said.

"You don't believe me? Come here."

He led me down the stairs, through the living room, into the kitchen, and down the basement steps.

"What?" I said, suddenly stopping and holding on to the railing. "Do you have a cage of some kind constructed down here? Are you planning to hold me prisoner? It won't work. I have plans tonight, just so you know. If I don't show up, they'll come looking for me."

"Shut up," he said. "Just look."

I descended the final steps, and we stood in the damp chill until my eyes adjusted to the gloom. The house was built only shortly after the Day Estate, one of the earlier houses on the island. Its foundation, like the big Day house, was made of flat slate slabs stacked into an intricate underground wall. But where it rose above the earth, I saw, it was leaning precariously inward, tilted. Over the years the leaning stones had actually pushed the basement stairs over, until they were slanted and cramped under the ceiling. How had we not noticed this? How fast was it moving? I tried to remember walking down the basement steps in childhood; had there been more room?

The adjacent wall was leaning outward, toward the bay. I saw the cracked and crumbling slabs all along the ground. A tomb by the sounding sea.

"You think the ground beneath your feet is solid? It's quick-sand. It will swallow you whole. Start seeing what's right in front of you," Cole said, "or you'll lose it all."

From then on, in addition to worrying about Cole, and Baby B, about my mother and father, about Lucas, about how long we could go on together like this, about what secrets the past was holding on to, I also worried about the house. It seemed vulnerable, both to Cole and to the degradations of time. I walked from room to room. I noticed suddenly all the ways it was falling apart: the pitted, scratched floorboards that seemed to slant toward the bay, the walls that almost sagged under the weight of moisture or salt, the rusty pipes seeping amber water underneath all the sinks.

Instead of sleeping at night, I lay awake and worried. During the day I walked to the graveyard and read the old inscription. SON~BROTHER. I sometimes felt there was someone behind me, over my shoulder, a little flash of movement. But when I turned my head, there was no one.

23

There was a knock on the kitchen door, as I was washing dishes, my eyes gritty from exhaustion. I stopped dead, my hands in the soapy water, and waited for something more—a long pause in the evening. Finally, I went to the door.

Tuck was on the doorstep. He held up his hands and grinned, like he was saying *surprise*. He was wearing the threadbare yellow shirt he'd been wearing the day I fainted by the Carson Cove information booth, a brown jacket with patches on both elbows. His hair was standing up all around his head, as mane-like as ever, and I wasn't entirely clear if I was looking at curls or tangles. "I came over on the nine o'clock boat," Tuck said.

"But—why?"

"I don't know. Wanted to see you, I guess. You haven't called in a few days, and—I don't know. Maybe they had you tied up in the basement."

The night was cool, and there were small bright clouds passing over the moon. I looked behind him at the lawn, the dock, the bay.

"And now I'm glad I came," he said. "Are you okay? You look—"

"But how did you know where I lived?"

"I just asked at that bar where the ferry comes in. Everyone knows you. I didn't even have to say your last name. Which is good, because I don't *know* your last name."

A gull screeched. From the living room, I heard the sound of something small falling to the floor, a spoon maybe or a comb. Tuck looked over his shoulder in the direction of the ferry landing, which was empty now. The boat was gone. It wouldn't come back until morning. He looked at my face. "Um. I can find somewhere to stay," Tuck said.

I smiled, shook my head. "No, no, I'm being stupid," I told him. "Of course you can stay here. I'm just surprised to see you. I mean, I'm happy to see you, too."

"Okay," he said. "That's a relief. Because I have no idea where I would go."

I was happy to see him, but there was more to it than that. A faint tension was growing between my shoulder blades, a strange little gnawing pain.

"I don't know how they're going to react." I nodded my head in the direction of the living room where we heard Lucas's and Cole's voices, a low rumble.

"Who cares!" Tuck said. "Anyway, let's go find out."

When he crossed the threshold, I reached out and touched the hem of his shirt. I don't know why I did it. Maybe to feel something that was real between my fingers. It felt rebellious, subversive even, to bring Tuck into the house. It was a house full of ancient and dead things, and his footsteps were already stirring up dust.

"I like your house," he said. "This place is, I don't know, haunted house meets beach shack."

Cole walked into the kitchen. He stopped inside the swinging door, looking at us. I couldn't read his face. I didn't know what he was thinking.

Tuck threw his arms up in the air. "There he is," he said. He went for Cole's hand and shook it so eagerly Cole seemed taken aback. "It is *great* to meet you."

Lucas came into the kitchen, and we all stood there looking at each other. Lucas was in a panic of shyness; Cole was stiff and formal. Only Tuck seemed at ease, as if he were honestly enjoying himself.

"This is unexpected," Cole said.

Tuck nodded in agreement. "I decided to come over on the spur of the moment."

"The spur of the moment," Cole repeated. I could see the little bone of his jaw, moving mechanically like a clock spring, tight and meticulous. I could see he was trying to smile and having a hard time. I felt scared for Tuck.

"So you're our girl Lydia's friend," Cole said.

"That's right."

"Making a visit on the spur of the moment."

"That's what I said."

"Now, how old are you exactly?" Cole asked him.

Tuck paused. Blinked. He seemed to consider Cole for a moment. "Twenty-one," he said finally.

We heard a quick patter on the roof. Sudden rain drummed and flashed outside the kitchen windows. Cole looked like he wanted to hit Tuck or maybe devour him.

"Let's go for a walk," I said to Tuck. "Right now."

"You do that," Cole said. "Take a walk in the rain. Take a walk on the beach. The beach is glorious in a storm."

"I know all about the beach," Tuck said agreeably.

"Maybe you do," Cole said. "Did you know how much Lydia loves a storm? Lydia loves the beach in a storm."

"Stop saying that," I told him.

We threw on yellow slickers and escaped into the night. I gulped cool air, realizing I'd been holding my breath in the kitchen. We stood at the end of the dock, looking out into the rain-pitted bay, our breath making strange little clouds around us.

"Pretty tense in there," Tuck said.

"You have no idea."

"So, are you okay?" Tuck said. He must have noticed how thin my face looked or how dark the circles were under my eyes. I considered telling him about the dreams that haunted me at night—the thoughts I couldn't shake during the day. But they were too private, too wretched. Tuck seemed to like me, he wanted to help me. How could I tell him that against my will I still dreamed of Cole almost every night? That in my unguarded dreams I sometimes loved him, and sometimes ran for my life from a monster that was him, and sometimes Cole wasn't there at all, just Colin, and I was the one holding him on the deck of the ferry, and I was the one throwing him over the edge and watching his body—with relief—as it sank.

"You're twenty-one?" I said instead. "Sorry, that's just younger than I thought."

"Why does it matter?" he said.

"It doesn't. I don't know. I guess I'm surprised you didn't leave home when you had the chance. Everyone leaves."

"I did leave. I went to college," Tuck says. "I went for three years. I have a year left."

I looked at him in surprise. "What are you waiting for?" I asked. "Why not finish?"

"Once you graduate, then it's time to *do* something, and I don't know what I want to do. Once I figure that out, I'll go back."

"So as long as you haven't graduated, then you're still technically a student? I'm officially a college student, too, then," I told him. "And I have been for ten years."

He laughed and turned back to the bay. The red houseboat rocked quick and fast out on the waves.

"Imagine living in that thing," Tuck said.

"Oh, I have."

"It would be like a miracle," he said. "Waking up every day like that."

We heard a splash and looked down toward the water.

"Seal," I said.

Tuck looked but couldn't see it.

"They're everywhere," I told him.

Then we heard—faintly—the chimes from the old clock at the bank on the landing, eleven small chimes.

"Eleven o'clock," I said.

"At midnight, I think I'll kiss you," Tuck said, turning his face toward me.

I looked at my hands, at my fingernails, at the white calcium deposits like specks of confetti in the pink nails. When we were young, girls said that each white spot on your fingernails was a boy who liked you.

"We'll be in bed at midnight," I said.

"Even better," he said. "I wasn't going to ask, but—"

"I mean—we'll be sleeping."

"Okay," he said, good-naturedly. "I get it."

"I'm twenty-nine," I said.

"So what?"

"So—I don't know exactly. I just don't want you to—get any ideas about something, you know, happening between us."

"Because you're eight years older than me?"

"Yes. Or no. I guess it's not that. I just don't want to ruin anything."

"Maybe there's nothing more you can ruin. I mean, think about it."

"You're obviously not used to this," I said. "You've probably never been turned down in your life. I mean, look at you."

"Stop, stop," he said, laughing. "I'm sorry. Don't be mad. I won't kiss you. I promise I will not kiss you at midnight. Nothing you could do would make me kiss you at midnight."

We stood on the dock, thoroughly chilled. I had a bad feeling about what was coming next but for a moment I couldn't remember what that thing was. I'd rather think about kissing Tuck at midnight.

"Can I make it up to you?" he said.

"Maybe," I said. Suddenly I wanted to tell him something true about me and my family, something to invite him closer. I wanted him to know more about me, even if it scared him away. I had to make that offer.

I began to tell him about my conversation with Mrs. Grendle, what my mother had said about having a third child who lived with another family. How uncomfortable Cole had seemed when I told him.

"Whoa," he said. "So what does that even mean?"

"It means—what if he didn't die after all?"

"You said there's a death certificate, though? And you found that article about it. And there's a grave."

"But—what if the whole thing was faked somehow? I know that sounds crazy, I know. Don't look at me like that. I went to get records from the funeral director, but he's trying to charge me an outrageous amount for them. I can't find anyone who was actually there when it happened. I mean, no one saw his body."

"Then what's buried in his grave?"

I put my hands over my mouth, felt my breath warm on the tips of my fingers. "We could find out," I said.

Tuck rocked back on his heels, regarding me. "No. No way."

"We won't find him if there's no body. But if he's there, we can put him right back."

Tuck ran his fingers through his hair. "You know this is fucked up, right?"

"It's the only way I'll know for sure."

"And probably illegal."

"It can't be illegal. He's ours."

"But you still can't just dig people up. Even your own people."

We heard splashing again and this time we both saw the seal, its smooth dark head popping out of the water nearby.

"Will you help me?" I said.

"I don't know," he said. "For fuck's sake, Lydia."

But he followed me back to the house. We rummaged as

quietly as possible in the shed, then walked to the graveyard in the rain, each of us carrying a shovel. I had a trowel in my raincoat pocket as well. I was glad it was raining—it would make the earth soft, and somehow make us less likely to be discovered, hidden by the soft pattering, hidden by the blur.

The only light we had was Tuck's key chain flashlight. There was no moonlight. Even so, our eyes seemed to adjust to the darkness, once we found the grave. Tuck shone his light on the headstone. He touched the letters. Son. Brother. I stood above him.

"This will kill the lady's slippers," I said.

"Well?" he said. "What do you want to do?"

"Kill them, I guess," I said and stuck my shovel into the earth.

Besides swimming in the Providence River with my freshman year friend Mary, I was basically a rule follower. I wasn't prone to wild abandonment of reason. I didn't follow my passion. I didn't dance like no one was watching. I didn't revere risk. I didn't need to! My home was on an island; I was brought up by a possibly insane mother, a pathologically shy brother, and a father who might as well have been absent. I was haunted by my dead brother. There were uncertainties of weather and tide to contend with in my life, and there was the unpredictability of strong personalities touched by grief.

Those things were all around me, so I stayed still, and quiet. That was who I became. Lydia, still and quiet. I didn't act, I was acted upon. I never would have gone into the Providence River, except that Mary convinced me to. I never would have gone to college in the first place, except that a teacher told me she could imagine me there, in Providence, and that was enough for me. I never would have come home except that my mother needed me.

But now I had made a decision wildly uncharacteristic of me and I was acting on it. I almost laughed, struck suddenly by the ridiculousness of what I was doing. And why was this important to know? What would it tell me? That my mother was a liar. I knew that already. That Cole was my brother after all. I didn't want to know that ever. I had made a decision all right, and it seemed like it might turn out to be a very bad decision in the end. But I couldn't stop now. I found my hands shaking as I gripped the shovel. I felt a deep hunger to know what was under the earth.

The digging took longer than you might imagine. We struck the ground again and again and only managed to unearth clumps of grass and lady's slippers. Then we heard our shovels tearing root masses, that terrible ripping sound, like muscles, tendons, sinews, coming unattached from their moorings, bodies ripped limb from limb. Then we hit rocks of all sizes. Although the night was chilly, before long we were drenched as much with sweat as with rain.

"This has definitely taken a very weird turn," Tuck said, pushing his wet hair off his forehead.

"You're under no obligation to stay."

"Shut up," he said. "I'm just saying it's weird. Sometimes you have to say things out loud."

The hole emerged slowly over hours. I had blisters on my hands, soft, raw, raised patches of puffy white. Everything about what we were doing made me feel like someone I didn't recognize, a stranger. A few times I stopped shoveling to laugh, but when I did Tuck stopped shoveling, too, and told me I was a lunatic and asked if I was done. No, we were most certainly not done. I didn't let myself think too much about what I was looking for, what I might find. I concentrated on the physical act of stabbing the earth with the sharp shovel blade, lifting as much dirt as I could out of the slowly growing hole.

Twice we heard cars on the road, but they passed us by, and although I didn't like the sound of tires on a wet road, I never stopped digging. I began to feel a growing excitement. I couldn't believe it had never occurred to me to do this before! The act of exhuming suddenly made such perfect sense. Wasn't this the culmination of all I'd been doing since Cole arrived in August? Every time I looked in my mother's drawers, the boxes in the attic, when I talked to Marlene at the police station, when I looked for articles in the *Island Sun*, all of that was a kind of gentle digging. This was simply more physical.

Tuck's shovel struck the corner of the coffin when the hole was only three feet deep. I shined the little key chain flashlight into the hole, saw the casket there. It was the same color as the earth. I climbed into the damp hole and touched the casket, brushed the dirt away. It was wooden, plain. We'd been digging in the wrong place, I realized, and had to extend our hole away from the gravestone in order to uncover the rest of it.

"Keep going," I said.

"Lydia," Tuck said. "Do you still want to do this? Are you thinking clearly about what you might see?"

I was sure there was nothing to see inside the coffin. It made powerful sense now. It explained everything. My mother hadn't dropped—or thrown—Baby B over the railing of the ferry. She'd given him away that night, left him in the care of some other family, and returned alone, and he was out there still. He might be Cole, or he might be some other man. But I had another brother, still alive, still in this world, which meant I wasn't alone. We weren't alone after all.

I realized I was crying. Covered with rain, and dirt, and now tears.

"Have you actually gone crazy?" Tuck said.

"Maybe," I said.

Once, at the booth, Kelly Cardoza had handed me her baby to hold while she ran into Jack's to make a phone call. I set it on my lap. It turned its head to look at me, curious, wary. I experienced a complex feeling. On the one hand, I felt comfortable, as if I were biologically programmed to know what to do, but it was like the programming was blinking in and out. One minute I found the baby beautiful. The next minute I was horrified by the drool and mouth empty of teeth. The baby rocked back and forth like an animal. But the baby also felt good to hold. Felt solid and right. Like the right-sized stone in my pocket. I held the baby for ten minutes. We looked around together. The baby put its hands in my hair and then on either side of my face. The baby touched my nose.

When we lifted the lid of the coffin, I knew we were looking at a baby right away. He was there, and not there, his bones skin flesh hair withered as a ghost. His clothing was only dark shreds now, like cobwebs, but he was a perfect shape there in his tiny coffin, the bones visible under the flesh. He was the shape of bones, even if the bones were covered.

"Holy fuck," Tuck said. We sat on the edge of the hole in the earth, both of us, looking into the coffin. I was shaking I realized. Soaking wet. The rain had poured down the neck of the raincoat, drenching my sweater.

"I can't touch him," I said. I wanted to pick him up. I wanted to hold him in my arms like I'd held that other baby. But I knew he might break into a hundred pieces if I picked him up. I knew the flesh would come off, and the bones would scatter.

"No," Tuck agreed. "Don't touch him."

His whole head was the size of my hand, smaller than my hand. He had eyes. He had lips. His nose, though, was mostly missing, two blank holes in a skull. I felt so sad about his nose.

The smell from the coffin was surprising. Not a smell of death. It was sweet and sour, an ancient primordial scent: earth, mud, leaves, and underneath that a faint chemical smell. And something else as well, something I wanted to understand. A smell that reminded me of a lost time, and I breathed in the air from the tiny coffin, trying to spark that memory, trying to send myself backward in time. But it was elusive, not a smell of death, but also not meant for the living.

"Baby B," I said, wondering. "He's so much smaller than I thought."

"Also more, you know, intact," Tuck said, reaching out for me, touching my soaked hair.

"Yes, that's really surprising," I said.

"What do we do now?" Tuck said.

"Put him back," I said. "What else can we do?"

But I didn't want to close the lid. He was ugly, his skin gray and desiccated. There was nothing cute about him. But still, here was his body, here were his small hands, here were his cheeks, his forehead.

"Little brother," I said.

I closed the lid, and, trembling now, we shoveled the dirt onto him again.

24

Cole was waiting for me at home. He would be forever waiting for me. In every house, in every room, at every table, in every chair. We came in through the kitchen, and stood there, soaking wet, our faces and arms streaked with dirt.

"Where were you?" Cole said, looking scared. Was this the first time I'd ever seen him scared? I couldn't remember. But I liked it. I hadn't thought about what I'd tell him. But I didn't need to think up anything, because Tuck answered for me.

"We were digging in the graveyard," Tuck said cheerfully, and Cole's fear seemed to deepen, break the composure of his face.

"Say what you will," Tuck said, "grave robbing is hard work."

"I have to wash off," I said.

We took turns in the shower. Cole stood in the doorway of his room, watching us as we passed in the hallway, furious.

"You really thought he wasn't dead?" Cole said. "You thought it was all a dream you could wake up from. It's not a dream. He's dead, Lydia. She killed him."

"What does that mean?"

But Cole disappeared into our ghost room and wouldn't come out again. Of course, that was the new question I had been asking myself. Had she killed him? I hated Cole for saying that, because we hate the things that give voice to our fears. We hate them and we're grateful to them—sometimes against our wills.

Tuck fell asleep on the couch, and I went to my room. From the window, I looked out at the dark lawn, serene now in a sudden patch of moonlight as the clouds cleared. The road, the woods, the cemetery, all quiet now. I didn't want to think about the tiniest baby, my brother, his fragile bird bones, the way he'd flown—just one moment suspended, levitating, and then—

I had to protect Lucas. That was the thought I couldn't escape from that night. I'd lost one brother, and I couldn't risk losing another.

I couldn't sleep, and I couldn't sleep. And I felt a kind of dissolution. I was crumbling like the foundation of the house. I longed for the past. Or the future. I wanted Tuck, and I almost went to him. I imagined kneeling beside him in the living room. I thought about kissing him at midnight. But I also thought, he may be helping now, but at some point, he'll figure out what he wants to do and go back to school. And I will still be here alone, just me and the demons down under the sea, brooking and bucking the pull of the tide, panting and clawing and fit to be tied, tumbling down by the festering side, of our darling, our darling, our life and our bride. In this tomb by the sounding sea.

★ ★ ★

We walked to the landing in the morning, Tuck and me. The beach felt disorderly, with piles of shells and rocks and seaweed, with small dead creatures strewn about. Everything was wet, and I breathed in the smell of rain and leaves, the smell of gasoline in the harbor.

Outside Mady's, the man with the cat greeted us gravely and politely.

"Do you see my kids?" I asked. "Do I have them with me today?"

"Just the one," he said. "She's standing right there."

"What does she look like?"

"She looks just like you. In fact—"

He studied my face for a moment, confused. Then shook his head. "Have you met my wife?"

"Yes," I said. "She's lovely."

"She's my whole world," he said. "She's my apple pie. She's the reason I get up every morning."

"Do you know who I am?" I asked. "I'm Lydia Moore. My mother was Cecily Moore. Did you know her?"

"No," he said, sadly. "I don't know your mother, little girl. Are you lost?"

"I hope not," I said. "Thanks anyway."

Not lost, old man, but different. When I looked at the landing that morning, it was as if I were seeing it through new eyes. I noticed things I'd never seen before, although they'd been there all along. Chips in the sidewalk. Rust on the old No Fishing sign hung from the post office dock. And there were other differences, too—the coffee we bought from Mady's tasted like bitter soil.

And I was different in a way I didn't yet understand. I

was separated from everything and everyone around me, as if I'd brought something back with me from Colin that had changed me. Not from the grave, not from the coffin, or from his body. From somewhere else, wherever death is. I'd brought back a shadow that fit over me, something transparent, undetectable, but *there*, every inch of me covered by it, like another skin. It wasn't a mood, an emotion, it was a state of being, and it felt permanent. I was permanently shadowed. I would never be without that shadow.

In the spring I would resod the grave. I would plant different flowers—daffodils and tulips. Until then I would visit the disturbed earth and say comforting things to that littlest of brothers beneath the earth.

When the ferry arrived, Tuck and I stood in line. The planks came down. He held out his hand and I took it. We walked onto the boat.

I remembered the smell of the grave. He was a child and I was a child. I remembered the tomb by the sounding sea. I remembered the dirt under my fingernails. I remembered the terrible days after my mother had died. I remembered my mother weeping in the night.

The ferry whistled. Its motors churned us backward.

Tuck and I stood shoulder to shoulder on the upper deck of the boat. I had nothing with me but my wallet and a wool jacket. I didn't watch the landing disappear. I looked instead at the wide gray water, the cape getting closer and closer and more and more real.

25

On Emily's Bridge, Tuck and I both fell asleep. We'd reached the bridge midafternoon, exhausted from the drive, and we'd sat down on the narrow bridge to wait, and without meaning to, slipped into sleep.

When we woke up, it was very dark, and we couldn't see anything but each other and the wooden boards we were leaning against. I felt a whirl of confusion, but it settled slowly, and I remembered where I was, and who I was with. I looked at him, messy hair, wide mouth. We scrambled up, since Emily's Bridge was so narrow there was barely room for a car, let alone two sleeping bodies.

"I'm frozen," he said. I nodded. I heard wind in the leaves, and cars on the highway far away. I felt stiff with cold.

I'd thought about Emily's Bridge obsessively for days, the smell of it, the sweet rotten odor of damp wood, and the sound of the river below. In my imagination Cole's identity was waiting for us here. We'd pluck it down as easily as sliding a jacket off a hanger. We'd go back home with that garment and throw it over the man himself. And he would disappear.

But I hadn't imagined this disappointment, as fast and chaotic as the water racing underneath us, at finding...nothing. No clue, no hint, no trace of Cole. I should have known, shouldn't have held on to such a thin—almost invisible—hope that the bridge was somehow the key to his identity.

"Where should we go now?" I asked as Tuck and I walked off the bridge. All was still and quiet now. No cars. No ghost. No shadow of a noose over the water. We climbed back into his car, the little rusted Honda Civic that had driven us here today.

"I don't know," he said. "Let me think. I had a weird dream on the bridge when we fell asleep."

"I had a weird dream, too."

"I dreamed I jumped in," Tuck said.

"I dreamed someone pushed me in."

"That's almost the same dream," he said. He looked at me in the dashboard lights. "We better find a hotel."

"Together?"

"Most rooms come with two beds."

I felt my cheeks going red. "It doesn't matter," I told him. "I won't sleep either way. One room will save money."

He glanced at me with a strange look—he was smiling, but sad. It occurred to me for the first time that I didn't know what Tuck was hoping to get out of all this. It had felt at first like a way for him to pass the time—to play detective. But now?

"One room, two beds," I said more gently. "We should stay together tonight."

He nodded and drove.

The motel we found had a big empty parking lot and little dingy rooms. The desk clerk was a middle-aged woman with a red face, angry and pinched. I was glad Tuck was with me, until we got into the room, and then I was suddenly overcome with awkwardness. I immediately climbed into one of the beds fully dressed and lay there looking at the ceiling, while Tuck took a shower.

"Sleepy?" he asked when he emerged from the bathroom, smelling damp and warm and like soap.

"No," I said. "Well, yes."

He grinned. "Was this a mistake?" he said. "You seem uneasy."

"No. I'm not. I'm just not used to being—"

"With a naked man?"

"I was going to say away from home."

"Want to watch TV?" Tuck asked. "That's a nice normal wholesome activity."

I sat up in bed, and Tuck gave me the remote. I clutched it, exhausted. I felt worn-out from the drive. Tuck's Honda Civic was a rusty rattling thing with a dented door and a missing mirror on one side. The rust and rattling didn't bother me, but the whoosh of cars coming past us on the highway, the flicker of highway markers as we raced past them, all the sounds of the highway and the reminders of how far away from home we were—those things nearly did me in.

Earlier, as we'd driven away from the cape, I'd sat in the passenger's seat holding a little blue hand mirror, something normal women use for putting on lipstick. I'd used it for the hypnotic effect of looking into my own eyes. *Okay, okay, okay*, I kept telling myself. And we *were* okay.

At some point in New Hampshire, my body gave up, too exhausted from two hours of adrenaline to do anything but sleep. I leaned my head back and sank into a tumultuous doze. And when I woke up, I was calm. The highway was still a flash of road signs and trees and other cars, and the sound of it was still the roar of another ocean. And I was still in the center of all that noise and motion. But I was calm. I was my own anchor, I guess.

"I'm okay now," I'd said to Tuck, amazed, and he'd beamed at me from the driver's seat.

In the motel late that night, we turned the light off. But I couldn't sleep. I listened to Tuck breathing. Long after Tuck was asleep, I lay in bed, feeling a terrible thickness around my heart. I looked at Tuck's face as he slept and felt separated from him by a wide gulf. He was too young, too happy, too beautiful, too optimistic, too good, too twin-less, too much of everything that I wasn't. The substance around my heart felt like a rubbery denseness. The shadow was there, even there, inside me—that darkness I'd carried away from Colin's grave.

I lay in the motel bed, listening to Tuck breathing, longing for home, and for Lucas, for my mother and father, for Colin, and for that old life that would never return. Mostly I longed for the old life, with its familiar griefs and those old beautiful fears that seemed quaint now, like things encapsulated in a museum display, not at all like the new fears that gnawed at me like hungry animals.

The town of Lindenberg felt familiar from all the poking around we'd done online. We parked the car downtown and sat there for a few minutes, looking at the sweet, carved signs hanging out in front of shops, bright leaves on the slender trees on the hillside behind the town. I felt tired, gritty eyed, impatient. Maybe just hungry, I thought.

"Where first?" Tuck asked.

We maneuvered through the sunny streets and finally found our way to a diner on the corner. We ordered eggs and toast and coffee, and a young waitress with a kind face, who reminded me of Diane back at Mady's, served us.

"May as well start right now," Tuck said. He pulled the snapshot of Cole out of his wallet, and handed it to our pretty waitress, who looked at him curiously. Her bangs were so long they kind of fell into her mouth, and she kept brushing them away with her little hand.

"Do you recognize him?" Tuck asked her.

She shook her head, looking regretful.

"Wish I did," she said. I got the sense it was Tuck she wished she knew. She smiled at him and kept on tucking her hair behind her ears in a charming way. I felt awkward, as if I were interrupting something.

"Why do you ask?" the waitress asked, her eyes wide with curiosity.

Tuck shook his head. "We're trying to track him down," he said.

"Good luck," she said and refilled our coffee.

Wherever we went, women were anxious to help us out. Maybe they liked the mystery, or maybe—probably—they just liked Tuck. They wanted to help, but no one recognized Cole at the beauty salon, the office supply store, the wine and spirits shop, the clothing boutiques, the sandwich place, the toy store, the consignment shop, the shoe store, the pizza parlor, the flower shop, the movie theater, the Thai restaurant, or the library.

We went to the police station.

"Is it an emergency?" the receptionist behind the counter said.

"Not exactly."

"We've got a retirement thing going on," she said, pointing through a door where we could see several men and women wearing pointed paper hats. "But if it's an emergency, I can get the guys."

"We just want to know if anyone recognizes this man. We emailed a picture a few weeks ago, but we thought we'd try in person."

"I'll see what I can do," the woman said, and took the picture and Tuck's cell phone number.

It was after one, and we were tired and hungry and discouraged. And there was still the drive home to think about, and what I had to face at the end of that drive. Life in the big, rotting house. Life with Cole.

"This is hopeless," I said. "You were so certain, I started believing if I could just get here, it would somehow be easy."

We sat on a bench outside the coffee shop. There were window boxes full of dead mums, their spidery flowers brittle and brown.

"Worst-case scenario?" Tuck said. "We don't find anything out. You go home and gather more intel."

"I can't go home." I slumped down on the bench. "I can't keep being around him."

Tuck stretched his legs out on the sidewalk in front of us. "He doesn't seem that scary to me. I feel like he has some sort of power over you, but to the rest of the world—"

"It's a nightmare," I said. "I didn't tell you everything. I didn't—"

I could feel the birthmark on my cheek catching fire.

"What more could there be? The ferry, and the grave—" Then all at once his eyes widened with understanding. He waited but I didn't say anything. "Wait. Did you—you slept with him?"

"No," I said. "Yes." I stopped talking and watched the expression on his face, the permutations of surprise and confusion and maybe betrayal. I wanted to tell him about the Island Inn, and Annabel Lee, about that night in the storm, the way I'd felt caught in some fierce current—how I'd wanted to hold on to Cole, keep him close, invade and conquer him—because he held answers I needed, and even the questions were something he had brought to me. How I hated him, but I was grateful to him as well. Even now. Even still.

"Wow." Tuck leaned back and ran one hand through his hair. "When did this happen?"

"Before I knew—before I realized—before I met you in Carson Cove that day. I feel so stupid."

He looked around at the cold, sunny streets, the Christmas lights in windows, the carved wooden signs. Classical music piped out from one of the shops across the street, triumphant violins and cellos totally at odds with the way I felt. I was the opposite of triumphant. I was triumphed over. I was tiny.

"You don't have to explain yourself to me," Tuck said. "Obviously. But I'm wondering what we're even doing here? Because now—"

"Now I have to find out who he is. Now more than ever."

"Because now you like him?"

"No. Because I—I feel like he's taking everything from me. He's taking my place." I leaned toward Tuck. "It's like I don't have a home anymore. We have to do something before it's too late."

Tuck stood up. He looked up and down the street.

"Maybe it's already too late," he said, cool and cruel. "I'm going for a walk." He went to the corner and then disappeared. I knew from being Lucas's sister that it's better to let someone walk away. They'll come back when they're ready, when the walking has cleared a good space in their thoughts, when they're ready to forgive, or agree on a truce.

But I waited for an hour, getting colder and colder, and Tuck didn't come back. I bought a sandwich, and walked back to the motel, where I saw with relief Tuck's rusty car still in the parking lot. In the dark motel room, I ate the sandwich and waited for Tuck.

I waited all afternoon.

Periodically I took a moment to catalog my situation. I was in a strange town, alone in a motel room, waiting for someone who may or may not actually ever show up. I didn't have enough money to pay for the motel room alone. And it was unclear how I would get home if Tuck never reappeared. Would I take his car? Could I find a bus? Did I even want to go home? I thought about waiting tables in the little diner where we'd had breakfast. I could change my name, dye my hair, start over again far away from any ocean.

And what about Tuck? I had no way to call him, no way to reach him. Was he at least inside somewhere? Or was he out in the cold?

I put on my jacket and stepped outside, walked toward downtown. The air was crisp and sweet smelling, and the whole town had a kind of Christmassy cheer. People with rosy cheeks were hurrying down the sidewalk. Children in mittens were trailing after their mothers.

I wasn't hungry, but I made myself buy a slice of pizza. I took it to the bench where I'd last seen Tuck, and worried half of it down. I sat in the dark, watching the happy people of Lindenberg holding hands and walking dogs.

Then I heard drums.

Not right away, but after hearing them for several minutes it occurred to me that Tuck was somehow responsible for the drumbeat. And once I'd had the thought, it became a conviction. He was communicating with me in that most elemental way, hands on skin, heartbeat.

I threw away the rest of the pizza and took off toward the drum sound.

But if you've ever tried to follow a drumbeat, you know it's almost impossible. The sound ricochets off buildings and trees. It echoes. It's everywhere. I walked to the end of Main Street, and heard it closer than ever, but when I turned a corner, it was suddenly so faint it was almost gone.

I grabbed someone's coated arm, a man, who looked at me in surprise.

"Where is that drumming coming from?" I asked.

"Dunno," he said. "Maybe Calderwood Park? That's what it sounds like to me."

He pointed, and I went in that direction.

I found the entrance to the park, a path into the dark woods. It was the right place for the drumming. I could hear it louder than ever. I had no flashlight, but there was a half moon, and the sky still looked blue-black, with the faintest light. I took the path, walking half blind, feeling my way forward tentatively. Then I saw brightness ahead.

And after a few minutes, the path opened up into a little meadow, where a small fire was sending orange and yellow sparks up into the night, and bodies crowded around it, swaying. I crept toward them, and no one seemed to notice me. There were about fifteen people, all young and stoned and gorgeous, and the air smelled like smoke and sage. Someone turned and looked right into my eyes, and then handed me the joint they were smoking.

"Go ahead," he said kindly, and watched when I held it to my lips and breathed in the ashy heat of it. More people emerged from another path and joined the fire, and people from the fire left to go into the trees.

"Excuse me," I said, to anyone who was listening. "I'm looking for my friend. Tuck. Does anyone know Tuck?"

Two people, a guy and a girl, turned toward me.

"He's beating the drum," the girl said.

"No, those are hammers," the guy said.

They looked at each other and laughed, their beautiful faces lit up orange. The girl's face was painted with splashes of color all along her cheeks and temples.

"Is he building something?" the guy asked.

"I definitely think that's a drum," the girl said.

Then more people came out of the trees, and with them was Tuck, no coat, his face painted with the same splotches of color.

"Oh my god!" he said, when he saw me. "This is amazing. How did you find me?" His eyes, what I could see of them, were pools of ink, irises swallowed up by huge black pupils. "Come on!" he said, and led me to the fire, where he lay down, so close to it, that I worried the soles of his shoes would melt. I watched tiny sparks leap from the fire and land on Tuck, one of them burning a hole in his sweater.

"What's going on here?" I said.

"It's like preparation for the solstice," he said. "It's a festival welcoming the dark." He closed his eyes and grew quiet.

"Let me take you home to sleep," I said.

"Not yet."

The firelight swirled, the leaves made their respiratory sounds in the trees. Everyone laughed. Someone started to dance. The sky was full of stars, and then the moon went behind a cloud, which was sad and beautiful, and then it came out from behind the cloud, which was just as beautiful and just as sad.

I finally led Tuck back to the motel, through the cold streets, and he took a shower. I had to turn the water on and tell him to undress and get in. Then after ten minutes, I had to turn the water off and tell him to dry off.

"What exactly did you take tonight?" I asked him.

"A couple things," he said. "I met a girl named Ramona, and she had this little silver bag, and it was full of pills of all colors, and they were so tiny, like fairy pills."

He lay down on one of the beds and looked up at the ceiling fan. I sat on the edge of the bed, not touching him. Looked at his face. His lips were parted in an ecstatic expression, as if he were trying to take a sip of the night.

"Why don't you like me?" I asked.

"I do," he said. His eyes widened, seemed to snap into focus.

"But no more than you like anyone else."

"What are you trying to say exactly?" He rose up on his elbows. "I feel like you're giving me some mixed signals. I mean, what is it you want?"

What did I want? Well, what was the opposite of loneliness? Twin-ness. Could he give that to me? Could anyone?

"You made me dig up a dead baby," Tuck said. His voice was thick and slurred. "That was a bad experience."

He rolled over and closed his eyes, and I thought he was asleep. But a minute later he started talking again.

"I wanted to fuck you as soon as I met you!" he said. "I mean not when you were passed out, but basically ever since. You haven't been very encouraging."

"Well. I don't think I want to just *fuck*. That's not my end goal."

"You wanted to fuck *him*."

"That was more complicated."

"Well, this doesn't have to be complicated. You're making it complicated."

"You're the one who's twenty-one."

"You don't like me because I'm young?"

I sat on the bed beside him, watching him. I opened my mouth to answer, and then realized he really was asleep now, his mouth parted, breath shallow and noisy. I pushed the hair off his temples. I leaned over him, put my lips on his forehead, smelled his scent of trees and liquor and earth. I watched him sleep for a long time, and all the while I felt the shadow, that same film of despair I'd brought back from Colin's grave. I felt it on me and on him. It was between us. I could almost see it, almost feel it like a second skin.

26

I felt Tuck's warm arm, his hair near my face. I had fallen asleep on the bed beside him, fully dressed. I tried to roll over and couldn't. In his sleep he'd thrown his arm over me. The smell of toast and coffee and the hot room and his arm, it all coalesced into an unformed understanding of something, a hint, a flash of the future. This body smelling of shampoo and old liquor. This falling asleep and dreaming the same dream. This is what people want, what everybody wants. This moment, the toast and heat and Tuck—*this* was the opposite of loneliness.

I fell asleep again, and when I woke up, Tuck was sitting on the opposite bed, wide-awake, looking at me.

"I just got an idea," Tuck said. I rolled over, rubbed my eyes. "You know where we have to go? I can't believe we didn't think of this. Bus station."

"You're right," I said.

"Right? We're transit people."

"We're information people," I said.

I dressed in a hurry, and we went out into the sunshine. Neither of us mentioned the night before, and that seemed best. There were no buses in front of the bus station, and inside only a couple of benches, a rack of brochures, a water fountain, and an information desk with an old man sitting behind it.

We produced the picture of Cole, and the man listened and glared, all the while smoothing his mustache.

"I told you, I've never seen him," the man said.

"You haven't told us anything," I said. "This is the first time we've asked you."

"Well, I can't help you," he said.

"Did someone else ask about this man?" I said.

The man said, "I thought it was you."

"Can you describe who you saw?" I asked. "Anything about them. I mean, old or young? Male or female?"

"I can't help." He wouldn't say any more.

Outside, the day was bright and cold and still. A long, slow day. We stood in front of the bus station door. "Someone else is looking for him," I said.

Tuck nodded. "This is how we find him," he said.

What a relief to think that we were not alone in this search, that we had *never* been alone. "Who is it, do you think?"

"I don't know," Tuck said. "But it makes sense, doesn't it? *Someone* from his past life would try to contact him."

"Don't say past life."

"Former life?"

"Real life."

We went back to the motel with a whole pizza and sat on

the bed, watching old episodes of *Who's the Boss?* as the morning passed and the afternoon unfolded out the window. Who was the other person looking for Cole? Every few minutes we said this out loud. But we never had an answer.

"I should call home," I said.

"What are you going to tell them?"

"Nothing," I said. "Just that I'm not coming back yet."

"Do they know you're with me?"

"Hopefully. Because then they'll just assume we're on some romantic weekend."

"It's kind of romantic," he said. "But I know how you feel about romance, so…"

I didn't have to answer him, nor did I have time to call home, because Tuck's phone rang and he answered it.

"It's the police," he said. He listened for a moment. "It's about the picture. Thank you. Yes, we'll go right over. This is really helpful." He hung up the phone and looked at me triumphantly.

"Well?"

"They don't know anything about it," Tuck said. "But someone's wife came in, and her uncle was in the hospital for a week recently because of…it sounds like kidney stones."

"Okay," I said. "But what about Cole?"

"She recognized him, but not because she knows him. She said she's seen a picture of him. Another picture. Somewhere in the hospital. It's like two towns over."

"In the hospital? That's strange."

"The whole thing is strange."

"Let's go to the hospital," I said.

There was a nurse sitting at the front desk reading. She was so engaged with her book, her mouth hung open a little, and she didn't look up until we were hovering over her. When she saw Tuck, she arranged her face to look prettier.

"We talked to Dan Graham at the Lindenberg police station," Tuck said.

"Oh sure, Dan," the woman said.

"And he thought we'd better bring this over here. We're trying to track down this man? And he said this picture might match a picture you've got here?"

"Um," she said, looking at us over her glasses. "Can you hold on for a sec?"

"Do you recognize him?" Tuck asked.

"Just stay here," she said. She slapped down her book and went walking away in her white shoes. Maybe this was what happy people looked like, I thought, this ponytail, this soft body in soft clothes, easy walk, paperback book.

We sat down in the little waiting area. There was a fish tank behind the row of chairs, and Tuck and I watched the fish do their laps around and around the tank.

"That's a tetra," he said.

"Look, that one's stuck in the castle," I said.

We watched a white fish with moon eyes poke in and out of the castle window, unable to move forward or retreat into the plastic fortress. His huge eyes were terrified.

"He's probably been stuck in there for days," I said. "He can't get to the food. He'll die."

I looked around to see if anyone could help, but the place was empty.

"This is a super small hospital," Tuck said.

"I'm going to find someone."

"You know what? If that fish has been stuck there for a couple days, it can stand another couple minutes."

A man walked through the big swinging doors, and I went up to him. "There's a problem with the fish," I said.

"I'm a doctor here," he said in alarm.

Then the nurse came back, with a second woman in tow. A small woman, with short hair and wrinkles around her eyes and her mouth. Some deep emotion registered on her face when she saw us. She marched toward us. She didn't waste anything. Not words, not energy.

"Let's see the picture," she said.

Tuck handed it to her.

"That's him," she said and looked up at me, looked me in the eye, looked completely and unguardedly for a long moment. "I don't know where he is either. Welcome to the club."

"We know where he is," I said.

She took a deep breath. "He's dead, isn't he?"

"God, no. What do you mean? He's very much alive."

She let out her breath. She swiped at her eyes with one tan, wrinkled hand.

"How'd you end up with this photo?" she asked. "Who even are you?"

"I'm Lydia. Who are you?"

"I'm his mother," she said. "That's who."

I stared at her. "You must have been out of your mind with worry." Then I felt the question tumbling out. "What's his name?" I asked before she could say anything. "His real name."

She looked at me.

"Anthony," she said, and I was sure she wanted to say his name as much as I wanted to hear it. "Anthony Evan Coletti."

27

The room at the end of the hallway was bright and sunny, with pink walls, and white sheets, and a vase of lilies on the windowsill. It was lined with machines and monitors, several of which were hooked up to the woman in the bed. She was sleeping, and Cole's mother didn't pay her any attention after giving her a quick glance through the doorway when we got there. We sat on folding chairs in the hallway just outside the room, speaking softly. My heart was racing, each beep and click of the machine in the room a little trigger setting off bursts of adrenaline. Anthony. *Anthony.* Anthony with a mother?

I looked into the room where the woman in the bed slept. Who was she? I looked at Cole's mother, and she looked at me.

"So?" she said. And when I didn't say anything, she shook her head. "Where has he been?" she asked us.

"Wolf Island," I told her. "Since August."

She blinked.

"It's off of Cape Cod," I offered.

"I know where it is. Why would he go there?" she said.

"I've been trying to figure out the same thing," I said.

"I haven't been there in a long time."

"We can take you there," I said. "We have a car. We're going back. We can bring you with us."

"I don't want to see him," she said, looking at me in surprise. "I never want to see him again."

"I thought—I was sure you would want to—"

"No," she said. "I don't want anything to do with him. But it's good to know where he is. Just in case."

"Just in case what?"

"In case she wakes up."

We all looked through the doorway toward the woman.

"But who is she?" I asked.

"That's Emily," she said.

I stared at her blankly. Emily's Bridge. Emily's Bed. Emily's Ghost.

"Who is Emily?" Tuck asked.

"His wife," she said, impatient with us. "Anthony's wife."

"His wife," I said. Anthony had more than a name. He had a past, a history, a home, furniture, pots and pans, and food in a fridge, and—I was swirling with the news of it—it made him a man, not a ghost at all, someone who was once a young man falling in love.

I felt these facts settle in me, with a mixture of emotions. To know something like this about him, finally, after so many months of only guessing, filled me with something like elation. But I felt sorrow, too, without understanding why. I felt that I was losing something. For instance, I knew suddenly with certainty that the history class he told people we took together in college, that was the history class he took with Emily. And the sound of the train, that was a sound he heard with her. And the crows were crows in trees outside the window when he was falling in love with her. I had always resented those false memories, but now they felt worse than false, they felt stolen. It wasn't that they didn't belong to me—they belonged to another woman, and I had no right to them.

I felt a surge of anger. He'd had—and left behind—the very thing he claimed to want so badly now. *Family.* All this time he'd been slowly leading my brother away from me, and he'd had a family of his own. A wife! When he'd held me, put his mouth on me. A wife and a mother! A *mother.* And my mother was gone and never coming back. He'd had everything, but he'd wanted more. I thought I might need to stand up and walk down the hallway just to keep from exploding with the pressure and confusion of feelings.

"Wait—what do you mean if she wakes up?" Tuck asked.

"Didn't he tell you anything?" she asked.

"She's in a coma?" I said, understanding suddenly. "He put her in a coma."

I stood up, and the folding chair's legs lifted and banged on the floor of the hospital hallway.

"He didn't put her in a coma," his mother said. "But he certainly didn't stick around to take care of her."

"What happened to her?" I asked.

"Only she knows. Anthony came home one day and found her like this. There's a police report—that's how I found out what happened. He got her to the hospital, but by the time I arrived he was gone. He vanished. He left her like this. They think she fell down the stairs."

Tuck and I looked at each other.

"He had nothing to do with it," his mother said. "He was at work. Neighbors saw him getting out of his car at the end of the day. And seconds later he was calling the ambulance. There wasn't time for him to hurt her. He called the ambulance and he rode with her, and he waited for an hour, until they told him she wasn't awake. Then he went home, packed a bag, and disappeared. He's weak, you see. He couldn't face it."

The machines in the room made a kind of electric drone. I could see the white bed, the pale hair.

"You go back and tell him what you saw," his mother said. "Tell him she's not awake, but she's alive. Tell him I'm taking care of her, and neither of us wants to see him ever again."

I stood up and went to the doorway.

"She can hear everything we say," the mother told me. "I don't want you to scare her."

I walked to the bed and stood over her. She had pale blond hair, and her face looked puffy and white. But other than two clear tubes snaking into her nose, there was nothing to indicate that she wasn't just asleep. The light came in the window and made patches of gold on the white leaves of the lilies on the windowsill. I wanted to say something to her— *I'm sorry. You didn't deserve this. You're safe now*—but nothing seemed right.

"She's a beauty," his mother said. "Maybe you can't tell now. But she is a beautiful girl."

"I'm sure she is."

She beckoned me ferociously into the hallway. "It's best if you leave," she said. "You don't know about Emily? I don't understand. Why wouldn't he tell you?"

"We don't know anything. We know he grew up here and that's all—"

"He grew up on Long Island," she said. "She's the one who grew up here. I brought her here once she stabilized. I thought she'd rather be here in the town she knew."

"You're the only one taking care of her?"

"She doesn't have anyone else," she said, and then an afterthought, "and neither do I."

We took Anthony's mother out to dinner. The restaurant she chose was dark with heavy olive-colored curtains and wood beams, a steakhouse. She ate an entire steak, and a baked potato, and a salad with ranch dressing. Her body seemed too small for such a meal, but she ate steadily and doggedly until every bite was gone.

She alternated between defending him and insulting him.

"I washed my hands clean of him long ago," she said.

She ordered cheesecake for dessert.

"He's been claiming to be someone else," I said. "He gave us a fake name."

"Why am I not surprised!" she said, then immediately put down her fork and looked at me angrily. "His life hasn't exactly been a bed of roses. Unless you've been kissed by tragedy, you wouldn't understand. But we were kissed by tragedy many times over."

I watched her eat the cheesecake. She seemed to derive zero pleasure from the act, but she kept at it. When the slice of cake was gone, she scraped her fork along the plate and ate the last crumbling remnants she'd collected.

"I would lie about my name, too, if I abandoned my wife," she said. "I'd be too embarrassed."

Here was one more person with a private grief so large and ungainly she could barely contain its bulk.

"Strange question. Did he ever mention my mother?" I asked her.

"I don't know your mother, so."

"Did he ever talk about someone named Cecily?"

She had just lifted a cup of coffee to her lips, but now she set it down and the liquid sloshed over the edge onto the tablecloth. "Yes, he talked about someone named Cecily," she said. "But I don't think that could have been your mother. Cecily was a friend he made as a teenager."

I leaned toward her across the table, feeling a swirling sensation, that terrible dizziness of discovery. "But it could have been my mother. I mean Cecily isn't a very common name."

"No," she said. "That doesn't make sense. How would he meet your mother? We were only there—we stopped vacationing that year. Cecily. Cecily was a girl. I'm trying to remember, but—I'm sure of it."

I felt certain that this was proof he had known my mother. I tried to imagine how they met. I pictured my mother grocery shopping, checking out books from the library, sweeping into yoga class, meditating at the end of the dock, draining spaghetti. Where in that life was there room to befriend a teenage boy?

"When did you vacation on Wolf Island?" I asked.

"You know what?" the mother said. "I'm tired. I don't much like to think about him, if I'm being honest. Why don't you kids go back to where you came from now. And give him this message. You tell him I don't want to see him anymore. Tell him Emily doesn't want to see him."

I pictured Emily, back at the hospital, still asleep, unable to tell anyone what had happened to her, unable to say if she wanted to see him or not.

"You tell him neither of us wants anything to do with him," the mother went on. "She doesn't and I don't. Tell him no one here wants to see him ever again." It seemed like she might go on forever saying it over and over if I didn't stop her.

"I don't think he wants to come back," I said finally.

"He can go to hell," the mother said. Then she looked frightened by her own words. "He probably thinks she's dead," she said, in a miserable voice. "He can't face it. But you tell him she's alive! She's still alive!"

28

In the hotel room, we didn't turn on the TV. I felt jumpy and breathless. The wind rattled the door. A moth hit the window screen and I jumped up and peered outside, terrified.

"Here," Tuck said. "Look what I've got. A sleeping pill."

I shook my head. "Something's wrong," I said. "Something is definitely wrong. I don't know what."

Many things were wrong. I tried to list them in an orderly fashion, silently numbering them to keep track of my fear. One, there were moths at the window screen. Two, I was so far from home. Three, the girl in the bed had been sleeping since August. Four, I had fucked someone's husband. Five, what were they doing at home without me? Six, the baby in his coffin. Seven, all those candles they were always lighting to bring him back. Eight, Cole and Cecily, Cecily and Cole. I mean Anthony. Nine, wind in the trees, and crows. Ten, the girl in the bed with her puffy face, her mouth parted, how she had plummeted down the stairs.

"We don't know what happened to her," Tuck said as if he could read my mind.

"I know what happened to her. He did it."

"It sounds like that couldn't have happened. You heard what she said about the neighbors."

"Of course his mother doesn't think that's what happened."

"Well, we're safe here," Tuck insisted.

I knew we were. Even wrapped in the shadow the way I'd been since the night in the cemetery, I felt that as long as we stayed in this hotel room we were safe. We could make a life here, Tuck and me. I looked up at him. I wondered what would happen if I touched him now, kissed him at midnight, took my clothes off and stood naked in front of him. I wanted to obliterate everything I was feeling, and fucking seemed like the best and easiest way. Fucking obliterated the mother, and the girl in the bed, and Cole and Anthony, and Lucas, and the lighthouse, and the candles, and the moth, and the shadow. Only no—I knew nothing so ordinary as fucking could have any effect whatsoever on the shadow, which was not a warm and human thing like sex.

And then from under the shadow's curtain, I felt something else, something tugging at my consciousness, like a memory. Like the strains of a song I was trying to place. What was it?

"You know what?" I said to Tuck. "Something's wrong with Lucas. I just, I don't know, I feel it. It's a twin thing. I need to go home."

"It's a five-hour drive," Tuck said. "And there's no ferry until morning. We can't go home tonight."

"There's something wrong with him," I said, suddenly sure,

the certainty like a dense black pit in the center of my chest. "I always thought I'd know, and now I know. What should I do, call the police?"

"You should relax," Tuck said.

"Shut up. I can't."

I dialed the island police, but no one answered. I dialed again, longing to hear George's voice. *Something's wrong*, I would say. *Again?* he would say sounding bored. It was his boredom I longed for, his reassurance that things were the same as they'd ever been.

"George!" I said, when he finally answered. "It's Lydia. You have to do something for me. Go over to the house and make sure Lucas is okay, George…No, I'm not there. I'm— I'm out of town."

For once in his life, George did what he said he was going to do. When I called the police station thirty minutes later, he said he'd talked to Lucas and everything was fine.

"Everything is not fine," I said to Tuck.

I went into the bathroom and locked the door and looked at my face in the mirror for a long time. I turned on the bath-water, and as the water ran I stared at my eyes in the mirror. My eyes were my mother's eyes, my brother's eyes.

I took my clothes off and got in the bath. I looked down at my body. So much of it didn't seem to belong to me anymore. My arms, my stomach, my chest—in some perverse way they belonged more to Anthony than to me. But why? I ran my hands over my skin. Why would I think such a thing? Did Emily believe she belonged to Anthony? I let my chin slide under the water, let the water cover my lips.

Strange how things come into and out of your possession in this life. People belong to you, and then they don't. Places, homes even, belong to you and then they don't. Memories, too. You might have no memory of birds and trains, and then suddenly birds and trains are everywhere, wrapped up entirely in some false memory of falling in love.

I stood up and the water shed off my body in rivulets, then solitary drips. The only thing I could think of that might be mine entirely was Tuck, sitting on the bed on the other side of the locked door. I wanted to go to Tuck and tell him he belonged to me now, or ask him if he did, or find out in some other more permanent way.

I wrapped the towel around me and went into the room. I sat beside him on the bed. I took his hand. He touched my wet hair.

"Let's just go," I said. "Please? We can sleep in the car. I'll take the first ferry over tomorrow."

He nodded.

I got dressed.

He handed me the sleeping pill, and I swallowed it, and we took our bags and left the hotel.

I climbed into the passenger's seat. But even though my eyes were closed I still saw her: Emily. And sometimes all at once she ceased to be *Emily* and was instead, terribly and completely and inevitably, Lucas; he was lying somewhere after a great fall, his body arranged in strange and unnatural angles, still as death. I was scared, for myself and for Lucas, now that I had an idea of what Cole was capable of—how easily he could hurt the people he claimed to love.

29

I took the first ferry of the morning, leaving Tuck in Carson Cove, and walked home alone. Then I stood outside my house, afraid to walk inside. The car was parked in the garage again. I imagined the inside of the house as I'd always known it, the furniture, dishes, wallpaper. Lucas would be tying flies at his old desk in the corner of the living room. I would be there, too, reading on the couch, feet tucked under an afghan. Only, now I knew it was Cole on the couch, and I was nowhere in the picture. A great swell of grief came rolling through my chest. How easily, how completely, I could be replaced.

I put my hand on the doorknob, scared I'd find it locked. But the door opened. I walked into the kitchen. There were two bowls in the sink. There was a horseshoe crab shell on the counter, and I stared at it, transfixed. Had they taken a walk together? Found this treasure in the sand, half buried.

I touched the crab, its brittle caramel-colored shell. Then I realized there was something strange about the crab. Its tail, that little dagger, instead of having one point, was forked like a snake's tongue. I touched it, felt the twin points pressing into my fingertips.

The house was still. As if no air from the outside world could get in. As if no one had been moving, talking, breathing the whole time I'd been away. In the living room, two mugs sat on the coffee table. The downstairs bathroom was tidy; it even smelled good.

I looked into the laundry room. On top of the washing machine was a little pile of clothes, damp with blood. I saw the blood immediately, the rich brown mud of it. Lucas's T-shirt, sweater. His corduroy pants. I felt a contraction of fear so sharp and deep I thought I wouldn't be able to stand. And from some place far away, my mother's voice urging me to take care of Lucas. I ran, afraid to find out how I'd failed.

I stumbled upstairs. Hallway. Bedroom. Afraid I wouldn't find him, that he would have disappeared the way so many things seemed to be disappearing, lost to time or memory. But he was there.

We faced each other across the doorway. Lucas looked at me, frightened. He was so handsome it took my breath away, his bright golden eyes. He was perfect, his left hand the only imperfect thing, tied up in bandages, a huge white mummy of a hand.

"I knew something happened to you," I said. I was crying, still holding the bloody clothes. "What did he do to you?"

"It was an accident," Lucas said.

"An accident!" My voice was shrill. "It was no accident."

I felt the air move behind me and whirled around. Cole was in the hallway now, calm, still, concerned.

"I was at work. It was the hedge clippers," Lucas said. "It was definitely an accident. You think I'd cut my fingertip off on purpose?"

Nausea rolled through me. The image of Lucas, and the blood, and the soft pads of his fingers.

"Why were you at work? It's the off-season."

"It was a winter work day," he said, and that made sense. At the Day Estate, Lucas shoveled walkways, raked leaves, and trimmed paths on an as-needed basis.

"How did you get help?"

"Walked home," he said. "There's a trail of blood all down the beach."

I sat down, right there in the hallway, and leaned against the wall. I set down Lucas's clothes, put my hands on the scratched-up floorboards, felt all the house's grooves and dents.

"I knew something happened to you," I said.

"I thought something happened to *you*," Lucas said. "You just disappeared. We didn't know if you were coming back or what."

"Of course I was coming back. I live here."

Cole had joined me, and I looked right into his dark eyes. I held his gaze. I was nervous he would immediately recognize that something had shifted between us. Even I wasn't sure what that shift meant exactly, but I held some power, now that I'd met his mother, his wife, now that I knew his name. I imagined it written on a slip of paper, folded neatly and stored in a box. Yes, I had the name, but I still didn't know what to do with it. It turned out a name wasn't powerful unless you understood how to use it.

"Where did you even go?" Lucas asked.

"I went to the cape," I said, which was true. "I stayed at a motel."

"Kind of expensive," Lucas said, holding his hands up as if to say why in the world would you do that.

"I was with Tuck. Anyway, I'm back now."

"I can't work for a few days, at least," Lucas said, holding up his bandaged hand and staring at it. "I'm just home again, I guess."

"We can all be home together again," Cole said.

"I was lying down," Lucas said. "But then I heard Lydia yelling."

"Keep resting," Cole said.

Lucas went back into his room. But I stayed where I was, on the floor, and Cole stayed where he was. When I first saw the bloody clothes, I'd imagined something terrible. Lucas's chest, his throat. Cole with a knife. A pair of scissors. I could see him standing by Emily at the bottom of the stairs. I still saw those things, even though Lucas was okay, even though the girl in the bed was far away.

"I'm so tired," I said to Cole, and I was. "Please let me rest."

He turned and walked away, down the stairs.

Tuck and I had agreed that I wouldn't confront him alone. "Just take your time," Tuck had said when we were back in Carson Cove waiting for the ferry that would take me home. "Let's take a few days and figure out the best way to tell him what we know. You don't want to put yourself in danger."

"Last night you were all like *give him the benefit of the doubt.* Last night you didn't think he was dangerous."

"I still don't think he's dangerous, not really—but why risk it?"

I had a vague idea that I wouldn't need to confront Cole at all. I would tell Lucas—and once he knew, once he *saw*, he'd be the one to confront Cole. All afternoon Lucas dozed on his bed, his wrapped hand cradled on his chest like a wounded creature.

I slipped into the room and stood watching him. He opened his eyes. We looked at each other. I was going to tell him, but he spoke first.

"You thought Cole did this to me," he said. He shook his head. His eyes looked so hurt. "Cole saved me. Why can't you see that?"

"I see that now," I said.

"You weren't even here," Lucas said. "You were gone again. I could have died. He was here to save me."

"What do you mean, gone again? I never go anywhere. You're the one who told Cole I'm afraid to leave the island."

"You left when mom was sick."

"I didn't leave when mom was sick. I came *back* when mom was sick."

"Cole said—I mean, I see it, too—it's actually pretty obvious, and I guess I should have seen it a long time ago—you don't *want* us to all be together. You've *never* wanted us all to be together. You couldn't wait to get out of here, don't you remember? You left even though Mom was sick. And now—"

"I didn't leave Mom here sick. I came back."

"I can't remember how it happened."

"I'm telling you how it happened."

"Cole says—"

"Cole wasn't here, so he doesn't know."

"It doesn't matter," Lucas said, his voice rising. "I found your folder in the pantry, okay? With all your applications and forms for college. When were you planning to tell me? You know what? It doesn't matter. Go to college. Or go off with that kid from Carson Cove. I can't stop you. You have a life to live."

My throat ached. I was so mad I had to leave the room—before I shouted or threw something at him.

I saw it again—like a dream—like a sudden head-splitting vision—the other life. That city I would have gone to, the street with its tall buildings, its doorways and windows, its people, all those faces, all those hearts moving their bodies toward inevitable outcomes. Every day that other life felt more and more unreachable.

Did I want something other than this life? Yes. Of course I did. But it was too late. *Just look what I gave up to stay here with you!* I wanted to scream it through the walls. My bedroom, with its tiny bed, it was too small, there was no room to move, no way to breathe. *Look at all I gave up. I gave that life up, and here I am, and there's no way out.*

I called Tuck from the ferry landing at lunchtime.

I told him about Lucas's hand. "I've been trying to talk to him," I said. "But he won't listen to me."

"Don't even try to talk to Lucas," he said. "Wait until I get there. I'll come right after work."

I tried to follow this advice. I walked around and around the island, staying away from the house. I was overtired from the night on the highway, overemotional from my confrontation with Lucas.

I wandered down to Tame Jaw Beach. It was chilly, and I buttoned my sweater up to my neck. I heard splashing in the shallow water, but I couldn't see anything. Then there were footsteps behind me.

The man with the cat was barefoot, traversing the beach, the cat stately on his shoulders, face into the breeze. He stopped when he saw me, and we nodded politely at each other.

"Thinking about ghosts?" he asked.

I laughed, a short intense laugh, the kind that is bottled up for too long. "Kind of," I said.

"That's what people do," he said. "They look at the water and think about the dead. Good day."

I looked at the water and I wondered, how do you tell the difference between the ghosts of the mind and the ghosts that are truly hanging around?

Finally, I stood and brushed sand off my legs, feeling stiff and cold. On Clara Day Street, the bouncer stool was empty outside Jack's. I went to the front window and cupped my hands around my face. My breath made a white circle on the glass. The place was full of islanders. Their heads were bent together, and they were talking softly.

Gordon and Sebastian and some of the other fishermen were lining the bar. I went in and stood behind them for a minute, studying their profiles. Gordon's skin was smooth-baked. Not wrinkly the way Martha the librarian's was, nothing that delicate. His wrinkles were broad folds of smooth skin. They drank beer and talked to each other and took little notice of me.

"Are there ghosts?" I said finally.

They all turned and looked at me. There was a long pause during which my ridiculous question hung in the air like a balloon that wouldn't rise and wouldn't sink.

"Hell, yes," Gordon said finally.

"Everywhere," Sebastian said.

"I had one put a pink pebble in my mouth while I was sleeping," Gordon said. "When I woke up, this pebble comes tumbling out. Smooth and flat and shiny."

"What'd you do with it?" I asked.

"Gave it to my grandkids."

"There are ghosts all over this island," Sebastian said. "They're always walking the widow's walks. They're still waiting on their husbands, but their husbands are ghosts out at sea."

"My granddad used to visit a ghost whorehouse," Sebastian said.

"My granddad did, too," Gordon said. "The one in New Bedford."

"I went once," Sebastian said.

"No shit," Gordon said, impressed.

"It's like this," he said, turning kindly to me.

Back in his granddad's day, he told me, they would come in after a few weeks out whaling and go to the place where the ghosts of whores would still fuck you for free. You paid for your bed and fell asleep and they would visit you in the night, ghostly, but gorgeous. They all died of syphilis pretty young, and their ghosts were young and pretty. You could feel them only faintly, but you saw them clearly, and they rode you until you came just thinking about what it would feel like if they still had their flesh.

"All true," he said.

Eddie appeared from the kitchen. "Look what the cat dragged in," he said, happily, throwing his arm around me and squeezing me to him. He smelled of the bar, the brine of beer and oil from the kitchen.

"You okay?" he said.

"Oh sure," I said. I wanted to hug him, to hold him for a long time, hold on to everything he meant to me—childhood and love and the simplicity of wanting something you can't have.

On the beach on the way home I saw a ghost moving toward me, larger and larger as it emerged from the fog.

No. Not a ghost. Cole.

We stood facing each other on the sand.

"You know what I like?" he said finally. "This." He touched the birthmark on my cheek. "It looks like the wind blew it there."

"Let's go home," I said, and we walked side by side.

In the doorway I paused, listening, because it was my habit now to pause and listen in doorways, even when the thing I was listening for was just there behind me.

"Where's Lucas?" I asked.

"He won't bother us," Cole said softly.

I looked at him in alarm. "What do you mean? Where is he?"

"Jesus Christ," he said. "I just meant he's out. He has an appointment at the clinic to look at his hand. They want to do an X-ray. He might be a couple hours."

"Someone should be with him."

"He can go to a doctor's appointment by himself," Cole said.

I felt sluggish and hot. Haunted by the ghosts of whores. By Cole sleeping on the other side of the wall night after night. By Emily. And Anthony. Lydia and Lucas and Colin.

And my mother, who seemed like a stranger to me when I thought of her now.

I went to my mother's room. I'm not sure what I thought would be in there. I don't know why I wanted to go into the room, and sit on the bed, and then lie down. The bed was bare, stripped of its sheets. But still it was soft, and the pillows comfortable, and the faint sweet smell of dust and sandalwood rose all around me. I felt for a moment as though I were floating—my body adrift in some ocean. Maybe, I thought with a start, this isn't my body at all, maybe this is somehow *her* body, my mother's—wasted and almost ready to die, giving in to the pull of its mortality.

I looked up and saw Cole in the hall. He'd followed me there. He came close and sat on the bed. I held my breath. His hands rested on the bed beside me. I saw a scratch on his hand, just beneath the thumb. I saw one fingernail was jagged, as if he'd torn it off.

"Hello, pretty," he said. I tensed, thought of the girl in the bed. "I'm glad you came back," he said.

"It's my home," I said.

"You know what I mean."

"I don't know what you mean."

"Listen," he said, softly, urgently. "We can find a way to be together without hurting Lucas. We can have all of this."

He took my limp hand and held it. He pulled it to his face and pressed his mouth against it. He put my fingertips between his teeth, and I let him. I thought about him holding hands with Emily. Eating breakfast with Emily at a corner diner. I imagined her body full of him on some expanse of sand somewhere. *She must have loved him*, I thought. *I bet she loved him so much.*

"I want to make you happy," he said to me. "I want to keep you safe, and happy. You and Lucas both. I'll find a way for us to be together."

Mom, I thought, *help me*. But I knew she couldn't. Then I thought, *I will say his name, I will say it over and over, like a protective chant. I'll say it in my sleep.*

"Cole," I said. "What do you really want? What do you want from us? Why us?"

Cole shook his head. "You think it's some big mystery. But there's nothing mysterious about what I want. I want to be home," he said.

Both our bodies sank into the mattress now. My heart was clumsy, flapping around in my chest. I felt a weight on my ungainly heart. It was all elbows and knees in there. Beneath, between, inside my body, my mother's body shifted a little and settled more firmly into place. She liked all this. She loved a ghost, she loved a stranger, she loved the dead.

"So—you meet a girl and get married," I said. "Start a family of your own. Make a home."

"It doesn't work out the way you think," he said, a profound sadness in his voice. "You think it's one way and it's not."

From underneath my mother's bones, a faint pulse. My blood reacting. Beginning to move.

"You know what your problem is, Lydia? You try to keep everything under control," Cole said. "You bind yourself with all sorts of rules you've made for yourself. But you can't keep that up for very long. You're too tired. You can't keep running. Someday you'll just—stop."

"What happens when I stop running?"

"Well, here you are," he said. "You're not running. What happens?"

My blood, my bones, my muscles, they sprang to life, inflated suddenly, shaking my mother's bones out of place, scattering those old ghosts of bones into the dim room. *What happens?* I felt my body filling up with something. I felt my heart pumping, regular, thrumming, warm.

I'd been quiet for so long, listening. Listening in the silent house. In the grocery store. Listening in the sound of the wind, in the sound of the waves, in the rustling of newspaper pages turning over. I was listening for it now. I listened for a sound to blossom out of the silence. His name. That name. I wanted to say it, just to feel that it was mine.

I turned toward him. I didn't expect to feel this way, sad, sympathetic. "I know who you are," I said.

I saw his body tensing, but it was with pleasure, with desire. He didn't understand.

"I mean," I said, "I know your name. I met your mother. I saw Emily."

30

The moment I said the word *Emily*, a change came over him. Swift and sudden. He darkened, his features changed. Something in him wanted out, and the name *Emily* called to it. I scrambled to my knees. Off the bed. He reached for me and grabbed a handful of my T-shirt. It ripped in his hand, but I didn't turn around. He could keep that shred.

We dashed out of the room and down the stairs. Into the kitchen, where I stood behind the table. The smell of sautéed onions was in the air, and a pile of shredded cheese sat on a plate on the counter.

Cole came toward me. His face was full of ugly rage. His chest looked strange—rigid—and his arms robotic. For one quick moment I thought he was reaching for a knife on the counter. I could see it shining there in the light from the bulb over the sink. But then I realized that what looked like reaching was a reflexive motion, an involuntary pulling back. His arms swung behind him, tensed, fists clenched, the veins in his wrists popping—his shoulders, elbows, everything pulled back as if an invisible presence were holding him back while he strained to come at me.

He didn't need a knife. If he wanted to hurt me, he could do it with his hands.

"Do not," he said, "talk about Emily."

"No one thinks you did that to her. I—I don't believe you pushed her—"

"Didn't push her? Of course I pushed her," he said. "But it wasn't *me* pushing her, do you understand?" He looked at me intensely, glanced down at his hands, and then back at me. "It was *my* hands," he said. "But they were just tools, the way we're all just tools. It was Divine Justice. She was a bitch of a liar being punished by the great hand of the universe. It was the tides moving her toward that punishment. Because you know what? I loved her with every ounce of my being, and she never loved me, not really. She kept secrets. She held herself secret from me. That's not what love looks like."

He moved toward me again, coming around the table.

"Everyone gets the punishment they deserve," he said. "I looked down at her, so helpless at the bottom of the stairs, and I was glad. I thought she was dead. I *hoped* she was dead."

"She's still alive," I said.

"You think I don't know that? You think I don't keep track?"

Naturally he kept track. He was a puppeteer, holding all the strings at once, twitching this way and that while we went through our routines. I wondered how he monitored her without being found out. But there were more pressing things to worry about now. His arms were still behind him, elbows locked, fists awkwardly out. I backed toward the door.

"Lucas will be home any minute," I said.

"You think so?"

I found the kitchen door behind me. The knob.

"Don't even think about it," he said.

I'd never seen him like this, with something in him set loose, called forth by the name of the girl in the bed.

Then I thought, *If* her *name calls out the monster, maybe* his *name calls back the man.* I knew his name, but I hadn't said it out loud yet. I'd been waiting to know how to use it.

This was how.

Help him find his better nature.

I said it softly.

His name floated through the kitchen.

Anthony. Anthony.

In the second it took him to process the name, I'd turned the knob on the door and slipped into the night. Where was Lucas? In my confusion I thought he must be out here somewhere.

There was someone at the end of the dock. For one fleeting second, the figure was clearly illuminated against the darkness. Lucas! That was where I ran—toward him, toward help. But the figure dissolved the closer I got. Became nothing, a ghost. And Cole—Anthony—was behind me on the dock. Advancing rapidly, his strange, awful arms still pulled behind him as if some force inside were wrestling him.

I turned and faced him. "What are you going to do? Put *me* in a coma?"

"If you're lucky," he said.

"You know you can't."

"Why? Because you've been so *kind* to me?"

"Because you'll go to jail."

"I don't exist," he said. "There's no such person as Cole

Anthony. Cole Anthony will disappear. Then you and I will both be gone."

There was no getting past him on the skinny dock. The only way out was the dark bay behind me. I did what I had to do. I jumped.

31

The water was icy, and the shock of it slammed into me, stopped my breath. I gasped. Breathed. Moved my arms and legs reflexively. My waterlogged shirt and pants weighed me down. But I didn't need to go very far. The night was thick with fog, and he wouldn't be able to see me when I resurfaced. I'd be nothing more than a rock, a seal, a sea wave.

I broke the surface, trying not to splash or breathe.

"I just want to talk to you," he bellowed from the dock.

I went under again and swam out into the deep water. The trick was to stay underwater as long as I could, but not so long that I'd gasp when I resurfaced. Everything depended on disappearing and reappearing in silence. Getting as far from him as possible without him knowing what direction I'd gone.

I felt something brush my body, a strand of seaweed I hoped. I broke the surface. He would think I'd stuck close to shore. That I was swimming along looking for a place to go ashore. But I was going straight out to where the water was deep. I had a destination in mind: the houseboat. That small red cradle of a boat I'd watched rocking in the bay every day of my life.

When I reached it, I held on to its sides for a few seconds, staying in the icy water. I looked toward the shore, and I saw the light of the house, but I couldn't make out whether anyone was standing on the dock or not. I listened, but I only heard the water lapping at the houseboat, and my own breath, and my own heartbeat in my ears.

Then I moved hand over hand around the edge of the structure, until I came to a ladder that led up to a narrow deck and the door of the house. The whole structure tilted when I pulled myself onto the bottom rung of the ladder, but I climbed up easily. On the deck, I sat shivering, looking across the water to my house, looking at the dock, which I could see now was empty. I went to the door of the houseboat. Obviously, it was locked.

I was freezing and scared. And the longer I stood on the deck, the more chance he would be able to see me, I knew. The fog that rolled in with the dusk was rolling off across the sea now, and soon my body on the deck of the houseboat would be clearly visible from shore. I felt the cold wind on my wet skin. The thing I wanted most was to get inside, but how? I tried the window to the right of the door. There was no way to open it from the outside. I pounded on it a little with my fist, but that didn't do anything.

But the window on the other side of the door—that one wasn't closed tightly. There was the smallest crack under the window, enough for my fingers to fit underneath and pry it up. It didn't move. When had these windows last opened?

I wiggled it and felt the window begin to loosen. The fog seemed to blow all around me, and above me the sky began to clear. Hazy light poured down, clearer and clearer. The moon, not full, but bright. I pounded the window with my fist and then wiggled it open a fraction of an inch. I hit it again. Soon, I could fit my hand under and push upward with more strength. Something seemed to give, and the window opened. It was a tight squeeze, but I pushed myself through, headfirst into the interior of the houseboat.

I carefully closed the window behind me and sank to the floor, breathing hard. The place was stale and warm out of the wind. Moonlight came through the window and lit the room. It was just as I imagined it would be: small and safe. The entire structure seemed to be one room. There were benches with cushions around three walls of the room, a table against the fourth wall that seemed to double as a bed—I could see the Murphy bed in the wall above it that lowered onto the table. Above me were two bunks, just big enough for beds.

I huddled there, catching my breath, with the smell of damp things all around me, a thick stench of mildew and disuse. I breathed in and out and tried to think how I was going to get out of this. There was only one way back to shore, that was clear. But when could I go home? How did I know Cole wouldn't be waiting for me, whenever I made my way back? I'd have to stay all night. I would strip off the sopping clothes and wrap myself in curtains. I could do jumping jacks until I warmed up. When it was day, when it was light, I would swim home, or even to the landing.

I concentrated on the sound of my breath, an almost violent rhythm. Then suddenly, I realized the rhythmic sound was not my breath. A slow even *thwack*, almost like a slap on bare skin. Then silence for two or three seconds, then *thwack*. It was a strange sound but also completely familiar. I struggled to place it, all the while hearing it become louder, *nearer*, with every *thwack*.

All at once, I knew. It was the rowboat. It was the sound of the oars slicing the water. The rowboat coming closer. *Thwack*. He couldn't possibly know where I was; he couldn't have seen, not through the fog.

Then the rowboat bumped up against the side of the houseboat.

I held my breath. I heard his footsteps on the ladder. The door was locked, I told myself. And he couldn't fit through the window. He would think I'd jumped back in the water. He would go after me again in the water.

He was on the other side of the door. His hand on the knob. I waited for him to swear when he realized the door was locked. Instead, a small sound of metal on metal. The doorknob turned, the door opened, and Cole walked into the cabin.

I don't know how much of me he saw. Maybe I was just a dark shape on the floor of the cabin. He was bright and clear in the doorway, illuminated. We looked at each other across the dark room.

"How did you get in the door?" I asked, as if that were the thing that mattered most.

"I'm not going to hurt you," he said. "Just shut up about her. I won't hurt you if you shut up."

"Okay," I said.

He looked around the cabin, then reached for something on a hook over the window. A flashlight. He tried to turn it on, and when nothing happened, he dropped it.

"Come here," he said.

I wouldn't. I stayed where I was on the floor, watching him.

He crossed the cabin in three steps and stood above me, his features all erased in the gloom now. I wouldn't offer him my hands, so he pulled me up by the armpits like a child. We crossed the room and squeezed behind a kind of half wall, into a small space with only a bench and an old-fashioned steering wheel, the kind that looked like a star. Cole pushed me gently onto the bench. He stood over me, looking out the window at the dark water. He reached into his pocket and pulled out a ring of keys, one of which he used to turn the boat on. The motor rumbled. The boat shook.

"What are you doing?" I asked.

The boat began to move. Beside me, Cole's body tensed. I turned to look at his face. His fast breathing. His strange look of fear. Afraid of what? Of me? Of what he was doing? Stealing a boat. Afraid that he would hurt me, after all, whether I shut up or not, that he wouldn't be able to stop himself?

The boat maneuvered through the dark water, around Bhone Bay's other inhabitants, the sailboats, the motorboats. It was slow and rough, rumbling through the water like some ungainly creature, half above the surface, half below. Cole steered with one hand, keeping the other on my shoulder.

"You are really something," Cole said. "You are about as selfish as they come, Lydia. Really, you disgust me."

The boat ground against something. A rock? A buoy? I couldn't see anything out in the foggy night. Cole didn't seem to hear it.

"Does it surprise you that I call you selfish?" Cole said, looking down at me. "It shouldn't. You don't think of anyone but Lydia. It's all about Lydia."

I looked from his face to the water we were moving through so swiftly, trying to gauge which was the bigger danger.

"I used to think you had the perfect life," Cole said. "Perpetual vacation! That's what I thought, but I was wrong. It's perpetual *childhood*. It's you and Lucas running around like children in your big house, with your little summer jobs and your little disagreements. You think that's life? No. That's playing house.

"There are people out there living real lives, Lydia. And when they have fights, they're real fights. And when they get hurt, they get really, really hurt. And the things you lose are enormous things, but you don't spend your whole life looking for them! You leave the dead things behind, Lydia. That's how it's supposed to go. But you couldn't have been more thrilled to have me be your dead baby brother. You practically laid out the welcome mat for me. You got what you wanted, didn't you? Here I am. And now I'm not going anywhere."

His face was flushed, his hairline damp. For once the heat from his body did little to warm me. The cold had seeped deep into my bones, as I sat there shivering in my wet clothes, watching the dark water be swallowed up by the slow-moving boat.

"How could I possibly start to like you?" Cole said. "But I did, Lydia. I really liked you. You thought it was a trick, but that was real. And what happens next? You fuck me and then literally skip town."

"That's not how it happened," I said.

"That's exactly how it happened. I don't go around feeling sorry for myself like you do, Lydia. But if we were going to have a pity party, I would win that party. From the very beginning, I've lost everything that mattered. You know what

I'm talking about. My wife is the living dead. My girlfriend fucks me over."

"I wasn't your girlfriend," I said. "I didn't mean to hurt you."

"No, that never even occurred to you," he said. "You never thought about me, not for a minute."

"I just want to go home," I said.

"I do, too," he roared. "But I don't have anywhere to go."

Then he looked down at me, and his face changed in an instant. His expression grew soft and melancholy. Even his grip on my shoulder softened.

"Let's go back home together," I said quickly. "I'll make coffee. And we'll find Lucas and just sit and talk. We'll talk all night. Just the three of us. Like you wanted." He shook his head, looking disappointed.

"Let's go to the house," I said. "Let's—I mean, you can't do this. You can't steal a boat."

"Steal it?" he said. "I'm not stealing. It's mine."

I glanced at his face to try to understand—and just like that I did understand.

"Oh," I said. "Oh no."

Because I knew who he was. I couldn't believe it hadn't been clear to me before. I'd spent all this time trying to learn his identity, when I already knew. I knew all along.

"Anthony Coletti," I said. "The little boy in the red houseboat. The boy with the straw hat. I remember you now." With the silent parents and the drowned sister. All those years in Bhone Bay when we were young. He must have seen us from his houseboat the way we'd seen him from our porch, our lawn, our dock.

"This is your boat," I said. "And you remember us."

He looked around the little cabin, his eyes resting on the mildewed cushions, the hooks hanging over the table with pots hanging from them.

"Oh god," I said. "That's how you knew about the shed door, and the way Lucas used to spin the net. And how my mom used to sit like that on the dock. You spent years watching us. You knew about the lady's slippers. Oh my god. And your sister. Your poor sister. You killed her."

"I didn't kill my sister," he said, disgusted. "Would you kill Lucas? A sister is sacred. I long for my sister every day. You of all people should understand that. Jesus Christ, Lydia, are you some kind of monster? Kill my sister! Like I would ever lay a hand on her. She was ten years old. Ten years old."

"I'm sorry," I said. "I'm sorry that happened to you."

"But Lucas still had his sister, didn't he? Jesus Christ, I hated him. Before I ever met him, I hated him. I hated you both. The way you were always together. Always! And I had no one."

"But your mother...your parents. You had them."

"No, I didn't have my parents." He shook his head at me, as though I were so stupid he couldn't believe it. "They were like invisible people after Holly died. They couldn't stand to be around me. They couldn't stand to be around each other. Luckily, I had *your* mother," he said. "She was the mother I wanted because she understood what it felt like to have no one."

"But how did you—how did you know her?"

"She swam out to me. She hung on to the edge of the boat and talked to me, said she'd been watching me. You know why she believed I was Colin? Why she was so desperate to believe? Because she was dying of guilt." He leaned toward me, his face coming closer and closer. So many expressions on his face at once. His eyes were angry—and then he lifted his eyebrows in a sorrowful way, a pitying way. But when he spoke next his mouth was malicious. "She killed him," he whispered. "She sacrificed him for you and Lucas. And then she couldn't live with herself."

And then the boat hit something. The jolt sent Cole against the wall. And in that instant, I rolled off the bench onto the floor.

Heart crashing, I scrambled around the corner and across the small room, to the door. I burst out into the night. Cole was behind me, reaching out for me. He was between me and the ladder, but that didn't matter. I climbed up on the railing, about to jump. But something was in the water beneath me. For one split second I saw—a face looking up. It was like seeing my reflection in the water, only I knew it couldn't be, not in this blackness. Cole was behind me, and the boat was lurching, and my feet were slipping. I had to jump. Right away. Then I felt a blow of pain on the back of my head. I plunged into cold water. And it felt familiar and right. To be suspended like that, a particle of light. A relaxed kind of darkness settled over me.

32

They say drowning is painless. People resuscitated after near drowning describe a deep chill, a feeling of weightlessness, then ringing in the ears and beautiful visions of light and color.

Yes.

Drowning is a good dream.

The lungs like full tumblers. Every other piece as light as air.

One time we'd stood on the deck of the ferry and had seen shooting stars overhead, Lucas and I. Nine years old, and we'd seen nine stars cross the sky. They seemed to be messages for us. Their light burned a long time before sizzling out into darkness. If you focused only on the stars, and shut out everything else, it was like you were the star, suspended in space, dazzling and bright. Heavy lungs, and all the rest flying like a star.

One time I'd fallen asleep on the beach and woken up underwater. I thought it was a dream, but it was really happening. At first I was scared. It was dark. I couldn't see my own body, but I felt my hair floating around my face. Which way was up and which way was down? Then I saw pinpricks of light, phosphorescence around my body, invisible creatures with their visible light, and I saw a pale glow, moonlight. I was able to move toward the surface.

Where was I now? This seemed to be the place of lost memories, this depth of water near the edge of the houseboat. What else was down here? My father's voice? That was something I couldn't remember, I could never remember, no matter how hard I tried. But apparently it had been here all along, and I heard it, a deep roar in my ears. *Take me out to the ballgame!* He was singing. I almost laughed in delight. Nothing was lost after all. It had been here all along. What else was here?

There was the baby, for one thing. I saw him suspended beside me, his naked arms and legs healthy and fat. I caught him as he drifted past, pressed his cold skin against me. His heart beat where my heart beat. His old memories were here, too, just like mine. I saw the light coming in a window onto a clean sheet. I heard her voice, my mother. I felt the electric shock of the cold water as he plummeted from the deck.

Glancing around, I saw a living room: couch and chairs and an end table with a lamp. Barnacles blistered the arms of the furniture, and seaweed drifted past. I thought I'd just arrived, but it appeared we'd both lived here a long, long time. There were my books, and there were my sweaters, and there was a mirror I could comb my hair in. The baby played on the sand, stacking quahog shells like blocks. I'd been taking care of him all this time.

Drowning isn't entirely painless. It doesn't hurt exactly, but the anguish of wanting to breathe, that's a profound and complicated pain, to want something with all the force of your mind and instincts, to feel *meant* to breathe and at the same time kept from breathing. To feel like you must breathe because the stars and the tides and the moon and sun have instructed it thusly. I opened my mouth. I felt the cold water. The baby grasped my finger with his cold, cold hand. His eyes were the milky white of the blind. He never cried. I took a breath. I tried to take a breath.

33

I was rocking.

That's what I knew first.

I almost drifted back to sleep, cradled and moving like this.

Then I heard water.

Then the *thwack, thwack* of oars.

I felt the water all around me.

My consciousness seemed to swim up from some deep place. I rose and rose and when I broke the surface it was with the sudden awareness that I was in the bottom of the rowboat, moving swiftly through the water. I opened my eyes and saw the winter sky all foggy and dark.

I thought, *I'm not dead, but I'm probably going to die tonight.* I didn't feel scared, but I did feel aware suddenly of how much I liked being alive. There were so many good, gentle things. So many nights like this with fog and stars. I loved fog and stars. I thought about how I hadn't yet had dinner and about how much I loved dinner, all kinds of dinner. I thought about how alone Lucas would be. And I thought about Ed Frank, and Jim Cardoza and Ferry-All, and Gordon and Sebastian and all the old fishermen, and the Grendles next door, and Martha at the library, and Elijah, and Tuck.

There were so many brothers, and who would take care of them all?

I would have to stand up and jump overboard. I'd have to be fast. The moment he saw me he would reach for me. I'd have to dive deep again, and swim underwater for a long, long time. And I didn't know where we were, or if I'd encounter the baby again. How long had we been rowing? The other trouble was that my head felt broken, with a sharp pain moving through it in waves.

And then—the rowboat swung, and I opened my eyes, and saw that we were at a dock.

I heard Cole say, "Oh no." I tried to lift my head, and the pain sliced through. I put my hand on my head. I heard Cole breathing. Then he said, in a different tone altogether, "Thank god you're here. Help me get her up."

"Who? What happened?"

I thought I must be imagining Lucas's voice. But no, there he was, looming above us on the dock, the bandages on his hand bright in the moonlight. "Lydia!" he said. "Oh man, I knew it. What happened?"

"She hit her head," Cole said. "She was climbing on the railing of the boat and slipped and hit her head on the deck. Here—take the rope?"

"What boat? Why was she climbing on the railing?"

"Running away from me."

I rolled myself over and sat up. My head was full of liquid that swirled and eddied and bumped over obstacles.

"Are you okay, Lydia? What are you guys doing out here anyway?" Lucas asked.

"I didn't slip," I said. "He hit me with something."

"Listen, man," Cole said, his voice strangely pitched. "She could have a concussion or worse. She fell hard, okay? I rowed from the—the boat—all the way…"

"Why didn't you bring her home?"

"I wanted—to—bring her to a doctor."

"He's lying," I said.

"All right," Lucas said. "Come on. Up you go. Grab my hand. Jesus Christ. Are you bleeding?"

I stood, and Lucas pulled me up. My head sloshed and burned. I was dizzy, nauseous. We were on the dock behind the post office, where the postmaster practiced bagpipes. I could almost hear the goose-honk of those notes. I could see through the buildings a slice of Clara Day Street. I saw half the sign from the T-shirt shop. I saw the window of Island Pie. I saw shapes moving through the streets. The people I'd known all my life. They were coming out of bars, they were eating ice-cream cones. God, I loved them, I loved them.

34

Everything happened in one fluid motion after that. Someone called Sean Alameda, the island's sole paramedic, who drove an old Subaru station wagon we called "the ambulance." He unlocked the clinic and brought me inside. Someone put a sweater around my wet shoulders. Dr. Lyle showed up in pajamas to check if I had a concussion or hypothermia. I kept telling them to call the police. I sat on the table shivering. Dr. Lyle felt my wrist, shined a light in my eyes. He listened to my heart, my lungs. Then Dr. Brent was there, wanting to know if I jumped in on purpose. "Were you trying to harm yourself?" Someone put a space blanket around me.

I said, "I wasn't trying to harm myself. He was trying to harm me."

I was still dizzy. It was hard to look at just one thing.

"He hit me with something," I insisted. "Maybe a flashlight."

Dr. Brent looked into the lobby, and Lucas and Cole both stood up.

"I'm pretty sure he was trying to kill me," I said quietly to Dr. Brent. "He tried to kill his wife, but no one knows. He confessed it, though."

"Is she okay?" Lucas asked. He took a step toward me, but Cole put his hand on Lucas's shoulder and held him back.

I remembered him calling me his girlfriend, the hurt and angry look in his eyes. There was something in him, some monster in there. I could see it every moment. A smaller, meaner creature concealed in the body we all saw, a creature full of wild rage. The Anthony inside the Cole. I could see them both, the two men, wrestling each other.

But then something amazing happened. All at once *Anthony* vanished and left only *Cole*. I saw it happening before my eyes, a transformation into calm, controlled power. And I realized it was because Lucas was there, that Lucas somehow had the power to make one man disappear and the other come to life. I knew one name, and Lucas knew the other, but now I knew that I'd been wrong about names all along; Cole was dangerous and desperate, no matter what we called him.

By the time George Samson showed up, Cole was gone, as I'd known he would be. George listened to me tell the whole story, skeptical but quiet.

"He has a wife," I told him. "Up in a hospital in Vermont. The official story is that she fell down the stairs, but it wasn't an accident—he pushed her. Her name is Emily."

George Samson wrote EMILY in a little notebook. I felt happy to see her name in his handwriting. I felt happy that everyone was listening, George Samson, and Dr. Brent, and Dr. Lyle.

"He hit me with something," I said. "I felt something hit my head, and I tumbled into the water."

"He says you hit your head on the railing," George Samson said. "He says you were trying to jump over the edge, and you slipped. Is there any way that could have happened?"

"No, no! I don't think so. He was trying to hurt me," I said.

George Samson said he'd call the police in Lindenberg and check in with them about Emily. "And I guess we'll bring him in for the night." He looked at Dr. Brent as if she'd know more about police protocol than he did. "I guess we'll find him and bring him in for the night and question him." He began to sound a little more sure of himself. "I definitely will want to question him, if we can find him."

"You won't find him," I said.

"You just get some rest," George Samson said, "and let us catch the bad guys."

Sean Alameda drove Lucas and me home, down the inland road. Dark branches hung over the road, fir branches, sweeping and dipping whenever a gust blew through. I kept looking out the window at the dark trees, thinking I saw a figure ducking behind each trunk.

I let out a laugh, and Lucas jumped, startled.

"I didn't know there *were* bad guys," I said. "Not here. Not until he came."

"There aren't," Lucas said.

At home, I saw someone in the bushes by the kitchen window, peering inside. My heart raced, and my hands went heavy with fear. But it wasn't Cole. I recognized the mane. It was Tuck.

Sean Alameda stopped the car and let us out. Tuck came loping over.

"What the hell happened?" he said.

"What happened to *you*?" I asked. "You're soaking wet."

He took my hands. "Is that blood in your hair?" he said.

We went inside and Tuck dripped all over the kitchen floor. His pants and T-shirt were drenched, and he was barefoot.

Lucas said, "Would someone please just tell me what is going on tonight?"

"Let's warm up first," I said.

Tuck got in the shower, and Lucas found a set of clothes for him to wear. Cole and Lucas were both considerably smaller than Tuck, so Lucas had to search the attic for a box of my dad's clothes. He pulled out a long underwear shirt, a sweater, a pair of corduroy pants. They had a faint musty smell but weren't as bad as you'd think. I set them on the bathroom counter for Tuck to put on when he came out. Then I stood outside the bathroom door, wrapped in the old chenille blanket, waiting for him.

"Why don't you lie down or something," Lucas said.

I shook my head.

When he was dressed, Tuck and I sat on the couch wrapped in blankets, and Lucas built a fire for us. We kept holding our hands out to soak up the heat. Tuck drank a beer, and I drank hot water with nothing in it.

"Who's going to start?" Tuck said.

"He chased me into the water," I said. "We were on the houseboat, and when I tried to escape, he smashed my head with something."

Lucas shook his head. "You fell and hit your head," he said. "Cole said you were balancing on the railing."

"The police are looking for him," I told Tuck.

"Listen to me," Lucas said, leaning forward. "You have this all wrong. There's a lot about Cole that we didn't know. He told me tonight. And maybe I shouldn't say anything, but it might help you understand. See, he was married, and something happened to his wife. She was in an accident, a bad one. She was in a coma, Lyd. So when you hit your head tonight, it brought back a lot of those old memories. *That's* why he ran off. He couldn't face that happening again. I'm actually really worried about him."

"You know who he is?" I said. "He's the little boy from the houseboat. He spent summers on that houseboat every year until his sister died... Holly."

"That doesn't sound right," Lucas said, shaking his head. "You're confused, Lydia. You're mixing up a bunch of different stories."

I leaned my head on the back of the couch and rested my eyes for a minute. When I closed my eyes I still experienced the sensation of rocking. I was in the red houseboat swinging on the waves; I was in the rowboat lurching toward shore. I opened my eyes and looked at my brother, at his golden eyes and hair. He was such a beautiful man. I knew not everyone would see him as I saw him; the sunburn, the chaos of clothes and hair wouldn't be beautiful to everyone. But to me, there was no one more lovely.

The way Lucas saw Cole, it was like he was looking at a photograph. He didn't see the real man, only the snapshot. He saw only what Cole wanted him to see. Or maybe he saw what he wanted to see. When we looked at Cole, Lucas and I were not seeing the same man, that was for sure.

I was too tired, too achy, too dizzy to argue with Lucas tonight. And in the back of my head was the thought that there would never be a time to talk to Lucas about Cole. Because Lucas wouldn't believe me. He wouldn't. I understood this so clearly. When he stood to go to bed, I felt a sharp, fierce loneliness.

From this point on, I kept thinking. *From this point on*. But I didn't know how to finish that thought.

In my bedroom, Tuck and I stood by the window, looking out at the lawn, the dock, the dark water. We leaned toward one another and our shoulders touched.

"Why didn't you wait for me?" Tuck asked.

"I meant to. But it just tumbled out. I don't know."

"Well, it's progress I guess. The police will find him; the whole story will come out. This is good news. We should have a party. We should make a cake," Tuck said.

Tuck lay on the floor beside my bed. I climbed under the covers and let my hand fall down to him. He held it.

"You never told me why you were all wet," I said.

"I got off the ferry, and I saw you immediately," he said. "I saw you swimming along the shore down by the landing. Yeah. I thought you'd gone totally crazy. And I yelled to you, but you wouldn't look at me."

I closed my eyes and leaned back on the pillow. I was so tired now, and it was that sweet heavy exhaustion, as powerful as a sleeping pill. "I was on the houseboat. And then I was in a rowboat," I said. "You couldn't have seen me."

"It was you," he insisted. "You were swimming out farther and farther. I went in after you like a fucking maniac. I followed you to the houseboat, but no one was there. I thought you drowned," he said.

I squeezed his hand. "Still alive," I said.

Cole didn't show up in the night, not even in my dreams. But I couldn't sleep for long. I woke up hearing voices. Tuck's voice. Outside somewhere, out where it was cold. Then I realized he was here, with me, my hand still in his.

In the morning, my head ached. I was hungry, and we ate mountains of scrambled eggs, slice after slice of toast. Then Kim and Eddie showed up with bagels and cream cheese and we ate those, too.

"I don't know exactly what happened last night, but it doesn't sound good," Eddie said. "I saw Sean Alameda this morning."

"I don't even know where to start," I said.

Later, once Kim and Eddie had gone, Tuck and I sat at the end of the dock.

"Is Tuck your real name?" I asked him. I wasn't sure why it occurred to me so suddenly.

"My real name," he said, "is Jonathan."

"Jonathan?" We began to laugh. "I don't even know why that's so funny," I said.

"Jonathan Edward," he said.

We howled with laughter. Laughed until tears rolled down our cheeks.

"It never felt right," he said.

"Maybe names don't matter after all," I said.

When the laughter ended, we grew serious.

"Do you know for sure he hit you with something?" Tuck asked.

"Are you sure of what *you* saw? Someone who looked just like me swimming in the water?"

"I had been drinking," Tuck admitted. "Did I tell you that

part? But I've never seen anything that wasn't there, drunk or not drunk. It was you."

We looked out where the red houseboat used to be. I didn't know where it was now, but I did know that the bay looked completely different without it, like a different view out a different window. A different bay off some other island.

Maybe there *were* ghosts: spirit swimmers, widows looking out to sea, the ghosts of whores, tiny faces at the window. I didn't know if Baby B was a ghost following me around the island. Maybe he did exist. But everything I had to fear existed in the human realm. It was the same stuff everyone here feared: lost love, loneliness, death. Slipping off the rocks into the cold water.

That afternoon, Lucas found me in the kitchen. He'd been crying. There was dirt smeared across his cheeks, and his eyes were red.

"He's gone," Lucas said. "He's not coming back."

"Did they find him?"

"They're not going to find him."

I looked at Lucas's face. "Is he dead?" I asked.

"Of course not," Lucas said. "But he can't be with us anymore. And he said I couldn't come with him either."

Would Cole continue this way, transforming himself into someone else's brother, someone else's husband or son? He would arrive on some other island, handsome and powerful, and I felt sorry for the girl on that island who he decided to love.

"He said he has to disappear," Lucas said. It seemed he was past crying, his sorrow heavy and immovable, the sorrow of rocks, of stones, of things that take years and years to erode.

I pitied Lucas, but there was nothing I could do. His grief, like mine, was a private thing. For the first time in so long, I didn't feel the need to grieve—I wanted to have cake and champagne. Walk on the cold beach. I wanted to go to the grocery store and fill a cart with food, enough for a month. I wanted to eat and then sleep, I wanted to shout, to laugh.

Cole was gone. Cole had disappeared. For now.

"Did I ever tell you about the ghost?" I said.

"No."

"I started seeing it in my dreams. This was after my mother died. Then I thought it was following me around, in my daily life. I kept catching glimpses of it, but then it would vanish."

"Wait, what are we doing?"

"I'm telling you a story."

"In the middle of the night?"

"I couldn't sleep."

"Okay," Tuck said. He looked around the room groggily. An almost full moon over the harbor was filling the room with pale light.

"Come up," I said. And he stretched out on the bed beside me.

"What did the ghost look like?" he asked.

"A seal," I said. "Sometimes. And sometimes like a skinny girl. Maybe that was what you saw when you jumped in the water."

Then I said, "Oh!" and a realization flooded through me, icy as ocean water. I closed my eyes and put my hands over my face, because I must have been an idiot not to have realized it long ago. That little face I glimpsed through the window in the bathroom at Jack's. The sense that someone was behind me. That flash in the waves. Those weren't seals. Not a ghost. Not Baby B either.

It was me.

It was always just me.

Little Lydia, lost all these years, wandering the island, haunting the Claws, swimming back and forth alongside the ferry, where I must have lost her to begin with, that spring I came home, when my mother got sick.

"I thought it was Baby B," I said. I felt something pressing against my throat and eyes, ballooning large and insistent. I was definitely going to cry. I lay beside Tuck and pressed my face into his neck. His neck smelled like ocean water. He put one hand in my hair.

"You're always seeing ghosts," he said. "How did you know it wasn't just a regular person?"

"I know everyone on the island."

"You didn't know me."

"I knew you weren't a ghost."

"Are you sure about that?"

He wrapped his arms around me, and I felt his body, strong and human and kind—a celebration. Then all my thoughts dissolved into a warm blur as he pulled me on top of him.

35

The morning light was steady and bright and almost green.

"Oh my god," Tuck said, waking up. His eyes were only half open, and he smelled warm and sweet. "Let's do that again." He found my body under the sheet and pulled me toward him. I felt myself relax against him.

I didn't feel compelled to be with Tuck. I didn't feel driven by external forces. Being with him felt comfortable, happy.

We went to Mady's for breakfast. Diane greeted me kindly, and she poured my coffee with the intimacy I'd once noticed between her and the fishermen. And I started to think: this feeling I'd had with Tuck these past months, this working together to solve a mystery, maybe that was being a normal person. Only usually there was no big mystery, it was just working together to buy a cup of coffee, working together to change the oil in your car, working together to take care of your home or your children.

Walking back to the house, I thought about how solid, how real he was, how warm and human, the dust-and-pollen scent of his hair, the seawater smell of his neck, the sound of his voice on the phone, the way life seemed to run through him like water through a sieve, coming out the other side cleaner and colder and better, his laugh, as refreshing as a cold drink. For several weeks now I'd known that I wanted to be the one to make Tuck laugh. But something new occurred to me. It wasn't just that I liked Tuck, it was that I wanted to be like him. I wanted to laugh. I wanted to be alive like he was alive. When I said I wanted to be a normal person, what I meant was I wanted to be like Tuck.

Lucas didn't come out of his room. All day there was the smell of Tuck grilling bluefish and scallops in the chilly yard. I stood outside Lucas's bedroom and begged him to eat with us. But he wouldn't. The dock stretched out into the blue water. The afternoon galloped into evening. We stood by the grill in the smoky winter light.

We made love in the dark in my narrow bed. In the morning we had breakfast at Mady's. After breakfast, we walked to the empty information booth and Tuck kissed me there, in the shadowy booth, near the empty brochure racks.

"You want to sit?" he said.

Jim Cardoza came out and stood near us. He shook Tuck's hand. Everyone knew something had happened. They knew Cole had hurt me. They knew he had vanished, and that the police were looking for him. They knew Tuck was here to help.

That night we walked to Jack's for beer. We sat so our

knees touched under the table. It went on like this for a few days. I felt again as if I were holding something fragile and precious in the palm of my hand. More precious because I knew any moment I might close my hand and feel it crushed beyond repair.

We waited for word from the police. We waited to hear they'd caught up with Cole—I mean Anthony—but as I suspected, they didn't.

Then one night in bed, Tuck turned to me, touched my face. "I have to go," he said. "I mean leave the island."

"Oh," I said, deflated but not surprised. "Okay. Of course you do. But I guess I just—when exactly?"

"Soon," Tuck said. "I've decided to go back to school. Spring semester starts in January."

"I guess you figured out what you want to do next."

"Maybe," he said.

After Tuck left, the weeks were lonely. Jim Cardoza would often invite us over for dinner, and when Lucas refused to go, Jim would show up at our door with small meals. On Christmas, Eddie and Kim knocked on the door early, ridiculous Santa hats on their heads and their arms full of packages. The gifts were nothing we wanted—a word search book, a shot glass from Jack's—but I held them, feeling like I was holding treasure.

"I don't even know what to say," I told them.

"We just wanted you to know—you've got a lot of friends. You've got us," Kim said. The look she gave me was uncharacteristically fierce. She didn't laugh even a little. I thought maybe this was her way of forgiving me, and I felt something give way in my chest, something hard and icy slipping into liquid. Warm and warmer, until it was all fiery gratitude and love for both of them.

I had friends. I felt it all the time now—a sense of community. I had Jim Cardoza, and Elijah West, and Sebastian and Gordon, and in the spring, I would have the information booth again, all the tourists with their questions. I had all this love suddenly—for the islanders, the tourists, for Lucas. *Home* began to mean something new.

After Christmas I made a decision. Although it scared me, I knew I had no choice. I needed a life of my own, a place that was mine to fill up. A place where I would make my own memories as pristine as a newborn's.

I found the folder of college applications, half-filled-out, and put them all in the fireplace one by one. That was a leftover dream from when I was seventeen, and I wanted to grow up, grow older, make a new dream. Whatever life had in store for me, it was here on the island—that seemed suddenly clear to me. But that didn't mean I was a prisoner to my mother's ghost, her dresses in the closet, the furniture she'd chosen. That didn't mean I was a prisoner to Lucas or the house.

The week between Christmas and New Year's was surprisingly warm. I went to the landing. Clint was practicing bagpipes again, and I thought, as I always did, of each note as a seagull, soaring out over the water. Behind the post office, I watched the postmaster, facing the harbor and holding aloft his bagpipes, with all the strange arms and necks and valves, that big heart of an instrument.

A little sign was hanging on the shingled wall just to the side of the post office's back door. This was what I'd come for. I reached up and took it down, held the paper in my hand. *For rent. One bedroom. Includes heat.*

I looked up the wooden steps to a closed door on the second floor of the old building. There must have been several apartments up there, since this was once a big, beautiful house, the home of a sea captain. I knew there were apartments above all the shops on Clara Day Street, like the one Eddie lived in. But this one. This door. These steps. The notes of the bagpipe suddenly became a story, and it was the story of a future, a real and possible future, and I could see myself walking up those steps and walking through that door and sitting on a couch and picking up a book. The couch and the book were both things I'd chosen carefully, and the cupboard was filled with cans and containers of foods I'd chosen to eat.

I could almost hear it, the ringing of this future. It filled my ears, shells crushed under a wave, the roar of a tide.

36

There are only three things left to tell you, what Tuck calls *miracles one through three.*

("I don't believe in miracles," I tell him.

"Are you sure about that?" he says.)

When I moved into the apartment over the post office, I left Lucas in charge of the house. Brother of mine, you can have the boxes in the attic. You can have the old bicycles in the garage. You can have the beds and the clocks and the blankets, you can have the ghosts. But all Lucas wanted was Cole. And since he couldn't have Cole, he didn't want anything. He stopped going to work. He stopped mowing the lawn. I visited him every day, but it took a long time before he wanted to get dressed, eat a decent breakfast, leave the house.

"Just come home," Lucas sometimes said. But I felt safer in the apartment alone. And even there I locked my doors at

night, and the circles under my eyes darkened from sleepless-
ness. So many nightmares.

The way Lucas felt about me was complicated. He missed
me. He wanted me to come home. But he blamed me for
Cole's leaving. He didn't come out and say so, but I felt it
when he looked at me. All his sadness, he thought, was my
fault. All that lost love.

I'd spent so many years taking care of my brother, it was
terrible to think that I was the cause of his misery. I worried about him all the time. I worried he wouldn't make it. I
didn't know how to take care of him anymore. It was a long
winter, the worst one we'd had.

But it didn't last forever. That's miracle number one.

In the spring, when the sting of Cole's leaving had dulled
for Lucas, he showed up at the information booth and told
me he'd gotten a new job, at the aquarium.

Yes, after all those years, Lucas had to find a new job. The
Day Estate had been sold, the whole deal somehow shrouded
in mystery. Developers, everyone said, whispered it like it
was a dirty word. I didn't know what would happen to that
old house, those paths and gardens, the long thin rocks that
made the claws of Wolf Island.

I just knew that Lucas was out of a job, and I worried.

But it turned out the change was good for Lucas. He started
off doing a bit of landscaping for the aquarium, then cleaning lobster tanks. He did some construction on the new seal
tank. He brought fish for the seals when the trainer wasn't in.

He began to talk again about refinancing, so he could fix
up the house. He wanted to add skylights to some of the bedrooms. He wanted to look up at the stars all night. He was
suddenly back in the world.

I love him as much as ever, but my heart breaks a little every time I see him. Breaks because we are not the brother and sister we used to be, breaks for the closeness we had that we lost. Perhaps hearts are supposed to break open—like acorns—so that new growth can green its way out. That's how grown-ups love, I suspect. And that's what I'm trying to be now—an adult. Someone who makes decisions for herself, even if they're sometimes mistakes.

I sometimes wonder about the shadow—that skin of despair I brought back with me from Baby B's grave. I've grown accustomed to it, almost grateful for it. I watch the other islanders; they all have shadows of their own. I thought the shadow had something to do with Colin, with my mother and what she may have done to him, something to do with secrets and lies, and the things we bury deep under the earth. But maybe the shadow has more to do with leaving childhood and a child's simple sense of the world far behind—finally. Maybe the shadow is the grief we feel for the children we used to be, not the children we bury.

Miracle number two is that Emily woke up.

Anthony Coletti's mother wrote to tell me so. I gathered from her letter that Emily wasn't quite the person she'd been a year ago. Neither are any of us, I thought, but I knew what she meant. It took her a long time to recover, to relearn what it meant to be human. To walk and talk, to do things like wash dishes and make sandwiches and write letters. By spring she could do all these things.

And then she wanted to talk about Anthony.

It was August when Emily came to Wolf Island, a full year since Cole first arrived. From far away I saw the boat that

Emily was on, a toy out there in the water. Closer and closer, and bigger and bigger, and it bumped up against the loading dock and let down its plank.

Emily stepped off the boat.

I saw her and she saw me. I knew it was her, and she came toward me and we stood and looked at one another.

I'd never met another person so exactly my height. I looked into eyes level with my eyes.

"Just start at the beginning," she said.

We walked along the shore in the dusky August light. The beach was so pristine it filled me with a great swell of nostalgia, as if I would never see it like this again. I looked around, trying to memorize what I saw: the gold sand, the hazy light on the water.

"It was August," I told her. "And I was working in the information booth."

We walked for hours. We went to the house, so she could see where he'd been for many months. I pointed at the place in the bay where the houseboat used to be. She shook Lucas's hand. "His wife," I said to Lucas.

He held on to her hand as if he couldn't help himself, gripped it so hard she opened her eyes wide in surprise. Carefully, as if it hurt him to do it, he raised his chin to look her square in the face. "Do you know where he is?" Lucas asked. She shook her head, and he dropped her hand, his expression of hope collapsing all at once.

Later, alone at the end of the dock, Emily and I watched the boats swaying. I still wasn't used to the look of the bay without the red houseboat. I still scanned the bay for it, even though I knew I wouldn't see it. So much of my life had felt that way, that more was missing than was there. I wondered if Emily felt that way, too.

"Do you remember it?" I asked her. "Falling?"

She shook her head. "Not really. But I remember him standing at the top of the stairs beside me, and he was angry. He was always angry. He was a deeply jealous person. It's like he wanted to possess me, and whenever he realized he couldn't, not really you know, he would freak out, become enraged."

"I can see that," I said.

"He thought I was plotting to leave him, run away with someone else. Whenever I got a letter, or a phone call, or came home five minutes late from work or the store, he'd be sitting there, waiting for me. He was always trying to catch me in a lie. I felt like I was under surveillance all the time. I just, I finally got tired of it—I started standing up to him. That was it, I guess. He couldn't take it anymore. I think he really wanted me to die."

"I'm sorry that happened to you," I said. I realized, with surprise, that I was crying. I couldn't remember the last time I'd cried.

"You know the really sad part?" she said. "I didn't want to leave him. I was never plotting anything. I wanted to grow old with him. There was never anyone else."

We would never, not one of us, tell the same story. We would never see the same truth. In that way, there was no escaping loneliness.

Before Emily left I asked her about my mom, if she thought Cole knew my mom at all.

"Her name was Cecily," I said. "And I found a letter from her in his suitcase. He said he knew her, that she believed he was Baby B."

"He had a friend who was an older woman," she said. "I don't think I ever knew her name. It could have been your mom. He said they understood each other because they both understood losing someone, and she was the only person he knew who had lost something big enough to—you know—ruin your life."

"But everyone has lost things." My mother felt irretrievably lost to me. I would never know the truth of what happened that night on the ferry, if she'd meant to kill Baby B, if she'd meant to kill herself. It was terrible not knowing, but sometimes I thought it would be worse to know.

"He never thought other people's griefs were as real as his," Emily said. "Except hers, this woman. He said *she* found *him*, that she used to watch him when he was a little boy, and that was how she knew about his grief. He said they'd been friends since he was thirteen. His parents never knew."

"That was her."

"People are weird," Emily said. "Love does weird things to people and so does grief. I still miss him. Every day. He tried to kill me, and I still miss him. I still think about walking home from the movies with him holding hands. I know I'm crazy, but I can't help it."

I understood what it was like to have contradictory feelings, that duel between what you longed for, and what was good for you. When Emily had gone, I felt empty. For weeks, I felt myself flounder looking for something to fill me up. A past, no, a future. A blue hat on a busy street, a wooden door with small black numbers outlined in gold. The bell tower in Carson Cove, a garden with star-shaped flowers. A bridge over a stream, where two people fall asleep and dream the same dream.

★ ★ ★

Miracle number three is Tuck.

He went away to finish school, but then he came back. And when he told me he wanted to stay, some little voice that I hadn't heard in a long time said *good*.

We made love in my new bedroom in my tiny apartment over the post office. The clean white sheets tangled up under us.

I woke up during that first night and looked at him in the dull light coming from the street. The waves, the hot golden sand, the cries of frogs and gulls: these were my sounds, my memories. This feeling—easy, plentiful, slow to blossom—this was the kind of love I wanted now.

Tuck has been with me for a long time now. "Five years?" I ask him.

"Almost five," he says.

He loves the apartment as much as I do. He loves a lot of things: dogs and dinner and beer and walking until his body is exhausted. Loves the taste of just-picked vegetables. Loves yoga. My mom would have liked him. He joined search-and-rescue and goes out on the water late at night. He writes poems. He grows a patio garden. A widow's walk garden. Tomato plants hang from hooks, beans climb up the old railing. Pots of basil and thyme and oregano spice the air.

Sometimes when we're making dinner together, or cleaning house, or grocery shopping, sometimes when I'm reading in bed waiting for him to come home, sometimes I still think, *This is what happy people do.*

We think about Cole often; we wonder where he is and if he's coming back. I think back to the night in the houseboat, and I remember drowning. The beauty, the stillness, the ache of wanting, with all the force of my being, one more breath. Sometimes now it feels to me that I was drowning all along—that the tumble into the water was only a culmination of a long, slow suffocation. Drowning in family, drowning in love, drowning in guilt and loyalty and loneliness. Drowning in a childhood I couldn't grow out of.

Now I dream about Baby B. I dream of what I saw under the water, little lost soul, living in his underwater home there for years. Little soul waiting to make his grand appearance. Water baby. Water baby.

The summer I'm thirty-five, I get pregnant. When we know for sure, we sit on the couch under a blanket looking out at the island. The streets are busy, the restaurants full. There is music drifting out of Jack's.

"I don't think I can do it," I say. "I'm afraid it's him."

Tuck holds my hand under the blanket. "Him?"

"Still wanting to be born."

Tuck nods. But I see what's there in his expression. He wants this, wants a son or a daughter. He has so much love—more than me.

"Not this one," I say. "Let's wait. This one's *him*, I feel it."

"Maybe it's always going to be him," he says. "Every time."

That night I walk up and down Clara Day Street alone. The lights are multicolored, reflecting in the harbor. I try to feel around inside myself, to feel him there. What is he after this time? I look deep inside and ask him, why me?

I have something of yours, he says.

"What is it?" I say.

Something you need, he tells me.

You really want to be born? I ask.

Yes! he cries. *Yes!* He shouts yes at the lights and the stars and the water all around us. He shouts yes at the buildings that rise into the night, the lit windows, the sparkling streets. He shouts yes at the parking meters and road signs and the music coming from the bars. Color and light and noise is what he wants. Smells and tastes and the feel of the wind. One more breath. He wants a sensory life.

"Okay," I say to Tuck climbing into bed with him.

"Seriously?" he says.

His body is a wonder to me still. I lie in bed beside him, not knowing what will happen now. I've never been so conscious of a future stretching out before us, a life reaching in two directions, into the past and into the future. Either way I look, there is sadness and loss, there is loneliness, inevitably. But when I look ahead, to the future that Tuck is part of, I feel prepared for all of that, prepared to have more than I ever imagined having, and prepared to lose it, too. Tuck rolls onto his back and stares at the ceiling. I look out the window at the harbor with its buoys and boats. The masts clang in the wind, like clocks keeping time. I think, *This is only the beginning.*

★ ★ ★ ★ ★

Acknowledgments

Thank you, Jenni Ferrari-Adler, my incredible agent, who labored over every line of this book in all its incarnations, and to Laura Brown, editor of my dreams. I'm forever in debt to both of you, with your sharp eyes, patience, humor and steadfastness. Thank you to Sally Wofford-Girand and Taylor Curtain at Union Literary, and to the whole team at Park Row, HarperCollins and Harlequin: Shara Alexander and Laura Gianino, Stefanie Buszynski, Mary Luna for stunning book art, Chris Wolfgang for scrupulous copyediting, Kristen Salciccia for supernaturally good proofreading, Erika Imranyi, Margaret Marbury, Loriana Sacilotto, Heather Foy, Linette Kim, Randy Chan and Amy Jones.

Deepest thanks to early readers of this novel: Nicole Griffin, Clarence Lai, Tia McCarthy, Sarah Madru, Jericho Parms, Carolyn Scoppettone, Robert Solomon and especially my dear friends Laura Farmer and Eric Rosenblum. Without Jessica Hendry Nelson, Sean Prentiss and Julia Shipley and their insights, I wouldn't have made it through the final drafts. Thanks to creative friends and colleagues who have inspired and supported me over the years. Your sweet friendship has meant the world to me: Lauren Antler, Julianna Baggott, Jedediah Berry, Matthew Dickman, Sian Foulkes, Vicki Kuskowski, Jeremy Lubman, Kerrin McCadden, An Na, Christa Parravani, Sonya Posmentier, Liz Powell, Jess Row, James Scott and Tolya Stonorov. Endless gratitude to Liz Knapp, who's been my champion and best friend for thirty years, the kindest person I know and the most fun.

Thanks also to my wonderful Syracuse teachers, Arthur Flowers, Mary Gaitskill, George Saunders, Mary Karr, Michael Burkard, Brooks Haxton, Chris Kennedy and Bruce Smith, from whom I learned so much about craft, kindness and generosity. For encouragement and inspiration from the entire VCFA community, especially the faculty, students and staff in the MFA in Writing & Publishing program, I am deeply grateful. Thanks to Clint McCown, Ellen Lesser and the Postgraduate Writers' Conference at VCFA. Mentors along the way, so much gratitude to you, too: Mona Simpson, Brad Morrow, Melissa Weidman, Barbara Stephens and Carl Phillips.

The Vermont Studio Center and the Vermont Arts Council provided the gifts of funding and time to write. A special thank-you to all the Vermont Book Award winners, finalists and judges these past few years. And thanks to the *Hunger Mountain* staff and writers, true superheroes of literature.

Endless appreciation for the Montpelier community, where my mailman, hairstylist, yoga teacher, neighbors and my children's dear after-school teachers have been supportive of my writing career. I am so lucky to live here.

Passionate thanks to my talented and wondrous writer

friend Robin MacArthur for reading and commiserating, and all that help with the bad list. Thank you to Ann Cardinal for daily pep talks and for inspiring me with your unrivaled work ethic; so glad we could write our predawn, naptime, lunch-break novels together, my writing sister. Thanks to Dan Torday, who I call almost daily with questions, who always has an answer and who works so hard he makes me want to work harder. My friends, I'm a better person because of you, and this book certainly couldn't have been written without your help.

Thanks to the Fournier and Hodgson clans, especially Dot and Bernie, Bug and Meg, Aaron, Darcy, Lucy and Rebecca. Thank you a million times over to my family, who fostered my love of art, filled my life with books, built me a writing shed on Oyster Pond and encouraged all my ambitions: Mom and Tom, Mary Jo and Peter, Dad, Auntie Ann and Aunt Mollyann—and Grandma Mary, who said, "Hitch your wagon to a star." So I tried to. Thanks to Teddy and River for their endless curiosity and love of a good story. Thanks to Lily, who once when she was little gave me a (step)Mother's Day card that said, "I love you like a magisine loves its edidor." And finally, thank you, Jeff, for your patience and hard work, for believing in me, believing in us. But mostly, thank you for defying expectations and breaking the rules. This book is actually a love story, and it's for you.